SLEIGHT

A NOVEL

Kirsten Kaschock

COFFEE HOUSE PRESS

MINNEAPOLIS 2011

Coffee House Press books are available to the trade through our primary distributor, Consortium Book Sales & Distribution, www.cbsd.com or (800) 283-3572. For personal orders, catalogs, or other information, write to: info@coffeehousepress.org.

Coffee House Press is a nonprofit literary publishing house. Support from private foundations, corporate giving programs, government programs, and generous individuals helps make the publication of our books possible. We gratefully acknowledge their support in detail in the back of this book.

To you and our many readers around the world,
we send our thanks for your continuing support.

LIBRARY OF CONGRESS CIP INFORMATION

Kaschock, Kirsten.

Sleight : a novel / Kirsten Kaschock.

p. cm.

Summary: "Sisters Lark and Clef have spent their lives honing their bodies for sleight, an interdisciplinary art form that combines elements of dance, architecture, acrobatics, and spoken word. After being estranged for several years, the sisters are reunited by a deceptive and ambitious sleight troupe director named West who needs the sisters' opposing approaches to the form-Lark is tormented and fragile, but a prodigy; Clef is driven to excel, but lacks the spark of artistic genius. But when a disturbing mass murder makes national headlines, West seizes on the event as inspiration for his new performance, one that threatens to destroy the very artists performing it. In language that is at once unsettling and hypnotic, *Sleight* explores ideas of performance, gender, and family to ask the question: what is the role of art in the face of unthinkable tragedy?" —PROVIDED BY PUBLISHER.

ISBN 978-1-56689-275-9 (pbk.)

1. Sisters—Fiction. 2. Dance companies—Ficiton. 3. Domestic fiction.

I. Title.

PS3611.A785S57 2011

813'.6—DC22

2011024142

PRINTED IN CANADA

1 3 5 7 9 8 6 4 2

FIRST EDITION | FIRST PRINTING

ACKNOWLEDGMENTS

An excerpt from *Sleight* appeared in *Action Yes Online Quarterly* and in *Xantippe*.

Profound gratitude to my siblings: Alex, Mary, Taryn, and Misha. Deepest thanks also to Ann and Alex Kaschock, Reginald McKnight, Jed Rasula, Judith Cofer, Sîan Griffiths, John Woods, Sabrina Orah Mark, Kristen Iskandrian, Mark Leidner, Heather Cousins, Alan Sener, Françoise Martinet, Sarah Jane Duax, Patrick Lawler, George Saunders, Mary Karr, Richard Cook, Ron and Mary Williams, Derek Ege, Ali Delgadillo, Marquet Lee, Maureen Smith, Mikey Rioux, Katie Zeller, Linda Koutsky, Sarah Yake, Anitra Budd, and all of Coffee House Press. Unabandonable love to my children—Simon, Bishop, and Koen.

This is a work of fiction: any Needs in this book that resemble Needs of the world
do so inadvertently and probably unavoidably.

To Danny (who pins me to this place) . . .
I have decided—I will let you.

Now, do you doubt that your Bird was true?
——EMILY DICKINSON

D.C. INSIDELOOP

JAN. 13, 2001, PP. 52-6

Interview with Clef Scrye, member of the sleight troupe Monk

INSIDELOOP: Clef—I don't think I've heard that name before. Not for a woman.

SCRYE: I'm sorry, was that a question?

INSIDELOOP: No . . . I'm sorry. Would you mind if—may I begin again?

SCRYE: You can try.

INSIDELOOP: Please, Ms. Scrye, I wonder how you might explain a sleight to someone who has never seen one?

SCRYE: I couldn't. No, I mean that. Sleight isn't . . . well, it's beyond anything it may have come from. Or out of. There's no disagreement about that.

INSIDELOOP: And what does it come from? What, exactly, is sleight made of?

SCRYE: It's impossible to say—"openings" is a term one hears, "suspensions," but that implies a bridge between things, and that's not quite . . . at any rate, at several points during a sleight performance—you've got epiphany.

INSIDELOOP: Let's step back. I go to my first sleight performance. What will I see?

SCRYE: Oh. You want me to lay it out. Okay, but it won't help. In most sleights, except West's of course, first a sleightist arrives in front and recites the precursor. Tedious, but if you miss it, the rest seems less—what? linguistic maybe? unlocked? Then, the curtains—just like at the opera or ballet or theater. It has nothing to do with the elements per se. Then, the lights fade up, illuminating the sleightists already onstage with their architectures.

INSIDELOOP: Which are?

SCRYE: Yes. Sorry. Transparent and flexible frameworks—moveable polyhedrons and so forth. Each sleightist (there are twelve in every troupe, nine women and three men) carries one of several architectures he or she has trained with. Sleightists manipulate these frameworks in and around our bodies, linking them up to create forms that span the stage. But you don't . . . I mean the audience can't . . . the sleightists' movements are timed, the works navigated in such a way . . .

INSIDELOOP: Yes?

SCRYE: Well, theoretically, you could examine the documents beforehand, know exactly the structures the hands have drawn—every form the sleightists will be moving through in a given evening . . . but it wouldn't matter.

INSIDELOOP: What wouldn't?

SCRYE: What you know about a sleight. It doesn't matter. What you'll see is . . . well, West calls it "the constellating empty." But West . . . I think West—West can be bleak.

INSIDELOOP: How did you become a sleightist?

SCRYE: [. . .]

INSIDELOOP: I'm sorry. Do you need a moment?

SCRYE: No . . . thank you. I think . . . well, I think I sleight because I always have. My mother sent my sister Lark and me, I guess for poise, and I was good. And when you are good and a girl at something, you stay with it—maybe for all the goodgirl words that come. Goodgirl words like do more, keep on, further—instead of the other goodgirl words—the if-you-are-you-will words—be nice and softer and you-don't-like-fire-do-you? In sleight there was less of that so more of me, until there was less. Once I tried to leave it, right after Lark did, and felt like half. Most people are satisfied with half, not knowing what it is to hold a thousand hungers suspended and you not feeling the hunger. After I quit I just wanted, all the time, to be in the chamber. To be stranded with my architectures— then, to abandon them, moving. To watch beauty, of its own accord. Yes. I think I missed my missingness.

A SOUTHERN.

You are living on the site of an atrocity

Lark stopped at the light. Her right hand, a severe blue, knuckled the wheel. Her eyes narrowed. Her left hand, also blue, impatiently pushed a nothing back into place behind her ear as if it were a loose, transparent curl—her actual hair cropped almost to the scalp, a silvering black. The billboard had been up for two weeks or more. That Wednesday it looked at her hard.

Lark hadn't been a sleightist for long, but she hung on to it. Few lead more than one life before thirty. Those few, Lark noted, tended not to bond. Lark's husband had always been who he was. He'd changed, but not into someone else. A harder else. Lark would come home and Drew would be reading to Nene or cooking dinner and he would look up and it would be him. Lark found that remarkable.

That Wednesday Lark came in and spoke billboard to Drew. She said, "We are living on the site of an atrocity." Drew looked at Lark, smiled as if from under a river, and said, "No, Lark—we're not."

Lark sold Souls at a kiosk in University Square. She did okay. Made enough for Drew to stay home reading, writing, minding their girl. He taught an occasional course at the community college, to keep himself whet. Lark did brisk business when it was warm. When it was cold, people made do with what they had. But Georgia winters weren't long, and she had a space heater. Januaries, she kept shorter hours, and when it got glacial—for Georgia, anything below freezing—she meditated on Paul Revere.

Her first summer at the academy, Lark had visited Revere's church in north Boston. A favorite instructor, Ms. Early, had suggested the trip: the interior of the church, she'd said, was a remarkable example. All the pews boxed, every family segregated from every other, and the minister pulpited up high, on an octagonal dais far higher and smaller than a stage. An eternal white stop sign. Lark thought these revolution-era Bostonians must've been cold—to wall off from neighbors even in church. It was some other tourist who asked the question, "Why are the pews boxed out like that?" The caretaker or security guard or unpaid, leisure-class but socially responsible intern explained that the church hadn't been heated in the 1700s; instead, families had stowed hot bricks under the pews. Short walls kept in heat, out drafts. Lark felt mean. A week passed and she forgave herself, figuring she'd still been right about the cold. Three Boston summers later, she decided centuries of heated churches had done and would do nothing for the city. The interior structure of the church, however, stayed with her. If she had been a hand,[1] Lark might have used it to draw.

Lark wasn't a hand—she sold Souls. She was proud of her Souls. They were pricey, but she wouldn't bilk or bicker. Her Souls were pocket-sized, responded to the warmth of the palm, had a good weight to them. Lark got a lot of browsers. A student might look at, fondle, then reluctantly set a Soul back onto its cloth, sometimes twice a week over three or four semesters before committing. Lark's daughter Nene adored the four she had, one for each birthday. She'd recently given them names: Fern, Marvel, Newt, and the Lacemaker.

[1] In sleight, a hand is recognized and promoted by a number of instructors. The child is studying sleight, has a deep love for it, but cannot manipulate the architectures. Some hands exhibit defects that make the most significant figurations difficult for them, if not impossible. Other hands simply seem to lack physical ability or to have problems with pain. Because of the intensity of the intervention by the instructors, certain members of the sleight community wonder if potential hands have been overlooked—nonfacilitated—because of their competence.

On the Monday after the billboard, a man came up to the kiosk and asked for two Souls—one for himself and one for the road. His dashboard? Lark was curious.

"What kind of car do you drive?" He didn't look like he drove a car.

"Not for a car—for the road. I'm gonna bury it under Space Highway."

Lark thought she was prying but went in anyway. "Can I ask why?"

"Because of the atrocity," he said.

A NORTHERN.

When what happened happened years ago, it happened quickly, and Clef had no time to care who was hurt. She took Kitchen from Lark. There were no jealous seeds. Clef, after all, had been the prodigy. At the time, they were all friends together in the same troupe. Kitchen was old, like a god, but they were all friends; Clef and Lark even had the semblance of best. As sisters, they were no such thing, but the semblance couldn't be denied. Clef took Kitchen from Lark because it caused pain, one of the primary substances. An original thing the world makes happen.

———

The metal door eked out a small intrusion (Clef made a note to prop it during performance), and there stood bright-morning Haley, a vapid bit of talent Clef could barely stomach, and not this early. Haley tipped her hotpink bag from a shoulder onto the nearest chair—a sloping gargoyle of kelly green plastic.

"Hey Clef, what's up?"

"Not so much." Clef was stringing together a new architecture with fishwire. It was only a few lengths long, but its configuration would create whole other potentials. The fiberglass tubes were transparent, as was the fishwire, which used to be intestines, and the tubes glass, of course, and fragile. Blown glass was still used for some opuses—the earliest works required a complexity of resonance. Recent materials (this was universally acknowledged) offered lesser song, but the control they gave the sleightists was astonishing. The best sleight, Clef thought, must hang somewhere between balance and exchange.

She could feel Haley waiting for her to look up. Angry at being interrupted and then telling herself she had no right, Clef tried to be civil—not looking up but raising her eyebrows expectantly. Evidently, this was enough.

"Did you see those awful billboards?"

"No, I slept most of the way across 80. Because of the corn."

(Pause.)

Haley was going to make her supply the line. Clef sighed. "Awful how?"

"I mean, what were they were selling? I thought maybe God shit— this is the Midwaste." Haley was from New York, and not the state.

"You'll have to tell me what they said before I can speculate, Haley." Clef pulled out nail scissors to trim the wire.

"They said 'you are living on top of an atrocity' or something. There must've been ten of them."

"Not, I think, about God. Could be Native American." Clef considered types of atrocities she might have lived on or driven near the grounds of during her lifetime: massacres of indigenous peoples, extreme cosmetic surgeries, executions of Chinese sojourners, rapes, terrorist bombings, genocides, suburbs, Three Mile Island, forced sterilizations, plantations, serial murders, baptisms of the dead, severe and avoidable industrial accidents. Clef had always liked being informed. She'd audited a couple of classes at Harvard while at the academy before realizing just how deep ran her loathing of paralysis.

"Is there a reservation around here?" Haley smiled. "I love roulette."

Clef couldn't help it, she had to strike the bunny. "You know, Haley, reservations are where people were driven after their families were massacred and their land was stolen. And I'm using the word 'driven' as in cattle—not taxi."

Haley, smile dropped, looked for it on the linoleum. "Right." Haley, none of the troupe, much liked this part of Clef.

Clef attempted not to care, couldn't manage, so eased up. "What did everyone else think?"

Haley took a few moments tersely upsweeping her flounce of bottle platinum. Clef's red was her own—her hand briefly left her architecture to grip a length of it. Still wet enough to braid.

"Mostly the troupe thought God shit. But Kitchen said it might be a car ad."

"A *car* ad?"

"Remember how Infiniti ads didn't tell you what they were at first?"

Clef nodded but couldn't stay quiet. "Only they didn't reference mass murder or genocide. Antagonism as a consumer strategy— not sure that'd—"

Haley, fishing bobby pins out of the side pocket of the hotpink, cut Clef off. "C'mon Clef, you of all people know Kitchen—he has a take on everything."

Clef stood up—she was barely a tick over five foot. She slammed her architecture against the cinder-block wall eight or nine times to make sure it was secure.

"Yes. He has his takes."

A WESTERN.

West is drift. West is sink and heal and halo. West is following orange all the way to whiskey. West was born West. But perfection being direction, not destination, he felt what he eventually worked out to be too much pressure. West, at three, knew he was a miracle. You don't get to be a miracle without knowing it early on. West took other names: Huck and Fret and Sin. Settled on Drift. Called himself Nomad-for-Hire. West was all about calling himself. That's how West got to be a religious, by working both sides of divinity.

AN EASTERN.

Byrne had been lullabyed beneath a tool mobile. A real wrench, hammer, Phillips and flat-head screwdrivers hung above his crib, and later from the defunct ceiling fan in the attic room he shared with his younger brother Marvel. Their father had wanted capable sons, sons who could fix a dishwasher, a dryer, a slow drain—sons for whom pleasure would come from the engines of cars.

When Byrne's mother skirted him and his brother along the edges of their father and off to the theater, it opened a geyser in him. It wasn't that the last defiant seed of her identity was contained in that act. It wasn't the cinema of murmur—the hush, then black. It wasn't even the sleightists: their tatted webs glinting against then obscuring their limbs, their perfect, blank countenances as they braided through one another. Nor was it the shock of seeing his first structure: helical then crystalline then "clotted," as "clotted" is indistinguishable from "containing life." For Byrne it was the words—the beginning of the sleight that most of the audience took like a vitamin. The words became the crime to Byrne in its entirety.

Byrne invited a girl up to his one-room.

"A drink?" Byrne headed to the mini fridge in the corner.

"Sure, what's in there?" The girl looked comfortingly like all other girls.

"Vodka, juice."

"What kind?"

No answer, Byrne one-handedly poured the drinks into two coffee mugs, brought hers, went back for his.

"Cheers," he said, lifting his drinking hand.

The girl tried not to look at the other one, the one clutching. Instead she tried recovering, tried trying out coy. She cocked her head, or tossed her hair, something before she spoke. Byrne didn't quite catch what.

"Cheers? What for?"

"For fellows, flowerbeds, muskets, olfactories, sects, flowcharts, squirrels, plots, deceits, blemishes, carp, blocks, barkers, sidereal freaks-on-fire." Byrne listed these absently and she giggled, uncomfortable, thinking she recognized this wasn't a joke.

Byrne wasn't really that way, not clinically. He was verbally sketching a precursor,[2] already bored and close to forgetting her there.

After she left, Byrne walked down to the corner cigarette, malt liquor, candy, diaper, and milk distributor. He bought a six-pack and some beef jerky, then sat on a bench maybe halfway back to his apartment. He held a can of ginger beer under one arm while he opened it, then shoved the jerky into his mouth and took out a pen and a folded index card from his shirt pocket. Once settled, he started composing on his thigh with his eligible hand. He was stuck on a string of words he attributed to the influence of the billboards. There was some disagreement online, but the first one had probably appeared almost a year ago. Some said outside Fairbanks, others insisted Wyoming. Now they were all over North America and Europe, Japan and India. All

---

[2] Before every performance one of the sleightists takes the stage. The word-list the sleightist recites is called the *precursor*. In the first works, the precursors had actually been written as marginalia, arrayed vertically alongside the diagrams. The choice to have the words recited prior to the performance rather than spoken concurrently with it is an established one. Lately, that tradition has come to be challenged by a radical troupe known as Kepler.

of the speculation centered on the author's identity. If there was urgency, a dire reason for the Gatsbyesque post, very few seemed to care what it might be.

Byrne didn't know why he bothered writing. If you weren't a hand, you couldn't write precursors. They were supposed to initiate the sleight. In truth, he shouldn't call what he wrote precursors—at best his work mocked. Precursors were supposed to pave the mind for a sleight, to bring the audience to capability. His did nothing close. They linked to nothing. *I make overtures to nothing*—it was a pathetic obsession. His father would've said, "I knew you weren't a man."

When Byrne had begged to take, his father had said sleight was for academics, which was a crock. Gil Dunne hated intellect, which he assumed was some kind of affectation, some trick. So no. That was it. Byrne was six then seven then eight, a hating child learning carburetors. His mother used to sneak him and Marvel to the theater before Marvel started telling. Byrne never liked cars. He didn't like working-class. His brother was anathema. And then he picked up his rock.[3]

---

[3] Some ancient American hieroglyphs contain depictions of "stone jugglers"; some of Revoix's original sleight structures seem to reference these forms. The figures are invariably shown with downturned faces and with one hand raised into the air, cupping a single rock. Initially, archaeologists thought this rock was a sacred object, perhaps even an original thing. But after enough ruins were stripped bare of their jungles, comprehension—even for archaeologists—was inescapable: the figures holding the stones were the center. Although their presence is integral to the calculations of time and shame in which they are found, the jugglers are separated from other carved forms (healers and mathematicians). Indeed, in pictographs with very little space wasted, left around the stone jugglers is a silent periphery.

In the South, Lark knows that dishes sleep. She knows this because she wrested the cabinet doors from their hinges and stayed up nights to watch. The dishes never woke. They sweated, they gathered dust about them like a personality, they quietly locked themselves against themselves. They didn't wake. Lark, indignant with vigilance, fell angrily asleep some nights herself. When five a.m. found her slumped against the oven, some roach's antennae in curious electric shudder at her ankle, the South became a certainty. And claiming to be unmovable, was.

East is the well that makes possible stone jugglers. Byrne was fated for it. When he first took up his stone, it killed his father. A stone is no tool to master, not in this age. But Byrne had an uncanny way into East. He could drop into East in the middle of conversation. Or while riding a bicycle. East was always half an articulation away. Byrne's access to East was what made him somewhat morose and frighteningly desirable. The time he spent East is what made Byrne more alone than the terrible granite egg he passed on the last day of each year from one of his hands to the other.

If you live on the site of an atrocity—say, the West—there is very little you need do. It never happened. If victims of that atrocity, or their children or children's children, make forgetting difficult, denial has been shown to be extremely effective. If denial is not deep enough (i.e., does not pleasure you), reversal of key factual information or misinterpretation of that same data may work. Reject history. At the same time, you must never admit to ugliness, never take a blood test. If ugliness seeps in along the baseboards—a sledgehammer. Then, reconstruction.

North was for Clef. North is pure, after all, docile. North is farm animals and true white, a color you don't come across. Clef was North in her thinness, in her daring punctuality to all events regardless how artistic, how "thrown together." She wasn't reached by dogsled or telephone, but over wire. You could tightrope to her. You might semaphore. But you couldn't gloss her. Any summation would end up two-dimensional, even were it four. Time slipped out of her throat like an orgasm or a chirp. When she said she missed you, what she meant was yesterday. She missed you yesterday.

Book 1

pain ≠ legitimacy :: nature of the subject :: survivor's gilt

edging ≠ the lily :: truth-afflicted ≠ envied :: jade elephant of

the cynic ≠ syntaxman :: atypical grace studies ≠ candy ::

dispensed (with/of) ≠ toileted ≠ separated-at-breath

:: quotidian ≠ woundings-clock :: life-pardoners ≠ correspon

/d/ensities ≠ remains glorious :: bruiseblack ≠ rose red

PAIN.

For Lark and Clef, the everyday injuries of sleight—pulled muscles, floor burns, fishwire and fiberglass cuts—came to both of them synchronously, as if they shared a single body or phantom abuser. Coincidence might have been plausible, until Lark left the sleight world and the unexplained bruises continued raising their greens and purple-blacks eventlessly upon her.

It had been six years since she'd left. Six years of minor aches and injuries not her own to tend.

And now—pregnant. Lark's breasts hurt, but she wasn't. Couldn't be, stitched, zipped up as she was. Nipples raw against t-shirts, sheets. With Nene this, yes, but else? A kind of calmly. Although she moved through it more like numbly, as during mending. Bones knitting. Her, pregnant, had been a broken state, and the child was a fix. A knot inside the wound. Nothing won, and when she gave birth, it was just another rent, another bit she wasn't getting back. The right mother would have made good, simple words at the in-fluttering thing: fly, go, be. You. The right mother could give and feel all sorts of right things she was incapable of. Whole joy. Resale-value joy. That store didn't like her. It was Clef who was pregnant. Had to be. But to live this again, adjacently, for her sister's body—how could that be fair? And how could she be thinking *fair*? Whose word was that?

Lark's dream woke her. Her, swimming in borscht.

"Drew?" she asked.

"Yes?" Drew was now awake too.

"I think I have to get out of here."

Drew's body nodded toward her, his eyes closed. "Was the ocean bouillon?"

"No. Borscht."

"Yes," Drew said, "that's no good."

NAMING.

On the flight to New York—to Clef—Lark had the aisle. The young girl beside her was maybe in high school, maybe not yet. She smelled like powder. Something about her assured Lark she'd never taken. She was lovely in a really human way. She wasn't, for example, aware of Lark staring at her. She didn't, because of the staring, extend her limbs against the short seat so her thighs wouldn't thicken. She slouched, but didn't slouch with length.

"What's your name?" Lark asked.

"Anna."

Lark smiled. It was a lovely, human name.

———

Lark's parents named their first daughter after a type of bird or adventure—an adventure lite. One that flew or flew by. Lark was supposed to grow into her name, to gather it round herself like an Easter shawl to keep her safe from every weighty thing. Forget that shawls don't protect against the elements, that only widows pin tight the neck, or whores—with gaudier jewelry. Forget that children kite them overhead in wind, that little girls taunt imaginary bulls with dirt-swept shawls, torn. To her mother and father, Lark's name was like an aria. They forgot that it rhymed with dark.

Lark had tried at light, lovely. To disappear. By herself with ten or eleven other girls daily for over a decade. The room she grew up in was the exact shape of a shoebox. On one side of the sleight chamber, a string of windows allowed her to look down on the suburban development where she'd never played but watched others play. The opposing wall was mirrors. Every childhood evening, after school before home, Lark had attempted sleight between sunsets. One might think this would promote an auspicious sense of beauty. Lark spent all her youth, penny by shiny penny, measuring herself against beauty and its mimic. Herself, she found wanting.

———

Lark looked at the girl again. Anna was now sleeping, and sleeping, younger—capable of pluck, of damage by fingertip. Out the window of the plane beyond her it was late afternoon.

———

By age twelve, Lark had acquired all of the normal self-hatreds. She became a meticulously ordered catalogue of ugliness. Repulsive to herself. Lark was uncertain, now, how repulsive she'd been to others, but a torturer cannot concern herself with the guilt or innocence of her captive. She'd had acne. It was mild, as acne goes, but ever-present. It had haunted her cheekbones and hairline, cropped up beneath her jaw and around her nose. Nights, in front of the mirrors that seemed to be everywhere—sleight chamber, locker room, her purse, at home in the bathrooms, bedrooms, hallways, and on the dining room wall—Lark had picked at her face until it oozed or bled, then splashed rubbing alcohol on the wounds and cried. Really the pain was unworthy of tears. They'd simply attached themselves, recognizing the uncanny way they completed the evening ritual. If she didn't shed a few each night, she'd been certain she'd wake the next day welted, leprous. She never tested the hypothesis—tears were too easily produced to forego.

Anna coughed. Lark reached over to cover her torso with one of the blue blankets. The orange in the sky was now orange in Anna's hair, and for a few seconds she looked like a softer, more manageable Clef. Clef had always had a wildly red mane Lark should have been too old to envy. Lark's hair was boy-short now, but she'd worn it long and silky black in high school. To keep it from separating into clumps, Lark had brushed it constantly and washed it with hard soap twice daily, which made the roots brittle, which meant when she pulled it back for sleight the hair around her face broke and small quarter-inch shafts spiked outward in an unintentional nod to punk rock. Lark had wanted to be Catherine Deneuve. She was nothing like her, and it had made her furious. She'd trembled all the time.

Lark stole another look at Anna sleeping, Anna folded in. And because she was aware of herself as mother, herself as failed sister, Lark decided the girl was still cold. *Is this how it will be for Nene? Thingness? Dolldom? Too many of the worst possible years spent being leered at and worried over?* Lark shivered. She rarely considered her daughter in the future tense. It seemed self-indulgent. Nene was so unlike her mother. Nene, despite everything else, had honest limbs.

As a child, Lark had hidden her potential among tendons. Specifically, her knees and elbows, always poised slightly bent, were prepared to let wrath exit through a swift extension of forearm and fist, shin and foot. She remembered living in that position for years, never exercising her anger except during certain of the fastest sleight manipulations, or in bed. The wall beside Lark's bed was battered by sleeping. To a social worker, she mused, the room—now Nene's—would've looked very much like the scene of abuse.

The pilot announced the landing. The ground was moving close, Lark's ears were blocked. Anna woke up and, noticing Lark awkwardly opening and shutting her mouth, stretched and smiled her barely developed embarrassment. It was too sweet. How unreal the girl was, how actual.

Lark had expected something different from life, something extraordinary. Public. That's why she had gone to the academy, and she had been good, very. But sleightists aren't known by name. Their greatest feat is an out-of-sight, a wicking[4]—the most talented hardly visible during a performance. She was never a true sleightist. But once she quit, Lark didn't seek out notoriety. People who want fame are willing to make other sacrifices, of a different kind. Lark only ever slaughtered a few Needs for her Souls. This last, she thought, peering into the indigo whorls of her fingertips, made eleven.

Anna walked behind Lark into the terminal. Lark held herself impeccably. She occasionally turned her head so that Anna could just see the left side of her face, the high cheekbone. It was a good angle.

———

In the middle of the final series—1st sefirot, fortress, sacri-fly, infold, purl, 2nd sefirot, j-ladder[5]—Clef felt the alien tug. The thing was too small to make noise, but she'd read yesterday that her body would start immediately converting itself into house. The tendons would start the realign without her say-so for this first crocus. She'd spent her entire life mastering her entire life, which lived bodily, continually bending the bodily toward what was not. Ad absentia.

---

4 At the pinnacle of sleight, a performer is snuffed out. At that point, the audience cannot perceive the sleightist. The surrounding architectures are always only barely visible—the subliminal flash of their apprehension/dissolution is a property of the art. But sleightists also vanish. The performers know when such a moment has been reached, and by which of them. They call it *wicking*. It quickens their skin. They taste metal. The best sleightists wick several times during a performance, though duration varies. The problem with wicking is known to them but never discussed: it can last too long. Time spent "out" corrupts a sleightist. The most talented retire after only a few years. This fact, combined with the traditional anonymity of the playbills, keeps the art form from developing stars. So sleightists are most admired, and most pitied, by one another.

5 Recent additions to sleight vocabulary have come from varied disciplines. Hands have reenvisioned structures from molecular biology, Kabbalah, psychoanalysis, physics, Vodou, baseball, astronomy, rock art, the I Ching, chemistry, and knitting.

She knew her torso. She knew the seven exercises it took to get the abdominals and latissimi dorsi warm quickly, how far she could drop a lateral (lower to her left than right by 2.6 inches), how the empty space felt, concave between hipbones when she extended full-length in hotel beds after sleight, too tired to eat for bad dreams. And she was supposed to end this knowing because Kitchen's condom broke. She was supposed to give up her body for eighteen months—nine flitting up to light, nine in burnt drift down—and Kitchen didn't want it, and said so. Nor did she. Did she.

There was taking care. Every fifth woman she'd known had taken care of some thing sometime. She'd always said she wouldn't because it was easy to say and seemed right. But the tug didn't seem natural to her. Would something change this? Would saying so? She tried it: You there, Child. No, it was still "it," a not, a bud—closed to her with no way in, no inside were there way. How was it possible for this to tulip? How does a fist shift into a cup of sun?

A light flickered in the back of the second balcony where no one could be smoking. *I cannot have.* Clef thought she smelled pot. A taut architecture passed sharply into her ankle, and it was like wind with blood, and she would not trip, did not, but made it in awkward, accidental flight to the curtain trailing a red whip.[6] When she came offstage, Lark caught her.

Lark went with Clef to the hospital. Although the Achilles was unscathed, Clef's ankle required six stitches. The sisters spoke little— a few words about Clef's upcoming schedule, the time she'd need off. A sullen cab back to Clef's apartment and it was two a.m. They limped

---

[6] Areas of indeterminacy—initially called *Unbestimmtheitsstellen* by the Polish philosopher Roman Ingarden, then baptized *Leerstellen* ("gaps" or "places") by Wolfgang Iser— are concretized in sleight. Thus, any timbre or posture left unspecified on paper, that which transpires onstage through the will of the performer alone, or accidentally, is embodied not as one thing or the other by the sleightist, but as *something wholly indeterminate yet perceivable.* In other words, there exist moments in sleight where potential is made flesh.

up the stairs to the second floor of the brownstone. Clef turned two locks and shouldered open the oak door. They went in and squared off across the coffee table, red and black; their father had called them Checkers—one nickname for both, an oppositional collective. Exhausted, they collapsed in eerie, familiar unison. Lark had never been in the place, but didn't comment on the high ceilings, live flowers, large, ugly art, or Kitchen's ancient, green leather jacket tossed over a lacquered Buddha next to the fireplace. Instead, Lark reached into a shapeless duffel, all she'd brought with her, and took out a wooden box—a cube that could hold perhaps a sparrow, a baseball. She placed it on the coffee table next to their injured, now elevated, ankles. Clef cringed.

"I don't need a Soul, Lark."

"It isn't a Soul, it's a Need." It was the first one Lark had had out since just after Nene's birth. Her sister sat forward and looked at Lark until Lark looked back. Clef's voice was low.

"I don't believe in those. My god, you're—you're still sick."

Lark swallowed hard. "I brought you one."

Clef looked at her hands and took a breath to settle, another to decide—not wanting to enable but needing to see the extent of her sister's instability. Finally, slowly, she reached for the box. The hinge was smooth and resistant, the wood almost white. Inside was a brown cloth, soft as a chamois. Cold. Unfolding it, Clef let out a small gasp. The Need was the loveliest, most repulsive thing she'd ever seen. Glimpsing a fraction of its anatomy, Clef snatched out the cloth and shook it so that the beast-husk dropped like a hand into her hand, the once-limbs falling in strange laces through her fingers. She looked up at her sister.

"What is this, Lark?"

"A Need. I mean—the husk of a Need. They're always empty like that." Lark paused, measuring. "I'm beginning to think, although I didn't before, that everyone has them. Maybe it's only that I'm capable of manifesting mine, or at least . . . their remains."

Lark had given up sleight. Not because she didn't love it—she'd loved it like a rope. Lark had given up sleight because of guilt. By the time she had been in Monk two years, she had slaughtered four times that many Needs. It didn't matter that they had hurt her—they'd been alive. It was again and again her reason.

She started off slowly, as if explaining something to her daughter Nene she wasn't even sure a child could believe. Something like God.

"I think maybe the first one chose me early on because I was so unhappy. I didn't know how unhappy until the eighth grade." Lark looked up at her sister. "Do you remember when I was in the eighth grade and Claudia Shale moved in down the street? Everyone hated her and we were best friends. We smoked cloves in the loft above the basketball gym. Friday nights, if there was a dance, she'd meet me in the parking lot and we'd swig vodka out of a copper flask before going in. Claudia said alcohol tasted better like pennies. Of course we didn't dance, just stood in the corner of the cafeteria. Being superior. Claudia lent me her entire Basque Liberation Front collection on vinyl, and some Delete." As she confessed, Lark allowed herself a smile. "I learned that I was very, very unhappy."

Clef didn't interrupt. She was intent on the grotesque in her palm, playing the fingers of her right hand above it as if to stroke it, as if it were a corn snake or a love doll. But then she didn't—uncertain of its relative frailty, substance. It was so light.

Lark denied herself the satisfaction of telling Clef that the Need wasn't really like that, that the thing obsessing her was just what a dead Need *felt* like, visually. When the Needs were alive, they were elemental—pure, shifting forms varying in size, complexity, character. But dead—Lark knew after dismantling the small corpses—except for subtle differences in color, one Need is all Needs.

Lark watched her little sister: her head down, her hair a bordello veiling the pretty monster. Clef, all caught up. Lark had expected this; she made a good living anticipating fixation. She went on.

"When the Need first came inside me, it felt impossible. Like love, maybe happiness. I could feel it behind my face, burning out fault, blemish." Lark pursed, then unpursed, her lips. "Clef, this is the thing—I couldn't tell anyone. Not you, then. Not Kitchen later on. Drew knows, but only peripherally. In high school, two years after the first one came to me, the night I killed it, I tried to tell Claudia and she stopped speaking to me. Her silence was quick and nasty—not a mistake. Yours was the same."

"You *kill* these?" The word had woken Clef from the Need in her hand—withered dragon-thing/dessicated moth; scaled wings split in four and shot through with iridescent indigo, and the body sickening, a large deflated condom, its milk-colored worm-skin trailing long, limp legs, legs with not enough structure to support what must have been the bulk of a live Need. A brief, comic image—her sister darting back and forth among Georgia pines with a butterfly net and a syringe—dislodged a nervous giggle from Clef. Then, a question.

"*How* you do kill them?"

"How?" Lark looked off, musing, as if she'd never considered the method. But she knew how. She swiveled back to Clef.

"I just make myself hate them."

———

Lark's twelve-year-old body had responded to her first Need with more pitch than she knew it had. She'd always suspected herself capable of things, but what frightened her was it was not her accomplishing them. It was Need. Her Need took her half in sleep onto her pillow and with her own hand got her off. Lark feigned disgust. Was disgusted. And her Need made Lark's sleight instructors finally take note. After struggling for years with her architectures, Lark's manipulations improved, and she had bursts of what she could only call focus. Briefly, she could summon something fierce in the sleight chamber. On occasion, even without her webs—in practice clothes—she would glimpse the mirrors only to see herself dissipate. The instructors said she was coming into her own. They'd had hooks in Clef for years, but now they talked of sending Lark to the academy.[7] With the Need, she had begun to wick. Her talent was abusing her.

Clef was barely aware of her sister. She was more interested in watching the Need for signs. She tried to imagine how Lark might've constructed it. Clef was the sister who made. Before, Lark had barely had the will to dream up. But this thing was physical, alluring. Clef looked at her sister, reassessing. Lark was more physical now. The last time they'd spoken, the night Lark had left Monk, she'd been stretched thin. Like cirrus. Clef had assumed the triangle had unraveled her—two sisters begging annihilation from the same force of nature. Clef had defended herself and Kitchen that night, but Lark had only softly spoken of her Needs. It had seemed odd at the time—an oblique, ethereal sort of anger—but it wasn't until Lark mentioned husks and wings that Clef grew worried. Still, she'd thought it was temporary. Rage and betrayal sprung into hallucination—that wouldn't last. Clef thought it could be dealt with in time. By time. But not this, not psychosis turned into cadaver. Her sister in front of her looked heavier to Clef. Or if not heavier, denser, as if the water in her body were under pressure. As if anything inside her couldn't help but drown.

Lark watched as Clef's face trembled through thought—a vulnerability her sister had learned to mask in early adolescence, though only onstage. Lark saw flicker there fear, shame, finally concern. She decided against euphemism.

[7] The academy, housed in an old brick warehouse near Emerson College, has lived quietly in that location for over eighty years. There is no sign, the building's façade unremarkable. Only locals are aware of the June influx of lithe bodies. Through the multipaned and translucent windows on the second and third floors, the students in class and in rehearsal are just beyond view from the street. If passersby could see, they might think they were witnessing a ballet or a cult, save for the presence of the architectures and the extremity of the sleightists' contortions. They would see instructors marking the margins of the chambers with long poles, driving them into the hardwood with metronomic precision, poking students whose focus has dropped to "recalibrate" them, and more rarely, passing the poles in sweeping gestures across the floor—to catch an architecture lazily manipulated and bring the entire linked structure, flesh and fiberglass, to ruin.

"Once I'm sure they're dead, I vomit up the husks."

Clef shuddered, folded the Need back into its cloth, pushed it into the box. Relieved of it, she shook her head too many times.

Lark broke the silence.

"Go ahead, call me insane. It's easier." Lark leaned forward and rubbed her ankle with both hands. "I don't like talking, but these things—she tapped the wood lightly with blue fingertips—are as much me as you are. As Nene is." Lark paused, looked to the floor. "I can't believe you don't know her."

"Listen, Lark, we need sleep. We'll talk tomorrow. You can have the left side of the bed.

"But that thing . . ." —Clef waved a blind hand toward the box— "that stays where it is."

CALLING.

West found Byrne on the beach. The beach of a lake—a big lake, but a lake. Byrne was riffing in his notebook. The odd interests walked slowly as they passed him in his folding chair with his eyes buried. For a few minutes West watched from behind, then wraithed forward and read aloud the words he could make out on the page: *disaster, starfish, crucible, pelt, stolen, end-machine, frictive, flight.*

Byrne closed his pen, slid it into his shirt pocket. He turned his notebook over and raised his face to his intercessor, his maestro. "What is it you want?"

The stranger handed him a playbill from the weekend's performance. "I'm West, director of Kepler. Might you help me with the obliteration of an oversight?"

Byrne looked beyond West's shoulder. An interval passed during which clouds felt the need to break apart. "Will there be much damage?"

West enjoyed Byrne's question before answering it. "I suppose it's possible—I've been lucky before."

———

West'd been thinking on Byrne for a month. The director of another troupe had told him about a kid doing performance art in Chicago and calling it she-ight. The director was incensed. "This kid," he said, "has never trained, is no sleightist. It's just words, a few crude mini architectures—get this: straws and tooth floss dangling from his arms—

a CD of Andean wind-sound, a rock." The director called Byrne over-educated trash. Then he called Byrne "a waste of a blackbox . . . a feck-less leech." West didn't say anything, and he didn't laugh, but he'd been thinking for a while that his art form could use a good bleed. West nosed around and found a review that called Byrne's work "a house for the irreverent and the waking: an antidote for poppies." By the time Kepler reached Chicago on tour, Byrne's show had closed, but West wasn't easily dissuaded from a prize.

If West was a proselytizer, it was with reason. The world was caving in, and West alone knew the way to reverse it. Sleight could save lives, but salvation alone was only bread. West wanted more—to offer the world more. He wanted to be out in front of it. He'd keep on changing up the structures until enough of them started dragging each other to the theater. Snake oil, movement: all the world really needed was a little removal.

West could see what was wrong—the audience was always too much at the surface of themselves. All those seeky mouths. Often, for minutes after his troupe was set onstage, West would stand at curtain's edge, eyes scanning the dark theater. He'd imagine how, if he delayed the performance long enough, they'd zeppelin. How the people would rise, hit the rafters. Go up like a matchbook. West was, admittedly, very fuck you.

It didn't take him long to convince Byrne to join his ranks. The boy was hungry. But now that he had him, West wouldn't allow Byrne's gifts to be squandered on parody, or worse: atrophy. West contacted a hand he knew had difficulty with precursors. But that hand wasn't relieved: he was insulted, hung up. One after another, seven hands slammed down the proposition. By the last, West's voice was starchy with his particular brand of persuasion. His own grand-mother, Fern Early, a respected sleightist—one of the few female artistic directors of sleight's recent history—had pushed West to become a hand. He couldn't do it. Though untrainable as a sleightist, he didn't want to study the documents either; he thought the history[8] too cloaked in myth, and more to the point, irrelevant. Nevertheless, in his early twenties he had studied, hard, eventually drawing and producing two mediocre sleights. But it was his highly involved approach to seeing them navigated that convinced Fern to first apprentice him, then leave him the troupe when she retired. He'd never drawn, nor wanted to, again.

West thought of the hands that Kepler commissioned—pinched, dry boys in their libraries scouring books and films, few of them ever at performances but always clamoring for video. Addicts, but to what? West hadn't seen or produced a remarkable sleight in over a decade. He had to get one for Byrne. For Kepler. And he wanted it navigated before their European tour. At the pit of him West felt, as he always did with a new idea, that death—the same white-booted white man on a white horse always—was riding toward him, trying to snatch the baby from his arms.

Byrne soon found himself in York, Pennsylvania—a working-class town that had, for nine brief months in 1777 and 1778, served as the first capital of the United States of America. While on a mission for jerky his second day there, Byrne read at least six plaques that told him so. He also saw one of his billboards mounted on top of an old

[8] In 1628, on the island of Santo Domingo, a French Jesuit named Pierre Revoix discovered a bundle of parchment secreted in a wall of his mission. These papers each detailed a series of theoretical structures, but none of them seemed to have been drawn by the same hand. In fact, the words on the hundred or so original documents were written in at least eight languages, among them Russian, Swedish, and Arabic. Revoix sent the documents back to Europe where they were copied and translated by members of his order. Only the copies survive. Revoix's journal of his life in the New World chronicles his intense interest in the papers he never saw again. He died in 1642 of fever. Recent academic theses have posthumously characterized him as a schizophrenic who almost certainly forged the structures himself. His notebooks show a Revoix who, though clearly trained as a linguist, also considered himself an amateur mathematician. But a deeper personal history—what called him to the Society of Jesus—has proved unrecoverable.

drugstore. Since meeting the driven and doubtless West, Byrne had begun to think of things as his that he never would've claimed before. The birthing of the nation as atrocity—the idea pleased him. He stopped to jot down a few words, among them: *mine, barrow, compact, hapless pursuit, esquire, shunt, gun, game, faithless, horde, species*. York was now, Kepler's director explained to Byrne on the third day as they ate three-dollar omelets at a hole-in-the-wall called Jersey's, plagued with failing schools, de facto segregation, outlying rural poverty, and an inordinate amount of designer drug traffic out of New York.

Kepler's studios were unbelievable—two stories high with skylights and sprung floors. Industrial meadows, they were full of ambient light, kinetic potential. Byrne had stood in the center of one of the chambers the day they first arrived, windmilling. Trying to create with his two arms and the momentum of his heavy hand something out of the vibrant nothing floating there. Byrne had never been inside a sleight chamber before, but he knew the ones in Chicago couldn't be as spacious, crowded as they were into church basements and old office buildings.

West told Byrne that Kepler's corporate sponsor had purchased the old cannery and converted it for a song. "Cheap space, cheap labor, it's why we're in York."

Byrne asked, "Which song?"

West thought for a moment. "It might have been 'Ode to Joy'— that, or 'Green Door.'"

"But not 'Don't Think Twice, It's All Right'?" asked Byrne.

West responded, coldly, "That's not how the business end is run." West's playful streaks, Byrne noted, had short lives.

When West wasn't around, he encouraged Byrne to talk to the sleightists, to mess around with an architecture or two, provided he was supervised. Byrne was, and did. He'd never had a Christmas like this one. His mother had spent teary, listless winters hating the trees. His father thought it irresponsible to give children what they wanted. At least Byrne, being older, had gotten new things. Marvel had received

Byrne's old toys, rewrapped. How strange, Byrne thought, how predictable, that eight years after his father's death, at the end of summer in a town that smelled like farm, Christmas had found and started rubbing up against him.

West, it seemed, was negotiating with the academy to get hold of one of the incomplete original documents: mere thumbnails of structures—not enough for whole sleights, and no accompanying precursors. Troupes had worked with them before, unsuccessfully, and hands were given one of them as an exercise at the end of their training. It was a negative lesson: to prove that compositional collaboration in sleight fails. The transitions between the hastily delineated structures were nearly impossible for all but the most fluid sleightists. In addition, these incompletes required the old blown-glass architectures. The one thing they seemed to have going for them was sound.[9] Byrne wasn't certain what West expected him to do if they managed to acquire one, but until then, he was going to enjoy his time. There was nothing to do in York but fool around like a child in the chambers, and then one by one with the very receptive and undemanding sleightists of Kepler.

———————

Over the four weeks they spent rehearsing, Byrne got a feel for Kepler's director. West was tall and gaunt and randy as any preacher. But he never seemed to have sex, at least not sex that got around the troupe, which bothered Byrne since West's energy fluctuations were unmistakable. Byrne wanted to know how, and more precisely with

[9] The music sleight evokes borders on the natural. Fast-moving architectures make approximations of birdcalls, or of the wind over wheat. Slower manipulations can mimic the hollow, charged air of the few remaining old-growth forests, or gustless snowfall in higher altitudes. Even sleightists' webs, crocheted from heavy metallic threads into patterns that hold mirror fragments in bodily eye-hives, contribute to the soundscape. A sudden cessation of movement by all twelve members of a troupe can paint a breaking wave, or the collapse of a doe beneath gunshot.

whom, West regathered focus. But the director was a model of non-disclosure and a certain type of restraint. He was quiet in most rehearsals. Even when he jumped up to run full-force at one of the sleightists to speed up a manipulation or a link, he never yelled at the members of his troupe. He screamed often otherwise: on the phone with the sponsor, with tour venues in France and Germany (in both French and German), at the two interns, at Byrne. But there was something nonthreatening in his raised voice, as if that wasn't the West to worry about. The calm West—that was the eel.

Because Byrne knew nothing of structures, West had been handling the navigation of the retrograde. He'd gotten permission to use an incomplete as a training tool, but not to perform it. So West decided to conform to the letter of the law and fugue the thing, torque it beyond recognition. So few were familiar with it in document form, he told Byrne, no one would be able to identify this particular order, especially if it were not only reversed but attenuated to fill an evening.

"But Byrne," West said, "you will need to find out why."

"Why what?" Byrne was often lost with West, but not unhappily. He was Gretel, brotherstruck.

"Why this sleight could not be made whole until this moment—backwards, slowly, with you writing its precursor."

Byrne flashed to breadcrumbs. He remembered it was birds who insisted that the children going home would finish the story too soon, before the fattening—before the arrival of Gretel's capacity to murder.

RECOVERY.

In the recovery room, they gave Clef an electric blanket for her abdomen. It was pink. They hadn't let Lark in during the procedure, but afterwards she walked into the room, droning with awful, soothing Mozart, and a row of girls—most with eyes closed—in vinyl recliners. She moved quietly over to her sister and handed her the orange drink in a plastic cup from the table beside her. She said she wanted to tell Clef the secrets of her birth.

"I was five, and there was a cardinal on the back gate near the day lilies. Red in the orange. I never fed cardinals, only jays. They were meaner, but I liked that their blue meant they could hide in the sky. I knew I was going to hate you because you came early, before my room was painted. They didn't bring you home at first—you couldn't cry right. Jillian had to rinse your eyes with a yellow bulb. I was the one who taught you to cry—how and what about. I only wish I had an old camera so you could see yourself. It'd have to be an old one. The grain lets you think you felt a thing—but hurt isn't lived. It's passed hand to hand until it goes . . . like soap."

Clef held the cup with both hands and took small sips while her sister spoke. Her forehead was a little sweaty, and a wisp of red hair curled just at the center, as if she had been horrid.

When they got back to the apartment, there were white roses from Kitchen.

"You know he knows that's death," Clef said.

Lark felt a shock of understanding that was sharper than the cramps she was also suffering. She didn't want to say anything more, but she did say.

"He's trying to acknowledge something lost, Clef."

"Like love?" Clef came back with this quick, more herself than earlier in the day. This time Lark didn't say, but went to cut the stems and find a vase. She hoped Clef still had the unsentimental one she'd bought for her in Oslo, the cobalt blue.

IN BRIEF: "POLAND"

BY GABE THIESSEN, ASSOCIATED PRESS
OCTOBER 2000, 12:43 GMT

LVOV (AP) —— In Lvov this weekend, Kepler performed a new work entitled *Poland*. Let me first say, *Poland* is most remarkable in its brevity. Although a full-length sleight—the customary three hours—*Poland* moves so slowly, sped up it might be performed in half that time. The beauty of the pacing is that the architectures seem to extend just beyond themselves before evolving into unpredicted forms. It's as if *Poland* threatens to pull apart at its borders, but then collapses back at the last possible moment into an exquisite contortion of its former self. Despite my misgivings about *Poland*'s elasticity and the unorthodox use of the precursor as accompaniment, there is no doubt that Kepler is a. technically masterful troupe and that the creator of *Poland,* a young hand Artistic Director West refuses to name to the press, is talented. The precursor, strung throughout the piece as it is—Kepler's trademark— is astonishingly subtle and seems at home inside the low architectural wind. Because of its lack of dynamics, at least in terms of speed, West must have felt it necessary to use the more resonant traditional instruments. However, their effect is haunting in a way that he could not have anticipated. *Poland* has a voice like black smoke, could it withdraw itself from the lungs of birds, could it return itself to the stack. My initial questions about its less-conventional elements are moot. I joined the audience in Lvov in giving Kepler a silent ovation—sleight's highest praise, and one rarely proffered in Eastern Europe.

When they first arrived in London, the last stop on the sold-out three-week tour, West immediately sent Byrne out to talk with two hands, a matched set who roomed together in Oxford. He arranged for them to meet Byrne at the train station and take him to a pub for mild illumination. West, thrilled with Byrne's first success—knowing, as the audience could not, that it was his precursor that had made the sleight—knew also that Kepler wouldn't be able to continue working with the incompletes. Besides, West wanted Byrne to find a partner. Neither of these two would be it, West knew, but Byrne had never met a hand. They took practice.

BYRNE: So, you two draw?

HAND 1: The boy is stunning.

HAND 2: I draw. He wanks.

HAND 1: Shut it, Leo.

BYRNE: I'm curious, when you sit down to do it—what do you think about?

HAND 1: Nothing. The mind must be cleared of refuse.

HAND 2: Easy for you since your mind is a void.

HAND 1: Come off it. My structures are just as complex as yours.

HAND 2: But they aren't well-reasoned, and they have no arc. Now—for weeks, months, before I sit down to actually draw, I've been making notes, thinking through transitions. My sleights have balance and composition. They're coherent.

HAND 1: No, they're not. Coherence comes from a moral center. I research. I read, I watch as much film, I'm at the microscope and the telescope and the needles as often as you are. I work in the garden and I'm better in the kitchen, particularly with Indian. But then, when it's time to draw, I empty my mind.

That is how one gets to a sleight. Yours are overdetermined, artificial. Yours are *clever.*

HAND 2: I'd rather they were clever than totally fragmented. You're self-indulgent and melodramatic, and so is your work.

BYRNE: I've never heard a sleight called melodramatic before. Wouldn't there have to be emotional content for that?

HAND 2: The audience can't see emotion because they watch the sleightists for it. And if the performers aren't well-trained enough to suppress their own, then one can't get underneath the thing, can one? The emotion lives in the structure. Clearly you don't understand the structure. Hardly any of the audience does—they aren't meant to—but what they do understand is intensity. They understand presence.

BYRNE: Isn't sleight about absence?

HAND 2: Oh, child.

HAND 1: Leo, there is no need for condescension—although *that* at least you're good at. And you aren't being accurate. It isn't emotion that's present. Sleight accesses something beyond both emotion and reason, which is why yours always fail. And don't abuse our guest, even the sleightists think it's about absence.

HAND 2: You're a prick.

HAND 1: I'm a prick?

BYRNE: What is it that's beyond emotion and reason?

HAND 1: Sorry, what?

BYRNE: You said they access something beyond emotion and reason. What's beyond?

HAND 1: You think we know?

HAND 2: Oh that's rich.

BYRNE: So you don't know. What exactly is it you guys do for a living?

HAND 1: It's more of a calling, actually.

HAND 2: We draw structures within a given set of limitations . . .

HAND 1: . . . what the sleightists are capable of, which architectures the troupe we're working for has trained with . . .

HAND 2: . . . and we bring all the figures we have personally and painstakingly harvested from the approved sources . . .

HAND 1: . . . which are expanding all the time . . .

HAND 2: . . . and which you take advantage of too often . . .

HAND 1: . . . and we set them down in their most significant order.

BYRNE: And that's a sleight?

HAND 2: Not yet.

HAND 1: It isn't a sleight until we drop in a precursor and it's navigated.

HAND 2: We aren't involved in that.

BYRNE: I thought you wrote the precursors.

HAND 1: Oh yes, those.

HAND 2: But we don't navigate.

BYRNE: Why not?

HAND 2: It just isn't done.

HAND 1: What Leo is trying to say is that it so often ruins all our work. We can't stand to be there.

BYRNE: So why give your work to the sleightists if they kill it?

HAND 2: We didn't say kill. We said ruin. Entirely different. I can't believe . . . is he really asking this?

HAND 1: I believe he is.

HAND 2: Because without the sleightists, sleights wouldn't exist.

HAND 1: They'd be documents.

HAND 2: Akin to the original copies, which lay two hundred years unnavigated, two hundred years dormant. Did you know, for a brief time they were here in England?[10] But no one knew how to value them. They were mere oddities.

HAND 1: And then we really would be wanking, wouldn't we? Thinking what we'd done was worthy of renaissance.

HAND 2: Resurrection.

BYRNE: But you do think that.

HAND 2: Sleight is the healthiest performance art on the planet. It has the largest audience, it's only somewhat co-opted by the sponsors . . .

HAND 1: I don't think they can quite figure out how to do it completely.

HAND 2: . . . the performers are the most highly trained, the troupes have as devoted a following as in football, and you're suggesting that we should refuse to participate because . . .

HAND 1: . . . we have some misguided sense of our own product as, what, pure?

BYRNE: Don't you?

HAND 1: Listen. Your father taught you everything you know. He loved you and he raised you. But he banged your mother and slapped you around a bit. He put food in your mouth and his foot up your arse. Did you ever hate him?

BYRNE: Every day.

HAND 1: But you never did kill him, did you?

[10] In the early eighteenth century, the copies of Revoix's documents made it into the hands of a Mrs. Esther Planck, an English widow who, after inheriting her husband's Wunderkammer—a curiosity cabinet with a great number of anatomical specimens—decided to display them in the Bloomsbury district of London, supplementing her meager pension with donations. A number of medical students record viewing the documents in this location. In various writings, they express bewilderment at the structures, some of which uncannily resemble materials they were viewing beneath a newly acquired instrument at the university: one of Leeuwenhoek's expertly ground microscopic lenses.

boy motionless :: boy unbemoved :: boy paralyzed :: newest ::
directionleast :: boy pensive :: boy spiral :: boysnail :: boy
undistinguished, unserial :: boy unboy :: madboywoman :: boy,
madwoman-desirous :: directiondesirous :: firecrackerboy—
firecracker-desirous :: boy-dud :: boy-slowlight, boy dogstar ::
boy glacial :: boybeing :: beboy :: bop

PILGRIMAGE.

Philadelphia. A day trip. Byrne would rent a car, drive through Amish country, take some pictures. Then Philadelphia. York was wearing thin. Actually, Byrne had only been back two days. Maybe Kepler was wearing thin. West hadn't bothered to return with the troupe; he'd stayed on in Manhattan after the flight. Business. Although everyone was technically on break, half the sleightists lived in York and were in and out of the studios, impossible to avoid. Extraordinary things had to be done for them stay fit: yoga, Pilates, aikido, ballet, contact improv, swimming, and—for at least one of them—tantric sex. Byrne was no athlete. He hadn't thought he was in lousy shape a few months ago, but he now knew that by sleightists' standards, his flexibility and stamina were nonexistent.

"Whatchya thinking, Byrne?"

This was T. T mumbled prayers over roadkill and had a face like a meadow. T's body lacked almost all swerve, was thinner from the side than from front or back. This was the result of the broad-shoulders-for-my-frame she frequently bemoaned. And T hated the taste of beef jerky.

"I'm thinking of leaving."

T's mouth popped into an *o*, a child realizing the Halloween candy has run out. Byrne reassured her.

"Not forever. For a few days."

T's face undid itself. "Good." She tried to look stern. T could only partly accomplish this, and only by placing her hands on her hips. "Byrne, you worry me," she said. "The way you say things."

"Don't be worried. How could I leave?"

T shook her head side to side, eyes wide in enthusiastic agreement. "No. How could you leave?"

Byrne at first had adored tour—watching from the wings as the sleightists eclipsed their own best work. And on the nights they performed *Poland,* he'd actually been onstage, suspended invisibly in black from black ropes, uttering at jagged intervals the words of the precursor. He was high up and not lit; the audience couldn't watch him watching them, couldn't see the trembling thighs entwined in oily hemp, the mouthing of the disembodied words. To them the language was a haunting, arriving from the structure raw, but sourceless. After a while, Byrne couldn't imagine his slow-motion scat without the structures below. It was beyond vertigo, this staring into sea.

But it felt wrong too. As if they were all just masks with nothing behind, or else wreckage. The sleightists moved slowly, but for Byrne there was no movement at all. *Poland* was not *Poland*—it was Easter Island. His rock bled into the joints of his left hand. He was dumb, although the words came and hung in front of him like nooses. He tried to offer the audience this same terrible stillness. And they somehow took it, and somehow they wore it, in the end, remarkably, finding breath. Byrne thought, *They shouldn't be able to breathe.*

On the opening night of *Poland,* Byrne had been scared. Once the curtains descended and his ropes were lowered, he bolted from the stage, barely taking time to leave his black face in a white towel before running out to the lobby where they all stood around—unmarred. Discussing it even. When he couldn't take it, had to go out for air, they were there too, hailing cabs with ringed fingers. How could they be there as if they hadn't been there? Byrne was even more shocked at how, for the sleightists, this was rote. "What is experienced at a sleight," West told him, "doesn't carry over." Sleight's addictive nature was tied to this, as were some sleightists' bouts with melancholy. West said these things as if he regretted them. Byrne's stomach was a graveyard. He'd adored tour. But did he also loathe? He did—and mostly West, for articulating this lack of weight. Their tracelessness.

Byrne wanted to get away. Not from the art exactly, but from the other practitioners, the disciplined and the unquestioning—T & Co. From people. He could best accomplish that in a city. He'd made the arrangements that morning. He chose Philadelphia because it was close, West wasn't there, and the two hands in Oxford had told him to go—it was the birthplace of sleight.[11] Philadelphia was also where Byrne's mother said Marvel had gone once he'd left Atlantic City. That had been after Detroit, which had been after Milwaukee and nearly a year ago. Byrne assumed it would be Marvel's last stop: his mother on the phone the night before—*couldn't you please check in on your brother just this once . . . not such a terrible inconvenience, is it?*—had been, even as she nagged, unable to apply her usual pale gloss of hope.

T's eyebrows were knitting. "Whatchya thinking, Byrne?"

"I'm thinking maybe I have time to go back to your place for a few hours. Game?"

T grinned, her meadow bright. As a rule, T didn't do melancholy. She clasped her hands behind her back and leaned forward, audibly releasing the zippered tension from her spine. She stood up. She teased.

"Why Byrne, have you been practicing?"

———

Byrne walked up the too many stairs. It had been a hike in cold almost-rain, and now someone wanted him to be Rocky. He didn't even want

[11] After traveling in and out of oddity collections across Europe, in 1892 most of the document copies were sold to a protomuseum in Philadelphia. It is there they were found and navigated into performance by Antonia Bugliesi, once a student of Marie Taglioni—the first ballerina to have stood en pointe. Charles Dodd, a Philadelphia merchant, owner of the documents, and lover of Antonia, built her a small theater adjacent to his museum, allowing her to maintain its artistic direction. He required only that the performers dress provocatively enough to ensure both a profit and his continuing interest.

to see art. He wanted a security guard. He wanted to ask about his brother and be done with it. Duty. When he finally got inside and paid the obliged donation—more stairs. He didn't start for them, but looked. Halfway up those stairs, a naked giantess was wielding an implement of death. A Diana. Furious modesty flaunting its stone skin. Byrne turned away. To his right stood a guard. Finally, a piece of luck.

"Excuse me, miss. I'm trying to find my brother."

"This'n't no lost and found."

Ah, this was just perfect. Byrne paused, and when he spoke his tone remained even, respectful.

"My brother, he loves museums, but he's . . . he's a junkie. He's probably been showing up here once or twice a month for six months or so. Maybe you've had to kick him out for disturbing patrons?"

"Oh, him. Yeah, I know him. Marvelous, right?"

"Marvel."

"He's a smart one. Knows his art. So, you looking for him? Let me see." The guard paused. "Maybe it was he hangs on South Street—that the kids treat him all right there. Yeah . . . I think that was it."

"Great. Thank you." Byrne almost left, then thought to ask another. "Is that all you know about him?"

"I know he does sketch. I've seen him watching the shadow people. In the museum they can get pretty bad, coming out of the corners like they do."

"Well." Byrne stood for a second, blank. "Thank you."

"Nothing to thank. You hold that rock for a reason?"

Byrne glanced down. People didn't usually ask. Usually, the question that hung thick in the air for hours or days or weeks was popped just before the sex, if at all. Sometimes the question, or its answer, put a real damper on the afternoon. Rarely did a stranger come out with it. Byrne slowly lifted his arm so that the rock nearly grazed the dark sleeve of the guard's uniform. They were that close. Byrne looked into her face for the first time. She was no prize.

"It's a sort of promise. Like . . . my word, I guess."

She smiled. An older sister's smile, Byrne thought, though he'd never had one. He was cowed. How did some women do that? Why was he never attracted to them?

"Needs proof that heavy . . . hmm." Still smiling, the guard turned away—first heading for the stairs, then up them toward the stiff woman with the drawn bow. Byrne noticed then that the Diana was balanced precariously atop a small sphere on one foot. Her arrow could never fly without her being brought down by the wrath she let go. By the time the guard reached the statue, Byrne was gone.

———

Walking through Philadelphia's Italian Market, off South Street, Byrne neared the black and red char of a spitted pig in an open storefront. He quickly reset his course, dropping down a side street to escape the immensity of spiced flesh he so adored in desiccated stick form. Embarrassed, he consoled himself: jerky was sterile and not from a pig. Byrne was still vaguely nauseated when he saw Marvel sitting on the far curb smoking a cigarette. Byrne wasn't surprised to see him. Coincidence was an illusion caused by proximity, and he'd worked hard to produce this nearness. Marvel, though managing to be alive, was spare—a stray girl huddled against the lean-to of him. His flannel shirt was faded, a red that couldn't seem to announce itself against the weather. Byrne didn't call to him.

"Byrne," Marvel said finally, handing the girl his smoke. He'd been staring from underneath loose curls across the narrow street at Byrne for over a minute. It may have taken him that long to place his brother's face.

Byrne crossed the alleyway.

"Byrne, this is my girl." He put an arm around the sleeveless, dark-haired shiver. Byrne thought about mentioning it was October, decided against it. A black, outsized crucifix swung between her negligible breasts.

"Hello," said Byrne, but he didn't have her name. Possibly, Marvel didn't have it either.

"Byrne is my brother." Marvel didn't seem to be saying it to her. "Aren't you, Byrne?" Byrne nodded. Marvel stood and pulled up the little breather. She was alternating between puff and fidget, unhappy, Byrne thought, to have been made to unfold.

"What can I do for you, my brother?" Marvel asked. If Byrne had needed a place to stay, Marvel would have offered up a corner of the laundry room in which better-placed junkie friends had been letting him crash.

"I'm fine."

"How's Mom then?" As a child Marvel had gotten their mother handled, sometimes brutally. He never failed to ask after her.

"She's fine. You been to the museum lately?"

"Yeah. But this one doesn't have enough Rothkos." When Byrne offered no sign of recognition, Marvel continued. "You know the ones, ten-foot slabs of orange on red, the breathers . . ." Marvel trailed off, his eyes looking somewhere—maybe somewhere warm.

"I guess."

Marvel refocused, fixing on his brother's face. "Not an easy thing for you—breathing?"

Byrne shrugged.

"I see you still have my rock." The girl's eyes shot up then, suggesting a first interest in the conversation.

"Someone has to carry it."

"Oh, I'm carrying it." Marvel grabbed the girl's ass. "Don't I carry my own rock, Ellie?" So he did have her name. Ellie cringed. Then, deciding something, she slapped his hand away and headed off down the alley with his cigarette. Marvel watched her go, shaking the sting from his wrist, grinning. He said to Byrne, "You should know by now there's more ways to carry it than in your hand."

"Our hands."

"Yeah. You go ahead." Marvel was revving some engine. "You *tell* me why they shouldn't be free."

Byrne hadn't shown up to be accused of responsibility. He volleyed. "Free to do what? You free, Marvel?"

"Hell yeah I'm free." Marvel ceremoniously lifted his arms, palms upturned, and started skip-stomping out a circle. A child's war-dance or rain-prayer, the movement had a certain flailing grace. Marvel's boots flung up oil and water from the street in dirty benediction. Byrne began to soften then, thinking, Some fifteen-year-old some-where—some future sleightist—is dropping acid for the first time, and she's seeing this. He almost laughed.

Marvel, meanwhile, was yawping into the drizzle. "I'm a shooting star. I fucking fly. I'm. Fuck. Ing. Fly. Ying." He spun and spun, obscenity swirling around him like cotton candy: no good for you, ill-colored, ache-sweet.

"It's not flying, it's falling." Byrne meant to mouth this, to quietly release his sarcasm into the air without bite—he wasn't angry anymore. He was, as always, a little dizzy from his brother's direction-less momentum. But Marvel was sober for Marvel, and hearing, quickly landed his pirouette. He looked with a strange pity at Byrne, as if his older brother were slow, or on something that was making him slow.

"It's not falling until the very end, my brother. Not until I taste the ground."

Marvel had been golden once. Marvel had done all that was wanted. Marvel had informed on his mother and kept Byrne in line with father-threats. Marvel, by age eleven, could take apart and put back together a '74 Mustang carburetor in under three hours. Marvel reviled sleight, lived for color. And in spite—or because—of her occasional and embarrassingly typical bruises, their mother loved Marvel with an effort that made the love enviable.

After Marvel effectively put an end to matinees at the theater, the art museum was the refuge of the mismatched trio. It was always just the three of them—there was no extended family, no chatty, cheek-pinching aunts to duck. Byrne sometimes wished there had been. Twice a week all summer long, once school was out, she'd take them on the bus into Milwaukee. Byrne's father was at work; the museum lobby was free and air-conditioned, and only rarely were they approached by an apologetic docent and asked to either enter or leave. On those occasions they'd hang out at the edge of the lake, Marvel whipping rocks at gulls, Byrne writing his name back and forth across the sand with a stick. Sometimes, their mother would have money for admission to the museum proper. Byrne often brought books, but Marvel could sit inside the same painting for an hour or more. Byrne couldn't remember what his mother did. Disappear into the art like Marvel? Nap upright on a far bench? He remembered how exhaustion strung her out like paper dolls—how thinly she held onto herself, to imitations of herself. Maybe she went to the restroom to cry noiselessly, like at the dishes. If so, she would've reapplied her makeup before coming out. She was always remarkably put together, considering. Her husband worked six days a week as a laundryman at the veterans' hospital, plus Saturdays at a friend's garage to get them by, to meet their ends. Didn't she have lip gloss that smelled like apricots? Byrne thought he remembered that.

Their father knew they sometimes went—the museum wasn't forbidden, not like sleight. He'd gone himself, once or twice. There were things he'd done for her. Rare, small things. Byrne remembered his father had liked the illustrators Wyeth and Remington. Even the room with the Hopper was okay because you could see what he meant. Byrne would've liked to ridicule this, but Gil's need for meaning had never seemed ridiculous to Byrne. His father cohered, having amputated the parts of himself that bled beyond the frame. Why shouldn't he expect the same from art? Others? And because his father's faults accrued with this truncated sort of logic, Byrne's hatred of him had always remained clean. Surgical.

His mother Byrne hated with less precision. The last time Byrne had been to visit her, at her suggestion they'd gone to the newly constructed monstrosity at the museum, and he'd worked to tune her out as she spoke not of his father's death or Byrne's own subsequent aimlessness, but of his brother's untapped promise. Under the great vault and spine of Windhover Hall, Byrne had felt that he was inside the ribcage of a massive leviathan, an ancient creature washed up dead and fleshless out of the bowels of Lake Michigan. Failing to be uplifted by white columns or the vertical thrust of the hall's backbone, he dwelled instead on how the opening of the brise-soleil, the structure above the building so reminiscent of a whale's tail just before a long submersion, left those inside both exposed—and trapped.

His mother had once given him words and Marvel color. She hadn't been projecting her own artistic nature—she'd never shown any evidence of a nature. She'd moved them through realms banned by and merely unnerving to their father. But for what? She told her two boys over and over how extraordinary they were, until that—along with the statement, *I don't believe anymore,* which Byrne had heard her say once in hushed vehemence over the phone—became to him the mantras of her identity. And his. Byrne's mother had given birth to extraordinary sons. And he didn't believe anymore.

Even when Marvel started going terribly wrong—soon after Gil's death—she would only say, "Your brother is not of the usual stuff, Byrne. He can't be held up to the usual mirrors." And when Byrne asked, "Mom, what other mirrors are there?" she'd answered, "Oh— glass at night, and tinfoil. And some people are. They're walking knives—you can see yourself in them, but you're cut up."

———————

The Theater of Geometry was a shabby one-story near the river. Its bijou was grimy and the graying varnish on its doors was cracking where it wasn't worn through. Byrne first noted the dilapidation, then turned a loose brass knob, walked in. An information desk sat in the center of a small lobby with a water-stained parquet floor. No one was there. On the desk were a few brochures—local attractions, two area sleight schools, some others—Byrne picked up the nonglossy one with the eyestraining font. He read its brief synopsis before entering the theater. It was succinctly put, if a bit irregular.[12]

The house wasn't lit, but the stage was. Byrne found himself a seat in the near-black of the second to last row. He looked down into the space—*there is a funeral here, a funeral for a church.* Byrne closed his eyes and took in the dust and the draft, things without scent that nonetheless trigger memory by moving through the sinus cavities. Byrne found himself remembering not the performances he'd seen as a child but winter in his attic room—hiding out with a book or a pen on the chill slice of floor between his and Marvel's twin beds. The room had proved an inadequate space for his mind. Like any theater.

[12] "Sleight is pure, a truly Western art form. Its seminal materials coalesced in the mind of one disturbed but blessed individual, the Jesuit brother Pierre Revoix, during his tenure at St. Magdalene's mission in Santo Domingo in the late seventeenth century. No other art form can claim such singular beginnings. No other art was created in such divine, misguided mist. Revoix wrote in his journal that 'these papers have great import, they weigh deeply into the crevices of my hands, but I cannot fathom them. . . .' Although he was author of the original structures and precursors, some psychological—possibly spiritual—impediment kept Revoix from disclosing their meanings for posterity, from even recognizing them as his own. Only translated copies of the original documents survived him, patiently making their way throughout Europe during the two centuries after his ultimate dementia and death. It was not until the papers reached Philadelphia, Antonia Bugliesi, and her Theater of Geometry—that sleight bore its fruit. Under Bugliesi's able direction, sleight attained its current bodily and theatrical incarnation. How she came to lift geometric forms from the page and set them on a group of novices training in ballet and acrobatics is unknown. How and by whom she had the first architectures fashioned is open to debate: a local glassblower named Cullen has been suggested (see area map); alternately, one of her students may have apprenticed in the trade. On the stage some of the original architectures (absent intestinal matter) are displayed, alongside webs (designed and executed by an anonymous but visionary tattress) and copies of the original document copies. Please honor these items as well as the prints lining the backstage walls. Recent vandalism has destroyed some of our most valuable objects. Your donations are appreciated."

Byrne stood and made his way down the central aisle. Not immediately seeing stairs, he threw his leg up and vaulted onto the lip of the proscenium, knocking a few footlights out of focus in the process. Screw the funeral. On the stage were three long glass cases, variously filled with the elements of sleight. Architectures. Costumes. Documents. Folded-over index cards with typewritten descriptions identified each item.

An architecture used in the sleightwork CARAPACE, first navigated in 1896. Color in the glass comes from the incorporation of iron and copper chlorides during the glassblowing process. The use of pigmentation was discontinued during World War I. A needlessly extravagant practice for minimal and tawdry effect, it was never reinstated.

Web worn by Agatha Spalding, founding member of the THEATER OF GEOMETRY and later, the first artistic director of BÖHME. The mirrors in older costumes were shattered and sanded down by the sleightists themselves in a charitable effort to withhold misfortune from the troupe lacemaker.

Accoutrements to Miss Spalding's web. A flesh-colored leotard and underlay. Modern performers wear nothing beneath their webs, claiming extra garments constrict. In the late nineteenth and early twentieth centuries, as today, the costumes were not specific to individual works, and so were worn repeatedly. Undergarments helped to maintain decency while minimizing the need to launder, and thus ruin, the intricate tatting.

A page from a Miss Spalding's diary. Professional diaries such as this one were kept by many of the founding members of the THEATER OF GEOMETRY at Antonia Bugliesi's behest.

A ticket from a sleight performance circa 1892. Within a decade of its founding, the THEATER OF GEOMETRY was attraction enough to draw private coaches from New York one Saturday afternoon each month, depositing their gentlemen back in Manhattan the following evening. According to the preserved correspondence between the Hon. Louis A. Lumadue and his brother Philip, the men returned from Philadelphia both morally intact and "unquestionably edified."

Three pages duplicated from the fifty-seven-page document copy for MUSIC 2, one of Revoix's original structures. Due to copyright regulations and in deference to their ineffable nature, these pages are partial (the precursor has been removed) and nonconsecutive.

Please Note: All of Miss Spalding's paraphernalia has been donated by her great-great-grandniece, Mrs. Johann Bauer of Bauer's Pretzel Emporium. We are indebted.

Byrne read these, and the rest. Agatha Spalding's uninspired prose seemed to consist entirely of one night's missteps due to "a nagging bladder that may require Miss Eugenia's nightshade-elixir and a week's bed rest." He was trying to avoid growing thoughts of Marvel, left on a curb similar to the one where Byrne had found him. They had ended up walking to a bodega together. Byrne had gotten his brother some smokes. There had been a hug. Marvel wouldn't take cash. He'd said he didn't want to compromise his brother, Mr. Rock Steady, and had launched into some ska backbeat. Byrne figured his brother must have had enough speed for the night, or maybe the week, to be so magnanimous. Byrne had left Marvel that afternoon feeling unsatisfied, bitter, tightfisted—and headed back toward the skewered pig.

Save for the scrape of Byrne's boots as he moved along the length of the glass coffins, the theater was dead, and dry. His throat hurt. Byrne coughed. He tucked Marvel into a less insistent part of his consciousness and walked backstage. Photographs lined the walls, but the light was dimmer. No matter, no captions to peruse. And no performance shots, of course. It was against sleight custom. The ones people managed to snap unofficially didn't capture much. An odd lighting effect was occasionally in evidence, but no sleightist seemed capable of truly inhabiting a photograph; the camera seemed always to be pointed in the wrong direction.

The prints on these black walls were more formal portraits of early sleightists: one seated on a high-backed wicker chair in front of a potted palm, ankles primly crossed; one standing at a backstage door in a long coat left self-consciously unbuttoned to reveal a flash of web; a male sleightist posed in taut arabesque, an architecture suspended between his right hand and flexed left foot. There was a filmy portrait of a woman Byrne could only assume was Antonia Bugliesi herself. He was held, for a moment, by the intelligent face—its large eyes unusually wide and dark, maybe impossibly so.

Byrne pulled out a small camera to lessen the sudden onslaught of nakedness: *what eyes she had*. He preferred the spy feel—Byrne unknown. He took his third one-handed photograph of the trip. The first: a blond and blushing Amish or Mennonite girl in Lancaster, her braided head lowered, a billboard in the distance. The second: a butcher (mistaken in his perception that this tourist was about to buy a side of pork) jovially presenting the rendered corpse that had a few hours earlier sent Byrne down the alley to Marvel. The third: the portrait of Antonia hanging beside another photograph, that of a fop (handlebar mustache) amid a chorus line of female sleightists, arms so tight around the two on either side of him that their smiles seem forced, pained by the pressure of his cupped fingers on their hipbones.

whisper-prey :: hold shade-cradle chase-cache :: mouthwork ::
lick :: color-warp waft withering :: gardenia-cum-rottedworm
:: purchased for/from——some/one :: charming nondisplay ::
only-thing-you-can't-connect :: only-connect :: only-can't
:: you——thing

SOUL.

Lark picked up a knot. Drew's participation in her craft was limited to this: he and Nene scavenged for fallen branches in the woods behind the house Lark had grown up in. They brought home the trees' deformities, tumors or abnormal sites of twist, dried them in the attic, eventually sanding them into silken cups with angry grains—evidence of the violent seasonal winds that had brought them down. More of these lined the house's bookshelves than Lark would ever use. She examined the one in her hand. It was from a sugar maple—a bird's-eye pattern dappled the knot. Drew had brought it to her almost four years ago; he had been carrying Nene in a sling, and when he tried to pull the gnarl out from beside her, she'd clung to it. Lark placed it on the oversized desk—once her mother's—where more than forty baby-food jars sat, vivid with cool-hued crystals. She opened the box Clef had refused to keep.

The night before, when Drew and Nene had picked her up at the airport, she'd looked at her daughter and felt it. She had been gone sixteen days; Nene had missed her gravely, was angry, was older. Lark spent the drive home atoning, telling Nene about her Aunt Clef, asking her about pre-k and the books she'd taken out from the library, about the two minor hurricanes her mother had missed. It hadn't worked. Nene was too quiet, and Lark, desperate, pulled out the box. She showed the Need to her daughter. Nene perked up. She wanted to hold it and Lark let her. After examining it with the grace of hands that have no agenda, Nene asked, "Mommy—why do yours hurt?"

That night, Lark put the box in the freezer, and in the morning the Need was ready for disassembly. She gingerly set the now brittle and painfully cold Need on the large square of wax paper that covered most of the desk. She hadn't done this in years and was surprised to find her hands trembling. She steadied herself, then picked up a pair of tweezers and grasped the edge of one of the wings in its pincers. She quickly twisted her wrist and the wing shattered, azure crystals scattering across the paper. Her eyes darted, attempting to follow each, lose none. Lark used the tweezers to recover and separate the fragments into the small jars according to color. Some were murky, others not. The jars varied in content from a soft willow past green through most of the known blues. The bodies of Needs, though originally colorless, all turned to some vegetative or oceanic shade with the cold, and fragile. This Need's central sheath was like moss, and when Lark tapped it, it came apart in pieces small as sea salt. It was a color she would use sparingly. She continued with her process—the ruthless aparting and assigning of the Need—before turning her mind as another woman might soil.

She stood up and stretched. She was tense. She went to the bathroom and bent over the tap for a few gulps of water. She looked out the window above the bathtub. The trail of an airplane was disseminating into noon sky. She waited until the evidence of its trajectory was diffuse, deniable. Until she hadn't seen it. She headed back in to the desk.

Lark sat down and placed the maple knot in front of her, along with a small can of varnish and an empty watercolor tray. This part, the painting, was familiar. Although she hadn't had a new one to dismantle in years, not a single one of her colors had run out. This vibrant powder—the last throes of her dying Needs—seemed inexhaustible. She began mixing, streaking, daubing at the thing with her fingers. Four years before, not long after Nene's birth, she had learned that the powders' tints weren't fixed, that they changed when they hit different qualities in the wood or paper. Then, she'd discovered the knots—how they produced the most variation in the least amount of surface area. Efficient.

Lark chose hues, knowing they wouldn't stay true. Early on she'd stopped questioning why she divided color from color at all—it was her chosen futility. Lark's failure to predict an end product was immaterial. She created patterns that ought to enhance the natural features in the hollows, but the results—through no design of her own—were unfailingly unnatural. Looking into the dip of a Soul, Lark's customers found dread. And had to own it. Lark watched them struggle with the cups, drawn to certain ones, transfixed. Whatever they saw they did not name. Lark could only guess what held them, not herself the author of her Souls. The colors played. They were frivolous and volatile, mutating to engine reds and dead-skin whites, or remaining infuriatingly blue, as on her fingers. There was no formula. The wrenching apart and recombination of Needs created something of its own. Lark midwived. For her, it was about listening to horror. Having rejected her Needs bodily, she couldn't abandon their infant cries to silence. They were hers to pass on. To foster.

When she finished she knew this one felt odd. Familiar. She went down the stairs and into the dining room where Nene and Drew were playing Memory and showed them.

"It's all gray," said Nene.

"It's really lovely." Drew took it from Lark and turned it over in his hands. "You know, you never have adequately explained how the varnish makes the wood so much heavier."

"I don't know how."

"Well, this one really is lovely. It feels like wind."

Nene reached over to touch it. "It needs a name, Mommy."

"Nene, this one isn't for you. Your birthday isn't for a few months."

"I know. But this one needs its name. It's Burning."

Clef smelled coffee. She looked out from beneath the down quilt, squinting. The digital clock blur was a yard—a mile—away on the dresser. Kitchen's leg was over her leg, her leg asleep. Sigh. How could there be coffee, and did it matter? Coffee was good. Someone was already moving. Purposefulness in her kitchen. Clef should go, host, but reminded herself she was naked. A pause in the hall, a knock on the bedroom door. Clef rolled out, stood cold on her waking foot, reaching to the back of the pine rocker for Kitchen's silk robe. It was the most unbelievable shade of violet. Things kept circling back to Lark, Lark's Need. Infuriating. Clef looked at her sleeping lover—in sleep the category applied better, she thought, than any individual name. It freed her, for just a moment, from the unique nature of her weakness. The rocking chair nodded her toward the door. Another knock. There is a stranger in my home who has made me coffee. How loved she was. Clef met her eyes in the full-length mirror that hung on the back of the door. She was purple with it.

She limped over and slid through the cracked doorway into the hall. The man had the decency to take a few steps back. She was shorter than she was onstage.

"What's wrong with your foot?"

"I sliced open my ankle a few weeks ago, but that's the other foot. This leg is asleep from the crotch down. *I* was asleep until a few seconds ago."

"I know, I'm sorry. This couldn't wait. It *is* almost ten forty-five." The tall figure glanced down at a bony, watchless wrist.

"We performed last night."

"I thought you were injured."

"I am, but Kitchen . . ." Clef gestured unapologetically toward the bedroom. "I mean—Kenichi, he isn't. I'm also pretty sure he's not going to be up for a while yet. Should I have him call you?"

"I haven't introduced myself."

"Jesus West, do you think anyone doesn't know you? You're here to recruit Kitch—Kenichi. I'm just surprised you haven't tried before now. He's amazing."

"He is. But he can sleep. Come in and have some coffee. I'd like to talk with you."

On the flight back across the Atlantic, West had recalled a sleightist named Clef who, it was rumored, liked to restring architectures and had even designed a few new ones—maybe she'd drawn something. It was rare for a sleightist to step outside the technique.[13] If she'd done so once, she might've again. The last time West had seen her perform, nearly two years before, she'd been dating an ex–butoh dancer named Kenichi Baba. Clearly they were still extant. That night, the two of them had been phenomenal—wicking twice as much as anyone else in Monk. But during the time they weren't "out," the audience was riveted to them. And that wasn't as it should be. West was certain they had been reprimanded, certain also they'd experienced a more personal shame. But since that night, West had become less certain their transgressions should've been swept from the stage. And now, he was beginning to think their methods should be embraced.

"Do you know why there aren't any female hands?"

Clef looked up sharply from her coffee.

"That's an interesting way to open a conversation. There have been . . . your grandmother, for one." Clef cared deeply about the gender division in sleight: the overwhelming number of female sleightists and

---

[13] The vast majority of sleightists are familiar with but scant history of their craft. They can recall a few names: Revoix, Bugliesi, even Dodd. But they do not know what transpired on the island of inception. They have read not one of the diaries left by Antonia, nor those of the bastard daughters of the Theater of Geometry. Most are divorced from other areas of their art. Expert at the handling of existing architectures, very few sleightists attempt the design of new ones. They know nothing of the work done by hands, the drawings completed far from theaters, the painstaking experimentation, the research. Their system of training suggests to the sleightists that they purposefully self-restrict to instrumentation. The technique demands so much of them: they are led by one another to think it is enough. Safely cloistered within the mechanism, sleightists choose not to reflect. On rare occasion, a talent, one who wicks often and with duration, cannot help realizing what has not been at stake. One might think these few would seek to reform their passion, but invariably, they withdraw from the sleightworld—quietly and culpably aware.

sleight students vs. the nearly exclusively male club of directors and hands. Instructors were split almost down the middle, although even that wasn't equitable—not the way she saw the numbers. But Clef had no answers. And Clef—who liked having answers—shut off after too much not-finding.

West acknowledged her correction. "Yes. Fern did draw. A total of five sleights."

"She was gifted. I'd rather have drawn her five than a hundred of the sort we're producing lately."

"No doubt, no doubt." West drank from his mug. "Do you draw?"

"What? No, of course not. I was never trained." Clef was caught off balance. West had put her there. She had heard things about him—that he could manipulate anything but an architecture. It was true she thought of herself as more than a sleightist, an instrument, but couldn't explain why without demeaning her own profession. West waited. He drew his middle finger along the thick rim of his mug. Clef counted three unhurried circles. She ventured a little further.

"This is the first real injury I've had. When I retire, I was thinking I might go back to the academy, but . . ."

"To teach."

"Yes. Why not?"

"I thought you might have other interests. I was—hopeful. I'm in need of a hand. A new one."

Kitchen was up. They heard him before they saw him. Coughing. He shuffled in wearing pale-yellow threadbare boxers, his hairless musculature leaner and longer than his five-foot-six stature and forty-odd years should allow. He went directly to the sink, hacked up some phlegm, turned on the spigot. They waited for him.

Kitchen lynxed himself onto the granite counter, cross-legged—there were only the two chairs.

"Hey West."

West nodded. "Kenichi."

"It's Kitchen. What's going on?"

Clef had been twisting her hair distractedly, frowning, but Kitchen's presence was a balm. She made up a small smile for her lover. "Toss me a couple of chopsticks, would you?"

Kitchen reached into the utensil drawer beneath him, and flicked two ivory sticks onto the bistro table in front of Clef. As she secured her topknot, she spoke directly to Kitchen, bypassing West as if he were out of hearing range, an incompetent, a child.

"West here is looking for something structural, and seems to fancy himself a progressive—but we knew that. Do you think . . . should we show him Lark's book?"

When Kitchen nodded, Clef left. When she returned, she was carrying it.

"My sister left this here." Clef looked down at the large, cloth-covered journal. The cover was worn, frayed at one corner. She set the book in front of West—and West's face was empty. She saw explanation was necessary, so she gathered up some air and dove.

"Lark was in Monk a while ago. Not for long. I've never seen any drawings—you directors are cagey—but Kitchen has. He says these look like structures, but for no architectures he's used. I don't think Lark knows what she's drawing. I think she's sick in a way I don't know how anyone would fix. You look at that. I see pain. I don't . . . I think . . . maybe she should come back to sleight. If you can do that, you keep the book. I don't know why she left it for me. I'm no good with what's not there. She should know that."

Clef was looking at West. She was waiting. He ran his hand over the book, taking time.

"I can't say I'm not curious. And sick isn't something that scares me, though you make her sound . . . ruined. I often find sickness to be the sign of a working mind. But why," and West looked bemused, "why so quick to trust me with this? Haven't you noticed? I encroach. I break enterings." His smile was light, almost coaxing.

Kitchen answered. "Clef doesn't trust you. She sees your use. When she showed me this, I told her we'd need to understand it if we wanted to help Lark. But I——knew——Lark once. I'm not the person to help her. Clef's happy to have you take an interest."

Clef stood to take her cup over to the sink. She stopped in front of Kitchen.

"You make me sound heartless."

"You have a heart, Clef. You just like to grip it with both hands."

LARK'S BOOK.

[On the first four pages, detailed pencil-drawn diagrams.]

Sketch one: Suggestive of a spiderweb with a central snarl. Cause unclear.
Or a game of cat's cradle with the children's fingers removed.

Sketch two: A family of trapezes. Horizontal bars with connective tissue every-
where indicating attempted and aborted support.

Sketch three: Parabolic. Small line fragments arranged to describe wave forms.
A digital tide that could be construed as the splintering of a single gull.

Sketch four: A machine with pulleys. All lines reach to a central form.
The proposed function either to raise up or to strangle.

[On page five, a newspaper clipping. A photograph with no caption. In the photo a bound man is being dragged behind a military jeep by his legs. His face is to the pavement. It is impossible to discern whether he is still alive.]

[On page six, Lark's handwriting begins.]

I'm back here. Have decided to stay. I have nowhere else. The ghosts aren't as
thick as I expected. I came two weeks ago to clear out, maybe sell some things. I
found my old papers. I recopied four drafts I did of the first Need. I got better
at putting them down, I think. Still, these first attempts aren't bad. I was only

thirteen. I can't believe Jillian never found these. Not that she cleaned. She never mentioned them. They were under the windowseat, just where I put them. It's helpful here. The dogwoods. I'm going to make soup tonight that should last the week. I went to the farmer's market yesterday and saw people. That girl from French class with the hips. The black boy I had a crush on junior year. He remembered me. I couldn't think of his name. I was rude, asked, my North coming out. Drew. We talked a little. He had the paper in his hand. This picture was on the front page—I kept looking down at it. I couldn't keep up my end of the talking. Drew noticed, gave me the paper, said he'd see me around. It's possible now, I suppose, that I could have that sort of life. Except—the man's face. I keep seeing how it must've left a trail of blood and saliva, skin and bits of bone on the asphalt—a screaming of. Itself. Into the asphalt. And so, now, I can't help thinking—what sort of life happens prior to that? What sort of life is possible with that death waiting?

———

West shut the book. He spoke to Clef.

"Do you mind if I take this with me?"

"I said you could."

"Your sister, where is she now?"

"In Georgia, where we grew up. With her husband and her little girl."

"Would you mind if I called on her?"

"*Called* on her?"

"I would like your permission, of course, but I'll do what I have to."

Kitchen knew what West had seen, but asked him anyway. "What did you see?"

West looked at Kitchen warily, but with eyes too tired to lie. "I saw a horse, legs buckling under, coming down. I saw white boots caked in red mud. And a child old enough, for once, to run."

enlightenment—the late years :: cancer reshuffling epiphany

:: the deal slow, inoperable :: a first study of cells ::

books / travel / tea / tarot / trysts :: cell art :: original things

breach :: primary substances fluctuate :: direction nexts :: pits

itself against :: entropy / overproliferation :: sleight-realization

:: mere &perfect

CELL.

Fern lived in a twenties-era apartment on the Upper East Side. The apartment was white. Everything in the apartment was white except for the wooden floors. But every white thing was a different shade of white, and every hard white thing was draped in volumes of white fabric. West had always thought of his grandmother's place as exclusively hers, not his at all, but warm. Warm and clean—a guest towel folded on top of the bathroom radiator.

His grandmother, perfectly rendered though wasting, was curled up on the couch in an ivory afghan, drinking tea. Her face was gaunt and glowy. She continued, even in stage four, to look twenty years her junior. *Good rouge,* West thought.

"How are you feeling, Fern?"

"Come off it, West. Why don't you just tell me why you're here?"

West went from shamed to defiant in three seconds, and so subtly Fern barely caught it, and she was the only one who could have.

"It's always money, isn't it, Fern?"

"It always is."

"Well, I need two extra salaries, and the sponsor won't budge."

"The sponsor."

"Yes, the sponsor, Fern. We could've been the only troupe in the world privately funded, unsullied by the Vice Corps,[14] but you had other plans for your wealth."

[14] Vice Corps: the nickname given by sleightists to the group of industries that have traditionally sponsored their art. Liquor companies, Big Tobacco, porn, the pharmaceuticals.

"I did."

"And how's that going for you? Your charity?"

Fern decided to ignore West's sneer. She looked directly at him, and answered the question as if it were honest. "I think we're doing well. I haven't been down to see the girls since the cancer took this turn. But I get letters."

"They write?"

"There's a school at the compound. Most of them are still school-aged when we get them off the street, West. They get used up pretty quickly."

West was done with the conversation. "So, can I have it or not?"

"When have I ever denied you?"

"You denied me the time I refused to ask."

"There you go."

—————

As West walked toward the park, he relaxed. He'd gotten the money. He would send Byrne down to meet Lark. He had a feeling they would work. What he needed now was to sit and think about next. Something bigger?—always a temptation. Maybe technology.

He was at Alice. He always ended up at Alice. Her, big and bronze on her big bronze mushroom, arms outstretched. Him—having run away from Fern at nine, ten, twelve, because she'd been making him listen about his father, or about practicing, or because there was another one of her women in the apartment. The summers in Boston while Fern taught at the academy had been worse. She'd tried to make him rehearse with the other students there—the best from small towns all over the country. Most of them female. And when he'd gotten frustrated

They advertise in sleight's playbills and use the goodwill they gain by erecting theaters (primarily in suburban communities) to garner tax breaks on other real estate ventures in those townships. Sleightists, as a matter of course, despise their sponsors. Sleightists also tend to drink, smoke, and have sex more often than many of their suburban neighbors—or used to, according to a Kinseyan endnote. These days sleightists are perhaps most anomalous in that they remain troubled, if abstractly so, about the ethical ramifications of patronage.

by his inadequacies, when he'd thrown down his architectures or tripped over someone else's—there was no Alice to run to. No big bronze girl blithely holding court among others' absurd expectations.

West watched as a little boy climbed onto her lap with the help of his father. West's father still lived and worked downtown, he assumed. It had been over a decade. The few times his father had been to see West, the three of them—Fern, West, West's father—had gone to eat at a place with dark green walls where waiters refolded his napkin every time he went to the bathroom. He'd always gone to the bathroom at least once during those dinners. Because the soap there smelled like other countries.

Fern had made West keep a daily journal since he'd turned ten. In it, there was a page-long entry about soap. Soap that didn't smell like his grandmother. She told him each night what to write in his journal, and that night he disobeyed. When they came back from the restaurant and his father took off—again—Fern said West should write about how he felt, and he wrote about soap. Musky soap. Soap that didn't smell like clean. Stolen soap he'd hidden under his bed in a small leather suitcase with buckles.

In his late teens, West discovered that the journal was a sleight tradition. He read around in several of the diaries kept in the academy book room. Sleight's founder had made her protégées take notes on every performance: imperfections, serendipities, suggestions.[15] Before they attempted their first tour, Antonia had her sleightists research the towns

[15] Her father wrote of her: "Antonia is brilliant like a polished egg." He had had her educated in Florence and then Paris while his aristocratic status allowed him to spend his own time on pursuits—chemistry, mathematics, comparative anatomy. A great many days of Antonia's vacations were given over to his dictation before she was disowned for her involvement with dance ("I indulged her interests, yes, but she was never to debase herself on an actual stage."). Antonia performed throughout Europe and Russia, and finally in America. It has been suggested that she came upon the documents in Prague and followed them, seducing Dodd in order to have him procure them. What is known is that she is the mother of sleight. Beyond that, Antonia remains an enigma who demanded a previously unseen caliber of physical dexterity and decorum from her charges—mostly young women plucked from callings grittier than the theater, and a few boys of like circumstance.

through which they would caravan, including chief industries, average per capita income, ethnic makeup, and weather. The performers became fixtures at the newly opened Free Library of Philadelphia. Their journals were dry, full of statistics and numbers—and for the most part, absent the authors themselves.

West supposed he was fortunate. His grandmother had only had him take notes on people: what they said, how they said it, how they moved, what they looked like, what they wore, what they didn't say. No research required, only a sound eye. When, as an adolescent, he'd toured East Asia as a roadie/techie/usher with Kepler, she'd quizzed him nightly on the composition of the audience and the demeanor of the critics. West, lacking the finer motor skills, lacking hand-eye coordination, gained a knowledge of humanity both indispensable and dreadful. And unlike Antonia's disciples, he was always present in his journal entries—as adjudicator. Fern did that for him.

West looked down at the dedication plaque embedded in the concrete below Alice. George Delacorte had commissioned this statue in memory of his first wife, Margarita, who had loved children. But Fern, facing her own death, hadn't bought art. Instead, his grandmother had abandoned her measuring stick to fix a bunch of broken Mexican dolls. The Queen adrift in the repugnance of the world—caring. The Queen drowning in decapitation, all the while ordering the pretty heads back on. Screwing them on with hands that had smelled always of lavender. At the end of a long selfish life, false selfless acts. Queen Hypocrita. Queen Early, too late, too late. West checked his empty wrist, headed over to Fifth Avenue, caught a cab to La Guardia.

West was trying to decide whether or not to go down to Georgia. As facilitator. He didn't know what to expect from this Lark. Her book was a singularity, an event. There was no doubt the things she drew—what she referred to as Needs—were some of the most complex, breathtaking structures West had ever come across.

T said she thought Byrne'd be back in York that day or the next. West had long before learned to trust T's clock, set to otherworldly yet intensely corporeal rhythms, so he booked two train tickets south for the weekend. Some time alone with Byrne might give him a chance to explain Lark's book, at least what he'd made of it. And to repair some small rifts. West wasn't unaware of Byrne's disillusion with tour—he would've had to have been blind, or extremely opaque. He was neither. West was rushing this meeting precisely because Byrne seemed so precarious, unable to juggle his talent in its new setting. *Crater. Roof. Abomination. Rock. Starless. Shorn. Devotion-blanket. Parallel. Ash.* Byrne's precursor for *Poland* had mesmerized. West would not let him drift off—not with things at stake.

West felt his heart gallop. He read its stop and surge not as his own demise but rather as a metaphor for the apocalypse. Bodies, he knew, housed the ends of their lives. Also beginnings.

SHARE.

Drew told Lark he'd invited them to stay, but West—Drew didn't know why anyone would name a child West—said he'd have to turn around once he got there, head back to York. Byrne, though, would be staying a week or two.

"You invited a stranger to stay in our home?" Lark wasn't incredulous. Drew was an open book, their house an open house.

"Not *exactly* a stranger," Drew tried to explain. "Clef called earlier—she sounds a little like you I think, sad like you—she said you knew West, and then West called from the train and vouched for the other one."

"I know *of* West," Lark said. It wasn't yet clicking for her. "Why would this other one want to meet me?"

"Apparently," Drew raised an eyebrow, "he has your book, and they'll be at the station in a few hours."

Lark shook her head. "I'll kill her."

"No, you won't." Drew stood up from the couch, pulled Lark into him. "Clef's as rootless as you are. In weather, you help, she helps—sisters."

———

"Can he stay in my room?"

"No, Nene. He'll stay in here."

"Can I sleep in here then?"

"No, Nene. You'll stay in your own room. Everyone has their own room."

"You and Daddy don't."

"No. That's true. Daddy and I share a room. But you have your own room, and so will Byrne while he's here. Take the pillowcase off that pillow for me, would you? Thank you. Why do you like this Byrne so much anyway?"

"He has a rock."

"I saw that. But maybe you shouldn't mention it."

"Why?"

"Some people don't like to talk about things like that."

"Like rocks?"

"Yes, sometimes the things are like rocks."

"I'm not supposed to talk about Newt."

"Not with your teachers, no."

"But Newt's your daddy."

"Yes he was."

"And a scientist."

"He and your grandmother both."

"Why is he little if he was married?"

"Nene, I don't know why you see the things you do. Newt was little once, not when I knew him, but once. Please don't tug at the quilt like that. Why don't you go down and see what Daddy and Byrne are doing?"

"Byrne thought I should be with you."

"He said that?"

"No."

———

Byrne spent the evening with Drew. When he had arrived, Lark had gone out for groceries with her daughter, then cooked for them—a lamb stew with curry and yellow tomatoes. After a subdued dinner, during which Byrne tried not to stare at her blue fingers, Lark had complained of a headache and gone to bed. Nene followed a few minutes later. For the second time since he'd arrived, Byrne was left alone with Drew, who was—though physically intimidating—a comfortable man. A large bald black to Byrne's small slouching whiteness—Drew was practiced at putting at least one artist at ease, and Byrne eventually let himself relax. They watched a cop show together while finishing the wine from dinner, and during commercials Drew asked a few questions about sleight, proving less knowledgeable than Byrne. His interest didn't feel like a test—he accepted the lapses in Byrne's haphazard education without judgment. At eleven, after the alleged child molester suicided, throwing the white cop deep into a well of ambivalence, Drew led the way to the guest room. A few moments later he knocked on the door, and when Byrne opened it, Drew handed him a mint green bath towel, face towel, and washcloth, with a bar of shrink-wrapped glycerin soap dimpling the crest of the cotton pyramid.

The next day, Byrne took a long shower. He preferred the feel of rock against skin, so left the washcloth folded on the sink, guiltily—he didn't wish to refuse any kindness in this house. He wandered down to the kitchen around nine. Nene was sitting at the table, sipping what looked like coffee.

"Cinnamon apple tea," she said before he asked. "No caffeine."

"Are your mommy and daddy around?"

Instead of answering, Nene took a bite of a sugar cookie that had suddenly emerged in a greasy hand from beneath the table. For a half second, Byrne had taken the cookie for dirty quartz. When she was done chewing, she said, "Daddy's out in nature because it's morning, and Mommy went to the kiosk to sell. There's coffee in the French press. Have some."

After fixing himself a cup, Byrne sat down across from Nene. She was a remarkably composed child. Her skin was lighter than her father's, but not by much. Her roux-colored hair was braided into tight rows, each secured with a gold band. Her eyes were open and gray. A gray like smoke, not storm or muddy ice. She studied him too, without reserve.

"What was your daddy like?"

"Well . . . he wasn't at all like your daddy."

"Why wasn't he?"

"I really don't know." Byrne grimaced, thinking. "Why do you want to know about my daddy?"

"Why do you want to know about my mommy?"

"I think I have some things to learn from her."

"Because she hurts? Do you want to know why she hurts?"

"Do you know why?"

"No."

Nene abruptly stood and left the table. She banged through the screen door and out into the yard in an oversized cardigan and leggings. It wasn't cold and Byrne could see her father through the window over the sink; nevertheless, he worried for her bare feet.

———————

What Byrne had seen in Lark's book during the trip down alarmed him. West had brought other diagrams of structures onto the train, both Revoix's and those of other notable hands, so that Byrne could compare. West had said that all hands were somewhat unbalanced, that the ones Byrne had met in Oxford had been two of the more socially adept. "I used to blame it on their education,[16] but Lark seems to have

[16] Hands begin training at the academies and then complete their studies in research enclaves—small rural communes replete with libraries and (to the uninitiated) seemingly idiosyncratic equipment: telescopes, blenders, astrolabes, harps, magnets, etc. In 1986, George Hirsch attempted to infiltrate one such community as part of his doctoral dissertation in sociology. Made aware of the vast number of packages hands accrue during the course of their matriculation, he posed as a deliveryman. A fascinating record of his conversations with his subjects can be read in the book *Eight Weeks with the Seven Hands of Preble;* his work underscores the elitism and paranoia that accompany the development of hands.

similar difficulties, if not worse. Maybe," West mused, "the education actually helps the hands retain and resemble normal—or feign it." And maybe, thought Byrne, education homogenizes their work.

Compared to the others', Lark's structures leapt. Byrne watched them shoot above the page to the visual rhythm of trees passing the train—running backwards and away—some on fire, some with newly naked limbs outstretched. Napalm. Alternately florid and stark, each of Lark's structures strived. That's what it is, Byrne thought. Lark's work crossed over—was synaptic. Her structures vaulted, though he didn't know what stood across the gap, nor how much distance needed bridging, nor what she meant to leave behind.

Looking out the window of the train, Byrne had seen, along the tracks, baseball fields. So many baseball fields. And because of late October they were vacant. Trains, Byrne had thought, make an earlier America, make world film: windows framing the glinting day-ends, passengers as captive audience, entering gold. To be inside a train is to be inside a gap. Inside the illusion of forward. They, all of them—and Byrne had for the first time in three hours looked around him at sleeping students, laptop-lit businessmen, and women of a certain age drinking wine from the café car in doll bottles—they were chrysalides. All of them, someone else for hours.

Byrne's head was light with thought. Maybe failure was sewn into such spaces: trains, bedrooms, the stage. In Lark's book, failure was the Braille of every page. The other hands' structures were more perfected, seamless. Theirs were relics, unearthed whole, while hers were prodded or drawn into defiant, living relief: needled.

West had watched Byrne's squint and ponder. West had smiled out into the landscape, and West had slept some. West excused himself to visit the facilities. West came back. West asked Byrne, "Well?" Byrne had kept reading, kept waiting, expecting to arrive at a group of words that looked like a precursor, that would make him beside the point, but he didn't. What he'd told West was, "I'm scared of her." What he felt was—relieved.

NOTES FROM A LAPSED HAND.[17]

When hands sit down to draw structures, each hand is its own—but common to holding, some notions follow:

It is good to draw on velum so that what is next appears as clouded-present rather than clear-present or blocked-present.

Many hands use tools—ruler string compass wedge whisk needle microscope. Other hands are not tool users, but arrive instead from an empty desk.

It is known that one note struck over and over facilitates (i.e., piano. i.e., alcohol. i.e., hymen.)

In a sleight more structures bind than tether.

Structures may be incidental, specific, remembered, fragmented, synthetic, grounded, or they may contain botulism.

Structures may be devised.

[17] This page is reprinted with permission from *The Pathologies of Performance,* an anthology compiled by the California psychoanalyst A. D. Statt, PhD. All texts within the book are the works of musicians, actors, dancers, painters, etc. This list was composed by a patient of Statt's, case number 33.2, a hand, as part of a decades-long treatment both during and after a semidistinguished career in sleight.

Structures may be taken in or let out for vision.

If a hand is beyond rules, no rules apply to that hand.

horsehead power $=$ vulva power

Drawing, it is right to keep the sleightists always in mind as they are unique instruments.

It is unwise to allow the unique nature of instruments undue influence.

By thinner spreading cover acreage, by centrifuge. Work always toward the original contraction.

Never hound nor hind nor buckle.

Bring about world-inside-world. Bring about ax with pine. Reinvest spare.

Respect what you do not know about what you do: efficiency, sweat-shop; fission, Hiroshima; church.

Lark was bruised. It was her state, bruising, blood welling up only to be blocked by membrane. Lark would've liked to let herself: dress in leeches, sate them, have them fall from her deceased. Leeches drank overmuch. She knew people like that: children. Children were feed-ings without end. But despite her daughter's insatiability, Lark will-ingly fed Nene. This was one part of her love for her child. Nene used her up, and without use, Lark was too much herself.

Drew had never taken advantage. After and during sex, yes, he made her less there—and she was, happily. Lovemaking was for them an act of subtraction. Drew knew when he was taking. In a way, Lark still wicked, was still performance; it didn't matter how intimate the audience. But Drew had never taken from Lark simply because that was what she was there for. Her daughter Nene had. Animalized her. Lark was grateful for that which she could not withdraw from. She was proud of how, after initial thrash and refusal, she had succumbed to motherhood—almost like a mother would. Thankful for how her daughter had, those first dark months, bruised and gummed the mythic breast. Until it was only and again sore and sour flesh. Hers.

Byrne was at her house now, a strangely passive figure, primal weapon in hand. He had been waiting for nearly a week. He wanted something and he was patient: an unusual combination. Though disquieted, Lark was coming around—thinking it was somehow right to give. Nene adored this Byrne, but Lark wasn't yet familiar. The idea of being perused frightened her—she was deeply uncomfortable with fingers, how they could open, how they read. But Byrne—what was he? A man. A man and his rock. Might he be as simply fed—as elegant—as a child or a parasite? She didn't see how.

During his sixth morning in her home, Lark invited Byrne to watch her work. Drew was teaching Faulkner at the community college. Nene was off at pre-K. The windows were open—it was almost hot. Something outside was burning. It had been a warm fall. Lark drummed indigo fingers: he was taking too long.

She wouldn't begin until Byrne came in. Her jars of hued dust were set out in order, but Lark had no Needs to show just now. All the Needs she'd killed were color. Before she'd brought up the last one, the one she'd offered to Clef, Lark had tried to assimilate it. To let it be in her until it was her. She was already a monster—why did she resist plurality? Perhaps because that Need wouldn't go quiet. Instead, it had kept at her, saying there was more. More. Lark was so tired of wanting—killing was better.

Still no Byrne. Her jars were nervous as test tubes.

Lark's father, Newton Scrye, had worked extensively with flies. Drosophila melanogaster. Red eyes. Her mother spent thirty years with diseased albino mice, red-eyed also. They had had their creatures, just like her, and killed them. The ten thousand deaths accomplished by her parents were made acceptable by crimson irises and an assurance of purpose. Because those deaths had been for knowing. Had been in the service of. Newton and Jillian Scrye's daughter Lark killed less. She killed only Needs, and only eleven, and she couldn't be certain they were actual. The difference: Lark killed in order not-to-know.

When Byrne finally got around to joining her, she would stain one Soul. That was it. She'd told him at breakfast that he could watch, and that because he'd been such a gracious guest, they could talk while she worked. She'd set a tall stool across the big desk. He would sit there where he could see, where she could.

After he slinked in and found his seat, Byrne watched Lark for a few minutes without speaking or moving. He sensed an edge. She had allowed him to examine the knot before she began: an elbow of locust branch. But she hadn't called it a locust, she'd called it a funeral tree. There was a locust over his father's grave—Byrne remembered the spiking vine that wormed beneath its fissured winter bark. And its black pods, long as his forearm, fallen, half hidden beneath a week-old snow. During Gil's burial, he'd leaned toward the tree to snap off a six-inch thorn from its vine. He'd inspected it, wiped it against his trousers, then sharply jabbed it into the cramped flesh between his thumb and index finger, newly knotted from its first few days gripping stone. Byrne wasn't glad for the memory.

"What is a Soul exactly?"

"Is this to be an interview then?" Lark mocked, slipping into a coy drawl she'd learned young. Though inexcusably tardy, Byrne was growing on her. It helped he had a deformity; a rock in the hand meant fewer available fingers.

"I guess. Sure."

"Then I'll say that a Soul is a vessel comprised of a unique combination of Needs. And that a Soul is a useless thing to buy. In fact, the idea of purchasing a Soul should disturb you. A person should earn a Soul, don't you think? Or grow one?"

Byrne laughed without noise, the sobbed chuckle convulsing him. "You're hysterical."

"Yes. A century ago, I'm certain that would have been the diagnosis." Lark's tone had gone from taunting to arch in one sentence. As had her posture.

Byrne straightened up. She was confusing him. "Right. So . . . why do you think people buy Souls from you?"

"Why is God lazy?" Lark's voice was a belle's again.

"Is God lazy?"

"Do you believe in God?"

"No."

"I submit that as proof of his laziness."

Lark was massaging color into the small wooden bowl. She didn't look up at Byrne when she spoke, but he watched a crooked smile walk across her face. She was playing him.

"You say Souls are made of Needs. I saw the Needs you drew. They weren't color, they were form. And they were plural."

"A Need . . ." Lark didn't want to answer though there was no question. She pushed herself. "A Need is what makes you . . . you . . . anything . . . do anything." She was losing control of her whimsy. She was embarrassed to find herself sounding sincere.

"It's desire then?"

"No. A Need is . . . let me think." She looked up at Byrne. "How's your grammar?"

"It's good."

"Good. Then a Need is like an infinitive, a passive infinitive: to be impelled, to be induced. Or no, that's not it." Lark thought, then spoke her thinking, which was wrong—vulnerable—of her. "Desire is what *I* do. A Need does desire *to* me."

"A Need is divine then? External?"

"I thought you didn't believe in God." Lark had found her way back inside the banter. Was she perspiring? She touched her forehead with the back of her hand.

"But *you* do."

"I most certainly do not." Her hand came down. She wasn't perspiring.

Lark held out the newly painted Soul for Byrne's inspection. Its hurricane of greens. Byrne remembered a punchline from preadolescence, *a frog in a blender*—but this was bloodless. She was. He looked into Lark's eyes, Irish with wrinkles, laughing and counting him. She made him feel young, like a young man. As if his skin were angry.

"Why is it you renounce them then?"

"Excuse me?" Lark, stunned. He'd hit something. She grew even taller in her chair, her vertebrae repelling one another. She tried to be scathing, fumbled it, seemed wounded. "Renounce—now there's a religious word. And I'm not. I don't. If anything, I *announce* the Needs. Announcing them fixes them, and they die for it."

"'Fixes them'?"

"I never wanted them to define me. And now, now I seem to be nothing but refusal."

"There's no escape for you then?" Byrne felt the need to catch her, pin her to some utterance. She irritated him—so few did. It was, he thought, her way of mocking herself, which mocked him better.

"I never tried to escape. I tried not to imprison them, but Needs die outside of incarceration. Outside of my body." Lark passed her hand sadly over the Soul, as if it were a small grave or a black hat. She looked up. "Only their color doesn't."

She wasn't hurting him, not really. And she looked like a bird now: sharp averted eyes, taut neck, instinct, arrow. Byrne tried to rescind. To be kind.

"The drawings you made look like sleight, you know. Like structures."

"I do know."

"Is that why you quit?"

"You mean, having found a way to rid myself of my Needs, did I then refuse to spend time inside their bodies writ large?"

"I guess that's what I'm asking."

"No. I quit because I was good, and when you're good and a girl at something, you should be suspicious."

"Of what?"

"Of what part of yourself you didn't know you were selling."[18]

. . . *grief-frog*   *thumbspan*   *subzero*

belly up   *bomb*   *organ failing*

piano slicker   *downpour*   *yellower-than-thou*

posthumous   *heavy-pocketed*   *earthwarm*

downed   *spinal plane*   *in-spire*

church pierced   *wordbloodied*   *slave*

slave   *hummingbird*   *slave* . . .

Lark read it. A dozen pages spilled over with words. She had asked Byrne to write her a precursor. She hadn't thought. It was what he did

[18] Antonia Bugliesi chose her students and then trained them in a manner that made their questioning of the underlying properties of sleight unlikely. Most were prostitutes, or at the very least destitute, without education or prospects. She offered them a living that required both unrelieved physical focus and obedience. In the few cases where a sleightist seems to have questioned Antonia, if that sleightist were a woman—she became pregnant (possibly by Bugliesi's lover, the lewd puppet-figure Dodd). If a man—he was asked to study the documents and eventually produce an original sleight: these were the first hands. In essence, when Antonia felt her charges were too close to the source, she shuttled them into acts of creation far from the well.

and she wouldn't. She'd never articulated the Needs like that. She had known that it wasn't possible, but also—that there was too much power in it.

When Byrne returned from his walk, Lark's daughter Nene was sitting cross-legged on his bed. A petite shaman. "Do you want to play cards again?" he asked her. And when she didn't answer: "How about I teach you Egyptian Ratscrew?"

She shook her head. "What I want to know," she spoke quietly, "is what you did to my mommy." Nene leaned forward then and placed her head into her hands. She was so old, and her head such a sad gift. When she completed the fold, she was the size of a large turtle he'd seen across the lake an hour before. Byrne didn't think she was about to cry—maybe because he couldn't picture it. He sat down next to her but kept his hand and his rock to himself. She wasn't the type of child one touched easily. She was the type of child who made one reconsider natural inclinations. As Byrne had come to know her over the past ten days, he'd started learning himself differently.

He tried to comfort her with an explanation.

"I just gave her some words."

"Why would you do that?" Nene's voice was muffled, spoken into her lap.

"She asked me to."

The little girl's head popped up. Hopefully. "She did?"

"Yes."

"I want to see them then."

"I don't think they'll make any sense to you." Byrne knew Nene could read, better than any four-year-old he'd ever known. When he'd first arrived, she had been in the middle of the *World Book Encyclopedia Yearbook: 1972*. They had briefly conversed about ecology and the fourth estate. Her grasp of the concepts was rudimentary—no better than if she had been twelve.

"Newt'll help."

"Your grandfather?"

"He helps when things are hard for me."

Byrne knew an adult shouldn't encourage this type of delusion, but Nene talked about Newt guilelessly. And the stories were enchanted.

"But isn't Newt a scientist?"

"He will be, when he's older, before he died."

"I see."

"But he likes words too. And he knows a lot about Mommy. He calls her Checkers."

"Why Checkers?"

"Because she doesn't have red hair."

"I see."

"You always say that when there's nothing *to* see. You can't see Newt. You can't see Mommy brushing Aunt Clef's hair in the bathroom. You can't even see the inside of your own rock."

Byrne stilled himself, tried to breathe evenly. If he didn't move too suddenly, or at all, maybe this creature would keep speaking.

"So will you let me see them too? The words?"

"Yes." Byrne breathed it. "Nene?"

"No. I can't tell you. But you didn't hurt him. Neither one of you did."

"Nene, who are you talking about?"

"You and Marvel didn't hurt your daddy. That's stupid to think that. Your rock is very tired of it all the time."

"Nene, how do you know my brother's name?"

"I have his Soul on my dresser. Do you want to see? I love that one. It's red and orange and it breathes."

LARK'S BOOK.

[On pages 17 and 18, fragments of graph paper pasted into the journal. The resulting pages are warped but the drawings—precise and depth-bearing.]

Sketch thirty-four: Bowel. A meander with searching inner filaments. And among the morass: unnamable occlusions.

Sketch thirty-five: A perfect and thickening spiral pitted against a cube. High, pornographic discourse.

Sketch thirty-six: A shutter.

Sketch thirty-seven: A tilled field, could all of its rows— its whole—be viewed simultaneously from within. Or below.

[On page 19, Lark's handwriting.]

It took me too long to figure out the things to hate. The word "plantation." Quiet boys who told me how I should. All my alien-withins: pity stones, unending suck, the impossible entrances into another, silver strangles—crotch to throat. After I had them figured, I killed them. I couldn't take how I couldn't take. How I was, am, girl. At twenty-five.

The first time, I was fifteen. They were drunk, some tripping. Eight of us. They made me drive Space Highway out to the res. I didn't drop that night, so even though the wine made the headlights talk so sad—white cryings, spider brides—I was the choice. We piled into a rusted-out Impala and some kindness took us ten miles to the spot above the river.

Got undressed. Claudia was the other girl, the one who'd dragged me in. My body, newly sprung, was still caving its chest into a sort of grotto: airtight, godtight. The boys were a year older, smart. They ranted about the breathing dark between stars, howled how willows swayed out essential seduction. Remember "essential" was all I could think. I tried to see it and the trying made me bold. That night I brought my body out—it, me, verging. Ready for shame.

Sleight had made my walking and standing better suited to intoxication. I had some balance. I half-tightroped, half-cakewalked along the lip of the dam. Spun a lopsided polyhedron. That night my limbs were limbs of hoary gods waltzing on the sea. That night, the boy I hurt for most begged a kiss—and I, naked, began it. But only seconds in, he stopped me. Grabbed my arms and wrenched them down. Off him. Said acid confused our lips, made it hard for him to keep us separate. "Besides," he said, "you're a pure and perfect child and I am a goat."

That night I learned what it was—a muse. A muse is to be relegated.

What I wanted didn't need to be taken from me. Was kept instead as if just above, not admitting my reach. I do not admit. So I, still throbbing with the silt-feel of muck between my toes, thighs slick and woken, started to kill the thing, the Need, that made me hope I was for something intended.

That was my first.

[On page 22, a clipping from a tabloid. The headline: HOLOCAUST SURVIVORS OPPOSE BAPTISM—MORMONS CLAIM DEAD JEWS AS THEIR OWN]

Two days after West's invasion, Kitchen found the note in Clef's apartment. She was off to Iowa for the last week of her recovery. She wanted to visit a friend of hers, an ex-sleightist who'd married an oral surgeon. They hadn't seen one another in years. Bea had three children under the age of six. Kitchen tried not to laugh at Clef's lack of self-preservation, but he did. Until two tears.

She called the next night. "They're beautiful."

"I've seen the Christmas cards."

"I mean, they're insane, all over the place, and Bea's a *mother,* but they're beautiful."

"Have you held the baby?"

"Emmy. Yes. But hardly a baby anymore. She's beautiful. She has such perfect . . ."

"Fingers?"

"Yes, and . . ."

"Feet?"

"Yes, and Clara Bow lips. Red. Her mouth is a bud."

"Rosebud. Of course—the mute enigma crying out. Unless . . . does this beautiful child not cry?"

"She only cries when she needs something, Kitchen."

"And how often is that?"

"I know. I do. I can't stay the week, I'm getting no rest. The toddler came into my room in the middle of the night last night."

"He's a bad sleeper?"

"Not really. It was six, but Bea and I'd stayed up."

"Drinking?"

"Stop it. She needed to talk—you wouldn't recognize her. Bea was always the gone one, remember? And now she's just so . . . there. She covers her tattoos, all except the asp and that's because it's around her neck. Jesus. Bea was the last person I expected to . . ."

"To what? Settle down? Settle for settling down?"

"You know, Kitchen, it's not always about us. Bea—she seems . . . well, she can't be happy. Can't be. But . . ."

"What?"

"She swears she is."

———————

Clef changed her ticket. Two days later Bea was driving her to the Des Moines airport. A few miles from the entrance, Clef saw the billboard for the first time: YOU ARE LIVING ON THE SITE OF AN ATROCITY. She made Bea pull over. Bea started to protest, but Clef assured her an hour was plenty of time for a domestic flight. Bea pulled onto the gravel.

"Clef, you can't *not* have seen one of these."

"I've heard of them, of course. But yes, this is the first one I've actually seen."

"They're not in New York?"

"There's one right outside the Holland Tunnel. Also on the BQE, the LIE, two on 95. I just haven't seen them." Clef was weirdly ashamed.

"I think this one's about pesticides."

"Pesticides?"

"That or the groundwater. The agricultural runoff around here is frightening. Especially what it can do to children."

"I bet." Clef had her own ideas, very few of which involved children. She got out of the car and walked closer. The yellow grass was tall there, just off the shoulder, and she bent to scratch her nonbandaged ankle. Bea had gotten out too—to follow her? Clef wondered. She turned quickly to her friend, to catch her in the act of mothering. But Bea was squinting up at the dark sign.

Clef asked, "Who do you think is putting them up?"

"I never really thought about it."

"You're kidding."

"Seems like a legitimate warning. Why be suspicious?"

"A warning? But according to this"—suddenly annoyed, Clef thrust her arm toward the black rectangle—"the atrocity has already happened. There's nothing left to do."

"Or is already *happening*. And there's always something left to do, trust me." Bea's hand went through her hair, worrying it, before it reached her neck and lingered there—covering the head of the snake like a cowl. She looked over at Clef. "Come to the car. I've got to get home before Jay's soccer game, and you're missing Kitchen."

After they were back on the highway, Clef spoke.

"Why did you say that? I told you how awful he's been. I just need to get into the city, into the chamber. Back into my body."

"Okay, you don't miss Kitchen." They were quiet together for a while. Then Bea reached across the front seat and laid her hand on Clef's stomach. She let it rest there. Clef did not think herself easily shaken, and not by so small a thing, the weight of a woman's palm. But—she hadn't expected it.

After a minute or so, Bea withdrew her hand and returned it to the wheel. Clef watched it go. Bea was by this time saying something— about finding a lost key in a spider plant, about potting.

"Do me a favor, would you Clef? You know that pep-squad twit they hired to replace me?"

"Haley."

"Could you be mean to her for a few days? In my memory?"

"Done."

"And give Kitchen my love."

Clef stared out across a blear of flatland. Nodded.

When the wind comes for Byrne, he notices time, exhuming . . . revisiting certain lost spaces, finding them lessened. His father's face has had, for some years, the blurred edges of a twelfth-century gargoyle—its granite angles sloughing off, one by one, degrees of severity. Deserts are not to Byrne location but pestilence: a desert is slower locusts. Instead of the quantum jazz of genius, Byrne composes thread songs. Eventually Byrne will sit on a high hill, a once-mountain, with his rock held out into the atmosphere. The air will eat it, and with the help of scavengers, his bones will finally move away from one another.

Underwater warble. Wings for fins. Lark called domesticity water, thrashing at its surface. When she could call. A phone sings. No answer—words instead lodge in the throat, a water chestnut at the Double Happiness. Drew knew to Heimlich. She'd rather drown anyway—Ophelia, daughter of Daedalus. Water damaged. Water-simple. Of course, water did not make one simple, nor husbands. Most days normal buoyed her up to breathing. Below, she swam like birds—lungs winding wet nests of sheet. Lark meant to catch her death in cotton. Twin, drenched, twists of bedding. Hotel thread-count. Smooth-as-lake.

Clef ground down. Pulverized. Mortar and pestle, gear, cog. Used up in the use—expended, hung out. Under the funnel, termite queens produce clones in endless peristalsis. A vomit of young. Queens do not choose. Do not live on in any next queen. The queen, then, is dead—call this gravity. Flesh of her flesh is not her flesh, but of it. Clef's body: all around her. To be of the earth is to be locked into it by a passing through. Earth is not inspired, taken in, transformed—only flung. Hard fought, Clef's battle against matter. Lost. Of the earth is to be the barren or bereft. Always, always mother. That is: doorway.

West is the end of his day. Down-slinking fire, a demolition ending in stars. West undoes the world each night in charcoal. How can a fire endlessly? From deep in earth, from chemicals, from neverending supplies: oxygen, woodland, people-made-of-paper. But whose day is West? Some fire signs: chameleon, moth. Together—dragon. But West is not fire-in-lungs, not fire-under-scale. West is fire in the belly. A furnace—West fuels the room. An engine at the end of the sun, burning miles through night soot, arriving hot before the next day blooms. And alongside the tracks—how singed the daylilies.

Clef made her way up the five flights to the chamber. The paint was coming off the pipe banister in large red flakes. On the way back down, sweaty from class or rehearsal, she often came out of the stairwell looking as if she'd just murdered some vagrant clown. Some balloonman. Today she wasn't winded when she reached the top, but she was no longer used to the climb. It had been over a month. She took out her keys and undid the deadbolt. No one would be there this early—she would have a chance to regroup.

Clef undressed in the cramped anteroom and slipped her shoes, coat, and sweats into one of the cubbies against the wall. She dropped her bag onto the floor, unzipped it, and pulled out an architecture she'd designed during her recovery. She'd adapted it from one of the more involved structures in Lark's book. The shape was an inversion: its center could rotate to the periphery and vice versa. The mechanics had kept Clef up nights, but she'd finally wrought it. She thought its novelty might help her ignore the unavoidable pain of reentry.

In the chamber, mirrors lined three walls. There was a small diamond-shaped window on the fourth, and two structural beams interrupted the room's flow. It was small for a sleight chamber, but that was because Monk, unlike so many other troupes, had maintained its urban presence, with chambers on Avenue A since the forties. Clef had been to other troupes' larger, more welcoming spaces, but there was something about grit and obstacle and a low ceiling that felt true to her field. Her art wasn't about expanse or breath. It had irritated Kitchen when she'd said it aloud, but she had come to see sleight as a death practice.

Clef placed her architecture on the Marley floor and curled her body around it. She lay there for a few minutes, eyes closed, to memorize the configuration of sharp lines and wires with the nerves and muscles of her thighs, inner arms, breasts, and abdomen. Keeping the architecture folded into her, her body protecting it from contact with the ground, she began to work her way back and forth across the floor of the chamber. This was kitten-play, Clef's preferred method of getting to know an architecture. She embraced it, scrapped with it, twirled it above her with feet and hands when she rolled onto her back. Then the play elongated, and when Clef went backwards, over a shoulder, she extended and arched her body, guiding the architecture down her spine in a spooling motion as she controlled the descent of her legs to the floor. She never allowed her movement to cease or gave the architecture over to static. For half an hour, maybe more, Clef used the rhythm of her breath to maintain energy. Then stopped.

Clef curled into her body again, without the architecture. This time the contraction wasn't maternal but fetal; the air—living, resistant tissue. When Clef released the position, her small frame expanded into an x that seemed to disengage her joints and send her extremities to separate quadrants of the room. Clef repeated the combination several times, inner withdrawal followed by the peaceable quartering of the body. Finished, she rolled onto her right side—this was called "relieving-the-heart"—and slowly made her way into the vertical plane.

Clef rearranged her leotard, then bent over to gather up the architecture. During performance she wore no leotard beneath her web, but in rehearsals the women wore them, while the men sported athletic belts or biker shorts. She looked in the mirror. Her hair, though pulled back, was coming undone around her face, which was growing red. She could already see blood pooled where a few bruises would be forming: one beneath her left knee, one on either hip. A throb told her of a fourth on her shoulder. It felt good—her—moving again. Tender.

Clef began to rotate her tubes and wires.

She started slowly, using mostly her hands, testing the limits of the architecture's flexibility, watching mirrors to the front and side to determine how best to accompany the shapes that came. Soon she was entering into the figure, inserting arm or head or leg through openings in the revolving form. Clef, during manipulation, felt as if each architecture were a symphony, and she—a child again, dancing in the grass at Piedmont Park during a Sunday concert. It was never only limbs. She pushed again and again her *self* through the architecture—when it was good, that was how it felt. With the ones she invented, she felt also a strange possessiveness. The not-wholly-oppositional senses of entrance and ownership clashed within her.

This one, though, allowed no conflict: each time she moved it into a form, there was only one way out—and that new form also coerced. The architecture yoking her shoulders demanded next to be swaddled in arms, then extended into a weapon form that required a telescoping downward, inward. The architecture—the instrument—in this way possessed itself of a willing Clef. As its shapes accelerated, sweat began to fly from the pools above Clef's collarbones, spattering floor and mirrors. She partnered the figures, leaning hard into thought until thought merged with skin and nerve and reflex, and all trained upon the architecture: how to maintain its escalating metamorphoses, how to offer it flight or escape, how to best exploit Clef as catalyst. And then, unexpectedly, and for what must have been a remarkable duration, she wicked. In the chamber, Clef was no longer.

———

Clef ate an apple as she walked toward the subway. The apple was a world. The wind that whipped a lock of wet hair into her mouth was inside the apple. She sucked salt from the hair before pulling it from her lips. Above her the blue pressed down coldly. She was taller now, and could pierce it. Clef cut a swath from the air as she moved down the street. First, someone noticed her passing. Then, someone else. Scraps of newspapers and neon-hued flyers drifted down to settle in her wake. She tossed the apple core into a wire trash can and peeled some red paint from her palm. It had the irregular shape of a continent. Some vagrant continent—brightly bloody.

———

"You did what?"
  "I wicked."

"On the first day?"

"The first day? Try within the first two hours."

"Wait. That's hardly possible."

"I know."

"It takes weeks."

"Months for most of us, Kitchen."

"Is this architecture like another one you've worked with?"

"Nothing like."

"Then how . . ."

"I don't know. But I was out for a while."

"How long?"

"I'm not sure. But the light from the window, the diamond . . ."

"What about it?"

"It moved."

"Are you sure? How far—what, half an inch?"

"No. Not an inch. A foot. Maybe two."

"You're on crack, Clef."

"No. I will admit to feeling a little high afterwards."

"High? Like post-performance high?"

"No—not *up*, not *on*. I felt, maybe . . . unencumbered? Like I'd left something inside the wicking. Something heavy. Cruel."

"Clef, I want you to talk to someone."

"I want to talk to someone."

"You do?"

"Don't get excited. I won't discuss my sleight with your butoh gurus—or anything else—so just please, don't. You left them, remember."

"I left them because—"

"You were tired of exploring your humanity. I know, Kitchen. And you certainly have excelled in that regard."

"You say something cruel fell away during the wicking? Not fucking likely. Okay. So if not Ito or Masaka, then who?"

"I hear she's dying, but Fern Early."

women die in Juarez :: men also die :: womenbodies scatterthedesert :: see internet :: see plastic-wrap :: debreasted&nippleless :: post-NAFTA-factory-shifted-women-bodies :: &girls :: sex tourism :: cum-American :: cum loud &documented :: see documentary :: sex workers or factory :: whores all :: otherwise—sisterhorror :: sisters factorywork :: sisters schoolteach :: see unsisterbodies :: see blame, buried :: factory-as :: die-way :: architecture-as-death-investment :: see. see. see.

COMPOUND.

Fern offered Clef a drink, and Clef took it. It was strong, faintly medicinal.

"What brings you here? I haven't seen you since the premiere of *Squaw King*,[19] have I?"

"No, and that was four years ago. You were only at the after-party for a few minutes—I'm surprised you remember talking to me at all."

When Clef had called that afternoon, Fern had immediately invited her over. Clef assumed this meant Fern had become addled, or—too old or sick for lovers—had grown lonely.

"It's cancer, dear, not Alzheimer's. Of course I remember. You were nervous that the audience had sensed your connection to the work, and I told you not to overestimate them. You were always such a pleasure in class. I taught you—what?—four summers? But so intense, everything taken too much to heart. You felt an obligation even then. Not at all like your sister."

Clef was thrown. She swallowed a mouthful of whatever sweet burning thing Fern had given her. Too quickly. Her face felt hot.

"You remember Lark?"

---

[19] The rules for naming sleight structures are obscure, even to directors, who must get approval from the International Board. The process is such that the rules differ subtly depending on whether the structures come from Revoix's found documents or were drawn by a known hand. Of the previous type, some of the most often performed are: *Musics 1 & 2, Carapace, The Face of Leaves,* and *Negligence.* The latter have been given wider-ranging appellations—titles such as *Hold, Iota of Crouch, Field-plate, Dart, Blastula, The Trepanation of an Orange, Grail-split, Hush a Day Late, Matadorsal, Cleave,* and *Dimebag.*

"As I said . . ."

"I'm so sorry, I didn't—"

"I know you didn't. Ignore me, I'm just old and mean. But you were asking do I remember Lark? Dear god, yes. She frightened us."

"Excuse me?" Clef kept losing her footing. She didn't remember Lark garnering much attention at the academy, especially not from Fern, whose interest in the more talented older girls had been fodder for gossip.

"After your sister wicked, she got weak. Every time. Not like the rest of you. That usually happens to a sleightist getting ready to retire. Am I right in thinking she stayed in Monk only briefly?"

"Two years. But what does that mean?" Clef remembered her sister's odd reaction to wicking—it was one of the reasons she never thought Lark very talented. Lark didn't return invigorated. When she managed to get offstage, she was a quiver of flesh—as if she'd been repeatedly shot through. After they wicked, other sleightists said they felt more present in their bodies, more alive. Not Lark. She hated it. And when Clef had pressed her for details, she'd said she felt eaten.

Fern stood up and walked toward the window. She motioned Clef over. Clef looked out at the taxi-strewn traffic below—too much of the wrong yellow—and then across the street. A sliver of park glinted from between two buildings: one art deco, one hidden behind scaffolding. She looked to Fern, expecting a tangential lecture on the buildings' construction or renovation, like the ones she used to deliver at the academy, but Fern was focused on the windowsill. There, set on top of a white silk scarf, was not what Clef at first took to be an ashtray, but a Soul. It was the palest Soul Lark had ever made, though Clef couldn't know that. Eyeing it, Clef wouldn't have called it white, but she wouldn't have called it another color. The gray light from the window collected inside of it and was drained of gray. The Soul seemed to pull the city in and through, leaving only light—thick like liquid.

"Where did you get this?"

"Lark sent it to me a few years ago. I believe it was one of her first."

"She gave this to you?"

"Yes. Your sister may be volatile, but she's generous. Since then I've shuttled quite a few collectors down to Georgia. Of course, they have to pretend not to be serious. Lark won't knowingly sell to a gallery. And she won't do an exhibition, you know. She's been approached."

"I didn't know."

"We've exchanged a few letters. She says she doesn't want her Souls to be another performance. I can't say I blame her."

"For what?"

"For wanting to know herself without the incessant doubling. Not that I think it's possible." Fern walked over to the coffee table and poured herself another glass. She gestured toward Clef with the decanter. "More? I don't suppose your sister is what brought you here. Shall we get numb before prodding about in you?"

They prodded for some hours. Afterwards, Clef couldn't explain to Kitchen exactly what had taken place. She tried. Retried. Fern had spoken of her overdue pilgrimage to Santo Domingo, about how she'd been made aware of certain unhistoricized practices: what Revoix couldn't stop seeing, what Fern could not. She had shown Clef pictures from her compound in Mexico. ("She calls it a compound, Kitchen, isn't that strange?") Fern had tried to tell her how little could be done against the deadened wall, and how necessary it was to do that little.

"The dead-end wall?" asked Kitchen.

"Just be quiet and listen—she is incred . . . an incredible woman."

Kitchen interrupted her, "Did you at least *mention* the wicking?"

"Shh, Kitchen—hush, please." Clef put her hand up to Kitchen's mouth. "It's because she is so sad from buying West . . . she says you shouldn't buy children, not even if they're yours to buy and you have the money, and that's the reason he will never stop hating her."

Kitchen removed Clef's hand from his face, gently. "Clef, I think we need to get you into bed." He helped her up and to the bedroom, and—while she talked on, gesturing obliquely when words were lost—he undressed her and laid her back onto the comforter. Once her eyes were closed and quiet, he sat down in the rocker beside her and started humming a leitmotif from a German operetta that had been grafted onto a Japanese commercial for long underwear, circa 1982.

———————

After dropping off Byrne in Georgia, after the train north, West headed to T's. A decade before, he'd taken over direction of Kepler from Fern and immediately moved the troupe to York. When he'd bought a dilapidated Victorian a few miles from the studio, he'd discovered one of his sleightists' hidden talents: T had strong thumbs and lips, the latter incessantly chapped from pursing nails between them. She had a husband too, Joshua, whom West liked. Joshua was a trial lawyer in DC and kept a modest apartment there where he stayed during the week. At the beginning, West didn't wish to complicate T's life with an ultimatum. Now, everything but the sex had been wrung out from between them. Besides, she'd taken on Byrne.

She was on her front porch just finishing carving ears on a disturbingly large pumpkin. A fluorescent light above her haunted her face. No matter how many times he'd hated it aloud, she hadn't changed it out.

"Aren't you running a little late? Halloween's tomorrow."

"Then aren't you early?" T stood up, wiped her hands on the thighs of her jeans and opened the screen door. She turned back to him. "Grab the knife for me, would you?"

Once inside, they headed to the shower. They ran the hot water into cold. The heaviness of two days on the train almost vanished from West's limbs, shuddered out. After T dressed, she said there was soup to heat up. She left to put it on. West, naked at the bathroom mirror, looked down at Joshua's things arranged on a wicker stand beside the sink: a razor, a comb, some man gel, cologne. They were familiar, these artifacts of the absent man. They made West neither sad nor jealous. He wouldn't open the cologne; he wouldn't shatter the bottle against the shower tiles in a cloud of citrus, or musk. He sometimes asked about Joshua, as he might've asked about T's brother. T had no brother. West would never complicate her life with an ultimatum. She was an excellent carpenter.

"This is good. What is this?"

"Leeks. And potatoes."

"Mmh."

"So you took your protégé down?"

"*My* protégé?"

"Yes, yours. He's just my sweet Byrne, he's your project."

"I did take him. What're the orange flecks?"

"Half a carrot. For garnish. And he was okay with that? Didn't balk or anything?"

"No. He was intrigued."

"You left the book with him then?"

"Yes."

"Didn't even copy those pages that were getting to you?"

"Which ones?"

"Please, West."

"No. I didn't."

"Well, you should've. There aren't many people I know bought or sold these days. It's okay it gets to you. Really. Do you think you'll want another bowl?"

"No, delicious though. And it doesn't. It's been over a long time now."

"You think? Listen. I'm sorry about this, but you can't spend the night tonight. I got a call earlier from Josh and he'll be home around eleven thirty. Missing me or some such."

LARK'S BOOK.

[On page 45]

I'm eight months pregnant. Am going to City Hall. I love, though an irrelevancy.

I found them almost a year ago. Mother's papers: Clef's and my pedigree. Funny, but when I showed them to Drew, not. I've been going it alone. For him, a wedding present. For our child. I've been using the Alberta May Library for the census. They request records from the LDS Library of Salt Lake City—the largest depository in the world. I've received dozens of copies of original documents from the early eighteen hundreds. Amazing—beautiful, beautiful penmanship.

In one document, the selection of names for the mare colts and horses are the same as for men: a bay horse named Sully, a man Sully; a gray mule Hal, a man Hal; a mule Georgie, a man Georgie; a mare Jim, a man Jim; a bay mule Dick, a man Dick; a bay mare Buck, a man Buck.

A document showing the date of sale of Drew's ancestors: his great-great-great-grandmother, Evie, his great-great-grandfather, Gus, and sister, Evangeline— sold by Silas Toomes to his daughter, Emma Toomes McCleod, on her wedding day, "for $15.00 & her continuing love and duty."

I am near the end. I went North to visit the DAR library. Drew's family didn't fight in the Revolutionary War. It was the Toomes men who were American patriots, "serving with distinction and valor." I have the Scrye, the Dolan, and now the white Toomes family trees alongside my child's father's—also Toomes. Black Toomes. The white Toomes's is, by far, the most detailed lineage.

My mother spoke of her ancestral poverty like a bedtime story: salad days and shanty Irish, whiskey beatings and potatoes. I don't doubt immigration was difficult—Northeastern coal mines didn't welcome micks. I've learned, from her papers, that when a Dolan died, the family gathered and scraped together funds for a photograph to commemorate the wake—all of them dressed in their best and only suits.

From the LDS papers I have learned that when a slave woman's age is listed followed by several children's names and ages in descending order and about two years apart, one might consider this a family.

MISSION.

Over the past few years, West had more frequently thought of his mother, imagined her harvesting wild rice on a small lake in Minnesota—though it was unlikely she'd gone back to her family. She was probably still in New York not far from Fern, in Brooklyn or Queens, past use as an exotic call girl, maybe doing the aging hippie thing. Fern had told West that the one time she'd met her, the whore had been wearing a string of turquoise beads.

West knew his mother was Native American, maybe in spite of the trappings. Moaning Wind was the name on the three thousand-dollar checks his father had made out to her, trying to convince her to drop West. The thought of him. His father had once envisioned himself holding a position in government. Holding a position—as for a camera, as on the stage. An illegitimate child to a buckskinned prostitute didn't fit any such tableau.

During rare visits, West's father never once mentioned the expensive indiscretion that had resulted in a son, but Fern said he'd been furious when she had retrieved the boy from Moaning's loft just off Amsterdam. Fern spent thirty thousand on her grandson—far more than fair market value for a child of any race. Later, Fern had tried to convince West that his mother was a doe-eyed Jew who'd ironed her hair and Siouxed-up for the sex trade. West didn't know why it was important to Fern that he was not the half Injun he so wanted to be back then. Loved being—at least until he was eight. But it was.

Recently, cancer had made his grandmother maudlin. Fern—out saving prostitutes, and native ones. West wouldn't have been surprised if this new, sick grandmother had tried to contact Moaning. But maybe his mother was beyond contact. A junkie now—a barfly. Or maybe she actually was on a Midwestern reservation, piloting a small boat through the reeds with West's half brother and two nephews, or dealing blackjack. He sometimes dreamt her on a corner in Chelsea with arms outstretched, filthy and deranged, waiting for her child to be returned. West didn't care that she'd let go. Money used in that way—to pry children out of darker arms—was no sale. It was pure and driven and one-dimensionally purchase. A clean, white thing.

West phoned the director of Monk. He set up a meeting. West had ideas about appropriation, about how stillness works, about pendulums, about the beauty of the obstacle. West was roused: he was going to break another rule and not think twice. The first hands (or one dear, mad hand) had been out to unveil physics. The bride. Like everyone, they'd been hunting primes, hungry for the irreducible. West viewed sleight's architectures as approximations that—combined with current culture (the words of the precursor), the anima of the human form, and the performers' will—create displacement. Escape, yes. Smallish death, yes. Latchless mind, yes. But also. Also. To West, the first sleights were the gunning-down-a-fast-road-through-salt-air to the bad but unimpeachable song from last decade that would become anthem for the next.

West had decided it was time for a new anthem.

The other director would be reticent, but West could call upon Clef and Kitchen. The most gifted sleightists in Monk would have pull with their mediocre leader. They didn't much like West, he knew, but he was recovering Lark—they'd be indebted.

West drove early the next week to Bucks County, Pennsylvania— farm country not far from Philadelphia. It was nearing winter. Still, the place was green with hills and ripe with cows, although sadly it had also come to boast espresso and beds, breakfasts, wine. He drove fast in his eighteen-year-old off-white Citröen—the last personal gift he'd accepted from Fern, a graduation present. He saw a billboard beside a barn adorned with a huge hex sign: YOU ARE LIVING ON THE SITE OF AN ATROCITY—★. *Yes,* he smiled. *Try to protect yourselves.*

For two hours he listened to the pauses in the conversation he was having in his head. The wet grays and greens rolled by too slowly. Color, West thought, is so often an act of revenge. That's why it's so frequently done with blood. Red pools of light. He could do that—and when sleightists passed through, if they were painted red, it would be like a half-wicking. A wicking that is truly illusion: color disappearing them.[20] They would eventually understand. Sleightists were brightly lit people. Invisibility achieved through something other than artistry would become to them something other than desirable. This would be an invisibility removed from talent, from choice. Yes—having them experience a different trajectory to nothingness would be first in West's order of operations.

He'd arranged to meet with the other director halfway between York and New York, inside the first hand sanctuary—the rural commune Antonia Bugliesi had created over a century before for her retiring male sleightists, to keep them in the family. Busying them with art that wasn't introspection.

He pulled up the long gravel driveway to the gray stone farmhouse. A low maple, hoarding the last of the season's blotched flame, hung a branch over the front of the car. West ducked beneath it to make his way to the side door—the one that led through the mud-cum-laundry room and into the original kitchen. A scrawny post-adolescent came to

---

[20] The illusion of distance—the illusion of illusion—is created and maintained in sleight by the very theaters in which it is performed. Distance is necessary to transform what is terrifying into what is pleasurable. For the audience, wicking is an illusion. They cannot explain it; they adore not being able to, but they do not believe for one moment that the figures onstage actually flash out of existence. No, the location of sleight—the familiar, deceitful stage—assures them that they are being happily duped. The eventual reappearance of the sleightists similarly pacifies them. Any misgivings someone may have while watching her first sleight vanishes when she witnesses the habitual complacency of fellow theatergoers.

and cracked open the door. Recognizing West, he flung open both the inner and the screen doors and gestured, disciple-ish, toward a kitchen lit yellow against lengthening evenings.

West said, "Thanks, we should only be a few hours." And then, remembering, he asked, "How many will that displace for dinner?"

The boy, looking threadbare in an undersized indie-rock T-shirt, frowned before answering. "In July we were eight, but now there's only the three of us."

"Look"—West's tone was sympathetic—"the same happened to my crew right out of the academy. I was one who eventually left, wasn't made for it—believe me, it's better to drop the untalented quickly." West put up a hand, stifling protest. "Here, take this." He held out a fistful of cash. "Is the Shot Clock still open? Go get some real food. I know how they keep this place stocked. Have a cheeseburger."

———

Monk's director was anxious. He didn't know what West wanted with him. West was legend. He was not. He sat unnaturally erect on a salvaged pew across the thick kitchen table from West. He nodded smartly, tried to ask the relevant question, but he was distracted. His eyes darted the room in a weak effort to stitch sense to what he saw: dozens of drawings on sheets of graph and legal paper scotch-taped to darkened oak in inscrutable systems. Arrows, grids, fountains of ink: the beginnings of sleights. Some of the structures, he noted, lacked what he would call verve; others were beyond ambitious, unnavigable. He felt uncomfortable passing judgment, however. Monk's director had never before been inside a commune; he hadn't been a hand. An ex-sleightist, he was insecure about his background—maybe it made his navigations too predictable, maybe he catered too much to the performers, maybe shortchanged the forms. That was, at any rate, what critics said of Monk. He tried to tune back into West, who was offering up a detailed plan for the collaboration but no reasons for it.

In front of the dead kitchen hearth, its limestone maw blackened with over two hundred years of soot, West crackled like kindling—this was the impression the nervous man had.

"Why color?"

"Why not?"

"Their skin, you say? What about the webs?"

"We'll glue mirrors to the skin itself, maybe even tint the reflections."

"Why two companies?"

"Size."

"Obviously, but why?"

"It isn't a massacre with twelve."

"Massacre?"

"Numbers. I need numbers. Twenty-four is barely adequate, but I think I can make it work."

"Make what work?"

"Look, I need your company. This is big. You have some of the strongest sleightists the academy has ever produced. Wouldn't you like to offer them something worthy of their talents?"

"Now hold on a second, West—"

"I'm not insulting only you. My own company has maybe two sleights worth its breath. We need this. Sleight needs it. It'll mean something."

"Mean something?"

"I'm not saying it'll have a story, at least not one to articulate.[21] No worries there. But it *will* have something for the sleightists to commit to other than their own vanity."

[21] Sleight is stringently antinarrative. Hands have been summarily dismissed from the academy for storying up their precursors, subconsciously or otherwise. Called the *mathematics of performance* and *visual music,* sleight forges its content from the medium itself. Whatever the original reason for its abstraction, by remaining nonreferential, sleight is able to be universally interpreted by its audience. Directors know that the moment meaning is attached to intent (the hands' or the sleightists') is the exact moment the audience begins to feel inadequate—and withdraws. The form is all. Sleight's function has always and only been the breeding, the perfection, the care and feeding of the form.

"Now you're insulting the——"

"No, I'm not. Why do they wick? Tell me. I mean, aside from proving their own techniques."

"I don't know . . . for the pleasure of the audience? A sense of community?"

"The audience can screw themselves and get just as much pleasure, for just about as much time. No. No sleightist wicks for the audience. And what did you say—a community? Of what, themselves? Working toward what?"

"I don't know. What would you have them work toward?"

"Exactly. *Exactly*. That, friend, is the first worthy question you've asked."

———

Clef was deep in practice with Kitchen when the director entered the studio. She was standing, heels in her lover's hands, her head nearly skimming the ceiling tiles, trembling with balance. The couple had skyscrapered two new architectures, linking them from Kitchen's ankles to her wrists.[22] Clef was trying to figure out how to add a next link, and then, how to bring the thing down kindly. She glanced over, saw killjoy in the doorway, and nearly lost it before regaining her focus

[22] In the syntax of sleight, an architecture is a word. A manipulation is a single defini-tion of an architecture; an architecture can be moved through several different manipulations—anywhere from three to thirty. A link is the method by which one architecture attaches to another. Links are phrases. A structure is a group of links that works together coherently: a sentence. When hands draw sleights, the structure is the most minute level they work with. Thus it is the director, not the hand, who chooses the architectures that best correspond to the structure on the page and then links them to create an approximation. The director is interpreter—wielding as much power as an interpreter chooses to wield. More. The product—the poem or the essay or the diatribe the director lifts out of the blueprint—is sleight. A hand, then, could be likened to a womb-deaf composer, arranging his notes not for instru-ments but solely in terms of color. It is the director and not the hand who transports prism to symphony.

in the mirror. She waited for his commentary. It usually upset Monk's leader—to catch Clef working with her own designs. Not today.

"You know, you should ask Haley in, if you need another body. She'd love to be part of this sort of thing."

"I'm sure she would, but no, that's okay." Clef tried not to show shock at the unexpected helpfulness. She smiled, maintaining her frozen posture. "Kitchen and I manage. How was your trip, by the way? How was West?"

Clef had knocked the wind from his sails—she saw it in his reflection. When she made a sudden jump down, the architectures clattered to the floor in dull violence. She hadn't meant to reduce him.

"I know him a little, West. It was me he called to get your number." Clef smiled apologetically.

"He's not trying to . . ."

Kitchen stepped forward to assure the man, whose ankles, like a girl's in patent leather, were starting to roll over his loafers. "No, he's not. He's interested in Lark."

"Clef's sister Lark?" The director took in a breath. "Why?"

"We aren't exactly sure."

"Hmm. He told me he wants to work with Monk. I'll be honest . . . I don't know what he's planning—but I'd be a fool, wouldn't I? I would. So I said yes. He wants to use your architectures, Clef. Says he'll get approval. I'll be anxious to see how he does that. But he gets what he wants, doesn't he? I wonder if that's his grandmother. The thing is, we need to start quick. He wants us in York Monday."

"What about tour?" Clef had been looking forward to South Africa.

"We'll be combining our schedules. West is handling it. Along with pretty much everything else, actually." The man grinned, as if he'd put something over.

Clef and Kitchen looked at each other. West was certainly adept. Their director was adrift in self-congratulation. Disconcerting—to watch him twitch like a glue-sniffing schoolgirl. West must have convinced him that he could be part of a singularity simply by surrendering control. Clef suppressed a smirk. But Kitchen, embarrassed for the man, looked away and down at the floor. At the long, taut tendons of his bare feet.

———

Kitchen and Clef were the only couple in Monk. A few of the other girls had boyfriends or fiancés, but these alliances wouldn't last, or the girls would quit. Elisa, Latisha, and Joan were dating brokers. Gretchen was about to marry a man named Hollis who had never seen her perform. Mikaela and Yael had split up years before and were now devoted friends. Haley was always happily severing from some man, attaching herself to another. Montserrat was a virgin.

Kitchen and Clef, a sleight couple, weren't typical of the art form. And Kitchen, because of his long meander toward sleight, and because he wasn't a graduate of the academy, qualified as curiosity solo.

Doug Terry's story was the more usual. Of Monk's men, he had begun sleight earliest because of four older, profoundly untalented sisters. Doug had talent, and even if he hadn't, he had been a boy and therefore would've been told that he had until he developed a certain self-confidence, enough to substitute for true aptitude. Manny— Emmanuel Vega—was the other of Monk's men. His case was also not abnormal. He'd started sleight as a teenager because his best girl friend was a serious but shy student who brought him along for comfort. She never made it—not with Manny, and not into a troupe. But Manny had.

Kitchen's experience didn't correlate. As a consequence, he spent little time with Doug or Manny, aside from drinking. He was older than them, knew more, was angrier. Drinking, he found he could stand them, and during tour each spring they watched the college basketball playoffs together. They were all American males enough to have been provided with that comfort.

Kitchen had come to sleight after butoh. Un-dance. To have un-danced he had trained in ballet for years—his mother had taught dance in San Francisco, his grandmother as well—first in San Francisco, then at the internment camp at Tule Lake. Kitchen had excelled, and ballet grew quickly intolerable. He abandoned it for postmodern modern. The German expressionist Mary Wigman, before embracing fascism, had taught—among others—a small cadre of Asian dancers at the commune at Monte Verità. Kitchen moved to Japan to study under not them but their disciples. During the late fifties a few dancers of this generation had moved beyond both Eastern and Western roots to create butoh, and in the late eighties, under their aging tutelage, Kitchen was carefully led to discover the correct questions: What is a dancer? What is it to dance? In his improvisational solo, *Pitted,* he spent time with each question—snaking vines of one around his calf, tight-fisting another inside his pelvis, dragging them along the floor like dead chickens guided by twine. This is where Kitchen got into trouble. "Butoh," Masaka had said to him one day after a particularly compelling performance, "is not dada." Kitchen knew then to stop. He wasn't interested in these particular questions, just in his own body's ability to ask. In fact, the less correct the question, the further his body could travel to it—the more and more various the dead animals he could pull along the floor. He could explore their weight, the quality of feather or scale as it pertained to drag. Kitchen crossed over to sleight and never once attributed a mechanical nature to the architectures. They were, for him, skeletal.

Since converting, Kitchen had come to understand that most male sleightists, although their physical skill might be comparable to his own, weren't dedicated to their craft. Male, they didn't have to be. They ate and drank sleight, but they didn't think it. That, originally, was how Kitchen had fallen in with the Scrye sisters, who also tended recklessly toward thought—an odd, unfruitful preoccupation for a sleightist.

Kitchen was in love with Clef, how Clef's mind worked. Once, he had wanted to be in love with Lark, and years ago had tried that. But Lark's thoughts were excruciating. Huge thorns. And cactuses, un-animal, would go unloved by Kitchen. He guessed he had been afraid of her, though it wasn't true. Now he lived with Clef's convolutions, no pale imitations of her sister's. The way Clef thought was feelable. She was angry like Kitchen, difficult, a bit of a crazy. She asked more of him than Lark had. Lark had asked for nothing but had been a chasm. Still, it would be a mistake to say that Clef these past years had been easier. Kitchen and she were together working and away from work. They kept separate apartments for this reason and because they didn't want commitment. Commitment murdered: this tenet they shared. But lately commitment had been in the room. Since Lark had shown up. No. Since the accident—no, call it a pregnancy, Kitchen. Since that.

Kitchen thought he must love her more now, and wanted to go away. She kept pretending. Clef's body, like her face, was a bad liar. In bed, that was when—or just after. The last time they'd made love she left the room the moment they—he—was done. She'd given a reason: wanted water or forgot her vitamins. Maybe she'd said she needed a shower. Whatever it had been, it had been a lie. She left the room to keep from breaking. When they had first gotten together, often after sex she'd collapse into his chest, crying. Her tears were quiet and thicket-like, and his torso those nights—above and below—had been slick with her. Now, with these new architectures, something was being channeled. Grief? Love? Kitchen wondered why he'd never known women with other hobbies. He wanted her to say it: that she wanted the child they hadn't. Lately, Kitchen couldn't keep himself from thinking about the rain. How good it could sometimes feel. How it felt all the other times.

And now, Monk's director had informed him that he'd bartered Kitchen's energies, his sweat and inquiry, to West—someone Kitchen didn't know, didn't trust, someone who had ideas about what things meant. Clef, invested as she was in private loss, seemed to find the maneuver unimportant, even droll. Kitchen, however, was beginning to feel a bit dragged. A bit along the floor.

Clef walked into chamber one. All of Kepler was there—and all of Monk filed in behind her. Regally she moved her diminutive frame through the loose gathering of sleightists, sleightists about to welcome her troupe into their space. She headed toward West, his back up against a mirror. As she got close, she said his name. And because he had already been looking in her direction—her red braid swinging angrily between the shoulders of the crowd—all he could do was say, "Clef?" At which point she kneed him in the groin with considerable force, having not, during the approach, slowed her imperial pace.

Gasps, and West doubled over. Kitchen ran up to grab her arm, but Clef was done. She pivoted and on her way out parted the silenced company. There was nowhere to go but back to the bus or toward town. She chose the walk. She left Kitchen there to speak with West. She had thought maybe her director would chase her down, beg her to apologize. Damage control. But his cowardice had predictably won out over appeasement—he wasn't after her. She turned down a residential street: brick ranch houses with carports and not much landscaping. She wanted to be alone for a while. Some shrubbery was all.

In the office, West nursed his testicles with a bag of frozen peas kept in the troupe refrigerator for muscle and joint injuries. Kitchen was with him. After the blindside, West had limped over to the office to speak quietly with an intern, who took a book of accounts and vacated. Kitchen had followed West and pointed through the open doorway. West let him in. But when Monk's director made a similar gesture from a few feet back, West offered only a puzzled stare and closed the door behind them.

"So. Your woman is insane."

"More furious. She thinks you're about to hurt her sister."

"Why? Because I've . . . well, not me personally . . . but because Lark's coming here?" West coughed, and grimaced. "I thought Clef would be pleased. No, ecstatic. In fact isn't that precisely what she asked me to do?"

"Yes." Kitchen saw how, for someone unacquainted with the sisters, Clef's actions might need interpreting. "Yes, she asked you to do that. Bring Lark back to sleight."

"So what's the problem?"

West's levity irritated Kitchen. Kitchen followed Clef's logic, but he didn't relish having to explain it to this near-stranger who, though puppetmaster, played at clown.

"As a hand. You're bringing her back as a hand. Clef thought that you'd make Lark what she'd been before."

"But the book, you were there—Clef gave me the book. And I *told* her I was looking for a hand."

"I know. You did. But this is where she has gaps. She never imagined. She doesn't see Lark's talent as . . ."

"Genius?"

"Just so. She doesn't see it that way. Her older sister was out of step. Problematic. Clef thought you'd bring her back and she'd quietly finish what she couldn't before."

"You're telling me Clef thinks Lark . . ."

"Failed, yes. Where Clef succeeded. And the book—proof that Lark regrets having left. Clef never imagined the sleights would pan out, or even that what Lark draws are sleights at all." Kitchen was shaking his head. He'd seen the book. He'd known what West would do, could kick himself for not trying to make Clef see it. He made an apology with his hands as he spoke. "So she sees this as a betrayal."

"But your director . . ." West was still unbelieving. "He told me Clef has been working on architectures based on Lark's work." West grunted, shifted the peas. He looked toward the door where he'd left the fidgeting man. "What a fucking idiot."

"No. I mean, yes. But he happens to be right. Clef has created over a dozen new architectures from Lark's sketches.[23] We've brought them. She's been obsessed, and the designs are—they're fantastic."

[23] Bugliesi began sleight with just under fifty architectures. Currently, there are sixty-odd institutionalized designs; preexisting ones are rarely altered—new ones are added to the official list at a rate of less than two per decade by a process both arduous and spuriously bureaucratic.

"So. I don't . . . I don't get it."

"Clef, she has her . . . gaps. I *do* get them. Eventually, they work out—or into—a sort of pattern."

When Clef came back around six, Kepler was packing up the bus for the motel. She headed to the restroom, where T cornered her. Clef's back was pressed against the wet sink as T apologized.

"We shouldn't have done that and I'm sorry we did."

"What?" asked Clef, a little taken aback by the moon-faced woman who stood so close.

"Once West heard you'd brought them, he made your director bring them in. We worked with them all day blind—your architectures. I wouldn't blame you for being upset, but I have to tell you, they're wonderful." And then T extended her hand. Simply that. And an invitation to dinner at her place. "Please bring Kitchen." Clef didn't refuse.

Though T hadn't said, Clef assumed West would be there. T had the sway of a negotiator, the fluid wrists, open face. Even the cold water on the small of Clef's back worked to T's advantage—Clef felt rigid: the woman in front of her was a move toward warmth, flexibility. And Clef, having spent the bitter afternoon wandering through suburban decay, was ready for wine, bread, a yielding. Her first fury was ebbing. She would offer West an opportunity to explain.

CLEF: I presume you can tell me when my sister will be here?

WEST: Byrne said they're leaving tomorrow. It seems there was some issue with arranging the nanny for her daughter, but it was resolved.

CLEF: My niece?

WEST: Yes, of course. I'm sorry—your niece.

CLEF: And for how long will you be asking Lark to abandon her family?

KITCHEN: (*from across the room*) Clef, come over here and take a look at this music.

MONK'S DIRECTOR: It certainly is an impressive collection. Are you from Mississippi, T?

T: New Orleans originally.

MONK'S DIRECTOR: Oh.

T: But Josh is the blues baron.

CLEF: Who's Josh?

T: My husband Josh.

CLEF: You mean you aren't West's?

KITCHEN: Clef.

T: No, that's okay. I'm not anyone's, Clef. But why doesn't everyone come to the table for some salad? The pasta will be ready in a few.

CLEF: Where *is* Josh?

T: He's in DC preparing for trial. He's a lawyer. It's a big case, I think—class-action suit, another insurance company. He likes this kind of work.

CLEF: "This kind" meaning lucrative?

T: "This kind" meaning punitive.

CLEF: Ahh.

MONK'S DIRECTOR: Are these sunflower seeds?

T: Pine nuts.

WEST: I think, Clef, that Lark will stay up here until she feels that she's accomplished what she needs to. She's welcome to bring her family. I'd be happy to help arrange that.

KITCHEN: Then you've spoken with her?

WEST: Not yet, but Byrne assures me—

CLEF: Who the hell is Byrne?

WEST: (*pauses, looks across the table at T*)

T: West found him. He's an unbelievable writer—Byrne wrote our last precursor. Phenomenal. But you'll get to hear it for yourselves . . . along with some new work, I think. (*pause*) Also, Byrne is my lover.

CLEF: Your lover?

T: One of them.

CLEF: (*laughing, lifts a wine glass*) To T. Faulty to her nest.

T: Thank you, Clef. I deeply believe in nests. Are we at peace then?

CLEF: Armistice.

WEST: Will you come to rehearsal tomorrow, Clef? We weren't entirely successful with your designs this afternoon.

MONK'S DIRECTOR: I tried to explain to them what I'd seen you . . .

CLEF: I'll come. (*to Kitchen*) What did you do all day? You didn't help them?

KITCHEN: I didn't show them anything. But I meant to tell you . . . the designs, Clef—they started elucidating themselves.

T: It's true. No one was having any luck—

MONK'S DIRECTOR: Despite my efforts.

T: —until we split up and started improv-ing in sepa-rate studios.

KITCHEN: I just watched. They actually came up with most of our links and some that we hadn't.

CLEF: Hadn't *yet*.

KITCHEN: Yes. You're right. Yet.

———

Lark spent the week before they left like something in a locked box. Byrne hung back, trying not to require the extra energy a guest requires, as she made preparations to join Kepler and Monk in York. Drew, Byrne saw, was sad but wanted a whole wife. Lark sat at the kitchen table those last days scribbling instructions and making calls, while Drew busied himself with the domestic space around her, drying the dishes, clearing crumbs from the mustard-colored linoleum, pausing often as he passed to touch her head. During these moments, Byrne looked away. He'd seen Drew make the same bear-like gesture with Nene. The man's hands lacked coherence. Though they clearly loved him, when Drew pawed at them, something inside his wife and child ducked.

While the couple spent their remaining nights up late talking and having, except for the bedframe, soundless sex, Byrne browsed the books lining the thin walls of the guest room—mostly history and theo-retical science written for the layperson. He skimmed an old volume on plate tectonics, newer ones on chaos and string theory, and devoured a biography of Linnaeus and his system of morphological categorization: naming bound by shape. Byrne kept study of Lark's book for the morn-ings, but waited to put down the words evoked by her sketches until the afternoons.[24] In the evenings, while Drew made dinner, he walked with Nene to the lake. He was teaching her to skip stones.

"You're getting good, Nene. That was four."

"I can do six." She leaned over and brushed the red clay off a thin oval rock. She held it up for Byrne to inspect. He nodded.

"When have you done six? I never saw that."

Nene let the stone go with a deceivingly faint flick. Six dips in and out of the calm. Across the water a jagged bruise of pines spread from earth to sky, in world and in mirror. She looked up at Byrne.

"My daddy taught me this summer. He's better at it than you. So's Newt."

"You didn't tell me you knew how." Byrne looked out over the vague, multiple rippling and dropped his next throw—a small yellow-white one—onto the bank. He brought the empty hand to his other and started massaging his wrist and forearm.

"You said you wanted to teach me."

"Nene, that's like lying." Byrne wasn't sure why he was upset. He struggled with his tone, tried not to accuse her. Of what, being four? After three weeks with Nene, he knew this revelation of her past history skipping stones was meant to hurt him. He asked her. "Why would you do that?"

"You're taking Mommy away." Nene wasn't sulking. She was answering.

"Yes, but only for a little while. She'll be back soon. I know she's explained this to you." Byrne was irritated to be comforting her— she'd wounded him. And he felt ridiculous, having wounds.

"Mommy doesn't always know how things will *result*. Newt says she wouldn't have made a very good scientist. She ignores certain *factors*." Nene enunciated these words as if she'd recently been made aware of their secondary definitions. "What factors is she ignoring?"

[24] Unlike the system of rules provided for the structures and even the naming of sleights, the writing of precursors is a fairly unfettered practice. A hand must not create narrative, but no word is off limits, and there are no guidelines to suggest how a precursor might match language with form. Precursors are the intuition of sleight, its curve. Hands who fall into formula with their precursors inevitably effect redundant sleights.

"For example: *before anything can mean, it must suffer understanding.*"

"Where did you hear that?" Byrne barely registered Nene's language as extraordinary anymore, just odd—like a streak of white hair, or an ominous birthmark. But this was aphoristic even for her. Byrne didn't like to speak of Nene's dead grandfather as if he were a playmate, but sometimes it was the only way to get a response from her. "Did Newt tell you that?"

"That's silly. Newt thinks that stuff is *bunk*. It's from Mommy's book, page forty-two. Don't you remember?"

"Nene, you shouldn't poke around in other people's—in my things." Byrne didn't know whether to scold or soothe. Parts of Lark's book, the photographs mostly, had given him nightmares. He hadn't paid as much attention to the words—journal entries, captions, quotes. They made him uncomfortable. He read just enough to assure himself they weren't precursors. "What do you think what you just said means, Nene?"

"It means Mommy's going to make people hurt. Because she does. Because she thinks it's right." Nene sounded, as she rarely did, angry. Byrne watched as her collarbones pulled forward, grew sharp.

Byrne felt cold. The air was wet with lake and the sun, low. Bits of trash at the water's edge were beginning to look placed—the right shadows adding significance to a candy wrapper, an abandoned sock. Byrne got down, reddening his knees in the mud to look into the girl's gray eyes. He was either forgiving or being forgiven, he didn't know which, and Nene's terrible smallness was starting to show. When it reached full pout, she kicked a Red Bull can into the water, then crossed the short distance between them. She bent over so that the top of her head pressed like a miniature cannonball into Byrne's chest. He reached out and with his clear hand took her shoulder. He didn't pull her any further in, and she didn't cry. His other hand and the rock it held rose and fell beside them, unable to settle.

———

For the first few hours in the car, Lark said nothing, although she did point out each atrocity billboard as they passed it. Byrne didn't mention his proprietary feelings toward them, or toward Nene for that matter. They were approaching the blue mountains—drunken giant-brides, sprawling and roomy. The morning was in mist, and the car had already begun pressing itself drowsily against the curves when Byrne asked if they could take a bathroom break.

Lark answered him, "That's a type of torture you know, an interrogation technique—not letting someone urinate."

"I did," said Byrne, "I watch TV." But the flippancy struck out, humorless, so he apologized by adding, "I've also heard a few war stories."

Lark eyes flickered from the road, appraising him. "Have you?" She wasn't being sarcastic, and Byrne blushed as if he'd been caught bragging.

"On Sundays, Gil sometimes took me to the VA hospital where he worked. I think it was supposed to be punishment."

"Gil is your father?"

"Was. I could take a bleach-and-urine sauna in the basement laundry with him, or I could pretend I was someone's grandson in one of the common areas."

Lark spoke into the windshield. "You chose the latter."

"I did."

Pissing, Byrne realized he'd had a favorite. There had been, always beside the aquarium, a powder-haired man who'd smelled of menthol cigarettes and Dial soap. Byrne hadn't been scared of this patient; his damage was less apparent than most. Once he had told Byrne how he'd been captured outside Dresden. How he'd been made to work with three other POWs in the German camp. Digging latrines starving. How one day, the soldiers had heard enemy fire—Allied fire—and this man, but not the others, had started walking toward it. No one had stopped him. How he'd walked, how he couldn't have run—he thought it must've been two hours, maybe four miles. And not been shot. How, hospitalized a week later in England, he'd weighed thirty-eight kilos. The old man had said that frail as he was now, he weighed double that. "And back before the war," he whispered to Byrne, "I boxed."

Byrne emerged from the interior of the truck stop. "Truck stops," Lark had explained before pulling off, "make more coffee more often." Byrne had noted only a burnt smell. His recovery of the old man's tale was like an itch, and as he recounted it to Lark, he felt a little too excited. She was filling the tank.

"Why do you think that one stuck?"

"He was an elegant man, didn't look tough. But the way he told it— it was nothing. Losing half his body weight was nothing."

"There are worse things."

"Yes."

"No." Lark was suddenly adamant. "There aren't. You can't do comparative suffering. It doesn't work." She ran a hand through her dark hair. "You just like how he didn't make you feel awful. Elegant, you said. You were eight? ten? He made you feel big—told you that story in a way that didn't make it seem impossibly far away or insane. But I don't admire pretty, or what's . . . self-abnegating." Her hand fell away from her head. "Of course, I'm not a man."

It pissed Byrne off a little, actually—Lark, condescending. As if he were much younger than she was. He wasn't.

"How about you? Vomiting up emotions—that's not self-abnegation? not denial? Christ then, what do you call it?"

Lark pulled out, gasoline dripping. She stared at Byrne blankly, then turned back to the pump to retrieve the receipt—glancing at, then crumpling it.

"What do I call it? I don't. You can't imagine what it's like . . . not to have desires but be populated by them."

"Tell me then."

It was a dare. She cocked her head at him. This was a confessional truck stop, perhaps. But she couldn't talk about it, not after that. He would compare. He would hold her story up against his war hero's and find it lacking.

Byrne was gnawing on some jerky he'd picked up inside. Lark watched his mouth, his jaw, the willful working of the flesh.

"What does that taste like?"

Byrne swallowed before answering. "It's a little like . . . like a beef raisin."

Lark laughed. She was pretty when she laughed, and it was electric, such an abrupt shift in the dynamics of her face. Byrne found himself smiling back, bits of jerky in his teeth. Then Lark opened the car door, signaling that the conversation was soon to end. She didn't converse well while driving.

"My mother would sometimes put raisins in our lunches. Press them into the sandwiches to make desiccated little eyes and mouths. Clef loved it, but I wasn't . . . convinced."

———

Clef walked outside the room to go find coffee, maybe a bagel, and saw a paper on the ground two doors down, big photo and headline font too large. She picked it up. As she read, her stomach knotted. And then a lower cramp, lower than her stomach. She dropped the paper. Ran back through her motel room into the bathroom, fell to her knees. She wanted to, found she couldn't vomit. She reached over to lock the door and then slumped, forehead against the toilet bowl, staring at the crossword of tiny black, white, and blue-green floor tiles for minutes. She couldn't identify the size or shape of the repeating unit, which infuriated her. Kitchen eventually knocked.

"I saw it, Clef. Come out. Please."

"I'm going to be sick."

"Then let me in." Kitchen waited. He tried again. "Or I'll huff and—"

"Children die all the time. Famine. War. So there're killers in the neighborhood. That makes it special?"

"It tends to."

That morning they barely worked. It was all over the papers and on TV. To report it was to encapsulate the current world-sickness, different from past world-sicknesses only in the viral speed with which things of horror could be repackaged for re-creation. Still, doorsteps mattered. These twenty-three, possibly twenty-five, had been killed in York, a few streets over from West's house—in a well-kept and mannered neighborhood, if such places were to be believed, which they weren't. They'd all been young, from what could be told, between five and eight. And these were recent killings, all within the past half decade. It was like bad cinema—the mug shots of the couple hovered, Bundy-style, around a-little-too-good-looking, but white like most and in their mid-thirties; the husband sang in the church choir every Sunday, and the wife was on her company's softball team—apparently, a solid second baseman.

The sleightists had drifted in behind schedule that morning, and then done not much. West ordered some salads for a late lunch. He sat both troupes down on the floor in the largest chamber. Still clutching the plastic utensils he'd handed out at the door, some of them stretched hamstrings and quads. But no one ate, as no one had worked.

"This has nothing to do with us," West said, "but we can use it."

Haley glared. Many of Monk's members nodded as she spoke. "I think we should call this day shot—I mean, you guys live here. We're just passing through, and it still feels like I've been kicked in the gut." She started, "Did you see how they . . ." then broke off.

Since the eleven o'clock news the night before, parts of the macabre video had played too many times in a row on the local stations, as if there were no children left but these. The couple, the Vogelsongs, had created a theatrical hive in their basement. A pageant. Voluminous curtains of pomegranate, tangerine, and honey hung around the room on six boxed frames just over five feet in height. The boxes faced into the center of the hexagon with a gap of perhaps eighteen inches at each corner. Each box had a different inner backdrop—detailed dioramas of the Serengeti, a rural Midwestern landscape replete with silos and combines, a mountain-pierced night sky, the mottled floor of a rainforest, Appalachian-style woodlands littered with birch, a thriving and technicolor coral reef. While giving the grisly tour, the eerily childlike and bearded Mr. Vogelsong floated in bust form as he passed behind the theaters, naming them as he circled—Safari, Farm, Stars, Jungle, Trees, and Sea.

Ray Vogelsong or his wife Melanie would have sat in a rolling office chair on the outer edge of the boxes to work the strings. The alternating puppeteers could have moved around the room with ease, while the interior audience—a bound, gagged child on a bar stool—would have been rotated from setting to setting, world to world. Her new surroundings. Maybe the child had been allowed to speak after the hours-long performance, to choose a habitat. Or two. Or all six. "Where would you like to live, dear? If you could swim or fly or gallop faster than the nighttime, which would you choose? Pick your pets. Pick the colors and shapes of your future. Such pretty homes we've built for you. Do you see?"

The news showed segments of the documentary-style footage: the camera scanned the basement shelves lined with plain brown shoeboxes—each labeled with a Polaroid of its contents, a date of completion, and a list of initials. The media had decided, in this case, to relinquish all but the most vestigial decency. So it was only in these cataloguing pictures that the Vogelsong's works were offered to the general public: in photo after photo, from the deft fingers of the couple were suspended their exquisite miniatures. Animal marionettes. Petite beasts fashioned from the boiled and bleached bones of past audiences: each one masterfully rendered—carved and polished but unpainted, as exemplary specimens of driftwood remain unpainted in the hands of discerning craftspeople.

It was impossible for a sleightist to stare at the television and not wonder—how had they configured the tiny rhinoceros skull, the bat wing? Could the horse trot? The monkey mouth swing open? It was this aesthetic curiosity that caused them to shrink bodily away from the television while their eyes remained, riveted in shame. The morbid fascination that other citizens could suppress or deny was, for the sleightists, much more compelling. It was professional interest.[25]

But it wasn't only the dozens of strung toys and the couple's workbench, with its precise divisions of unused bones and fine, clean tools, that impressed them. The very character of the space demanded admiration. The killers had reversed the concept of theater-in-the-round. Like many brilliant ideas, it was simple and elegant and it borrowed—wrenching function from an earlier model. The victims, had they not been too frightened by the kidnapping, might have at first delighted. In how just-for-them it was. Eventually, the spinning would have disoriented them. Some might have gotten sick on themselves. And if they weren't too tightly bound already, their accumulating complaints and struggling to be undone would have earned them more rope: a cocooning. The transformation from child into animal would have begun long before the Vogelsongs picked up their long knives for the reincarnation. It was all there—in the space. Any good sleightist could read it.

"Listen. I know it's gotten to you. But Clef graciously decided to put aside our differences to come in today and help with her architectures, and Byrne and Lark are on their way. We don't have much time before tour." West was looking around at the two dozen faces, polling their expressions.

"I'm not feeling that hot, West."

---

[25] Sleight is not routinely perceived as grotesque, despite its recorded adrenal effect: a heightened sense of threat. In a study done by Dr. G. T. Theva of the Hookings Medical Institute, puzzling chemical phenomena were documented in a third of the study's participants—all seated audience members. Indeed, the number of heart incidents occurring in sleight theaters prompted managers to equip them with defibrillators far before it was fashionable. Beyond the effect Theva noted in its spectators, sleight has also been described as "a carnival of self-annihilation" and "a compulsive reenactment of the death-wish." This is to say that, despite its continuing success with the general public, there are a minority who find sleight theoretically abhorrent.

"I wasn't feeling so hot yesterday, Clef. And that had something to do with you."

A couple members of Kepler sniggered and immediately fell silent, embarrassed to have found humor in this climate.

"What do you want us to do? Create links about this? Improv on the dismemberment of children?" Clef's voice, though caustic, was not up to its usual fire.

"Actually, yes. I think yes."

"You're a sick fuck. I can't believe I put you in touch with my sister."

"Maybe. But you all know that it'll feel good to move. Better, even, to wick—though with the new forms, you probably won't get that release. And if you work with some sense of purpose—for these children . . ."

"All . . . the . . . pret-ty, lit-tle hor . . . ses." T mumble-sang this with her face hidden in her hands. Then she bought them down, folded them in her lap. She lifted her head. "I agree with West. Action is preferable to nonaction. If we don't practice, I'll just go home and chop wood all afternoon. Oh." She put her face back into her hands. "Jesus."

"I just can't." Haley shook her white-blonde tresses in a no.

"It's beyond exploitative." Kitchen said this.

"What else are we going to do?" One of Kepler's women stood up. "I don't want to go home, I don't want to see it anymore. Do you?"

This was what it took. They slowly stood: one, and then another, and then a few. They dropped their forks and knives in front of West, who sat cross-legged in the middle of the space. With each piece of plastic, his look of satisfaction grew and his presence faded. Cheshire. The sleightists migrated to the edges of the chamber to pick up the various architectures. They decided quietly among themselves who would work where. Some resisted and went to sit in the lounge, but eventually, even for Haley, the idleness became suffocating, and those few reentered the chambers.

After nearly half an hour spent watching Clef, brutally numb, Kitchen pulled her to her feet. "West's right about this," he said.

Drained of heat, her voice atonal, still she attempted a refusal—
"You said it was exploitation."

Kitchen kissed her damp forehead. "Yes, Clef. It's art."

West knew it was wrong to see this as a stroke of luck. But he wrestled with the moral dilemma not at all. This was what they needed. Impetus. Emotion they couldn't rid themselves of as they worked, and imagery. He'd thought he would have to dredge up something historical—Dachau, Nagasaki, Kibuye. But today was history, closer and more vivid than anything he could bring them in a book. He would not have to work to have them haunted—and not merely by the children. The details would catalyze them: the painted fantasies of place and those pale animals, and the idea of each child alone in the midst of it— alone in the center of his own disappearance, watching milky creatures court his bones to soaring horn and bullfrog tones. It seemed the Vogelsongs, at least on their basement hi-fi system, had been partial to early recordings of Satchmo.

The husband had gone to the police station to confess. The wife, simultaneously, to York's Channel 8 with their homemade footage—a sympathetically filmed and narrated journey into the couple's world. There was no reason. No one had found them out; not one had escaped or nearly escaped. They were tired of their work going unremarked upon perhaps. His eyes were no longer attentive enough, hers no longer admiring. They were obsessives who had honed their skills while craving difference. They hungered for a wild-type reaction. It wasn't possible to switch up the victim profile or method, everything having been perfected. So they varied the response the only way they could: they went public.

West understood their quandary. The scales had tipped. The pride in their work had finally won out over their need to continue performing: it had come time for fame. He wondered who had been the first to fall. He didn't assume it had been the man.

For West, horror was a natural throe of childhood. These children had just escaped a longer set of convulsions. They'd gone off like honored guests—wined and dined and performed for. All children were slaughtered into adulthood; these ones had been thrown a party. West was unable to stop analyzing—disavowing their pain with analogy, swerving it into commonplace, an American cliché. In the media, the Vogelsongs would be called monsters, but he knew better.

Although his mind might be fringed in a bitter light, that light allowed West a pitiless clarity. At the edges of his worldview the cowboy had always stood: a pure looming, a reversal of gypsy, tinker, the Goodguy who swept all dark children up and away. That's who the Vogelsongs were. Sweet wranglers who had saved these unwanteds from future treachery. That's how the couple saw it. That's how much of the country would see it soon, after repeating to one another, with far too little embarrassment, soundbytes from Melanie Vogelsong's oddly poetic monologue:

Each one of our animals was an adoption. They were lost. They call it a system—my Ray worked in that system. That system, it didn't work. We took them in, gave them spirits. Now they are strong. Proud. Beautiful. Free. They belong to Christ. Christ was the lamb. They are what they wanted to be: Christ's. Ray asked them. Ray gave them choices not many animals get. They didn't want to be what they were. Their hair, for example. I couldn't use the hair of all but two. Those two had to do for every mane, every tail. We have eight lions and five horses. And now the bones are clean. You can't tell anything at all from the bones. I'm very happy about how clean they came.
—transcripted from the Vogelsong tape as it aired on *Channel 8 News*

The links were breathtaking. In all four chambers, members of Monk and Kepler were speaking with the architectures—invocations of animals that didn't exist. A calling forth of alien life: sky-whale and tree-elk and earth-sparrow. Montserrat, Doug, Manny, and Yael joined a member of Kepler in a low structure. They alternated taking two small stutter-steps with a quick carving motion to make the floor swarm with skittering fish, then shot the structure overhead so that mice seemed to spiral along the architectures before moving up into the rafters. Strange mice, smooth as icing. Haley and a pair of Kepler's men were lumbering gracefully—a two-trunked elephant clearing ground and air as if in preparation for the planting or burial of thought. Latisha and T were bound by their architectures in what seemed a vegetative embrace, until the link began to rotate, arcing them across the floor in a velvet bestial waltz. And they were all wicking. All of them—flashing in and out like the evening news in a July thunderstorm. There was an overpowering static to it, a haze in the chambers that lasted hours.

Kitchen and Clef weren't themselves inside of it. They walked slowly, slowly between the chambers, disengaging each foot with care each time it left the floor. Mute. It was Kitchen silently crying. Clef, reaching for his hand. The second time they entered chamber two, they saw across the field of sleightists a man and a woman holding hands at the other entrance. This was not a mirror. This was Lark, but the man was white, not Drew. Between the couples, sleight was giving birth. Creature after creature tumbled forth in a discontinuous river of forms. A dumb show. Eden unnamed.

West watched, rotating through each of the four chambers from the office. A door and small tinted window on the fifth wall of each chamber led into the small gray room: file cabinet and telephone. There he had gone, to sit in the dark like a child, choosing the fauna of his next life.

Book 2

Anna   Adam   Clay   Tara   Bethany   Jamal

Lark   Hava   Rory   Ruben   Midori

Dahlia   Cole   Oscar   Rashanda   Sarah   Jenny

Krystal   Ari   Omar   Trent   Sissy

Ziad   Wilson   Machete   Edmund   Lesha   David

Mikaela   Alix   Dominic   Jesus   Maya

Serena   Kate   Ayde   Misha   Tomas   Dante

Carter   Boy   Tiffany   Mireille   Angel

Sebastian   Malcolm   Fran   Sy   Chloe   Vice

Flora   Miles   Joan   Jeremiah   Allen

Sariit   Taryn   Holly   Dago   Sunny   Ariel

Xavier   Alice   Denzel   Jean   Glock

Quentin   Undecided   Martine   Lourdes   Brandon   Ronald

Trent   Ho   Barbara   Cassandra   Francis

Sapphire   Kyle   Elizabeth   Ira   Zelda   George

Maria   Eleanor   Zeke   Troy   Penny

Vincento   Ula   Bree   Daniel   Axe   Sofia

Chink   Claudia   Wyatt   Isaiah   Lilly

Riley   Adania   Dylan   Elliot   Jude   Spear

Mace   Isabel   Window   Michelle   Seth

Knox   Frederica   Bo   Izzy   Lance   Tasmin

Dirk   Hope   Dreyfus   Ruby   Sinner

Orion   Pace   Fallon   Ennio   Garrote   Keith

Roberto   Priya   Lowell   Sylvia   Marianne

Gail   Siobhan   Kevin   Ethan   Karl   Moses

Jonathan   Noelani   Grant   Joy   Gook

Calvin   Moron   Joshua   Tanya   Simon   Eric

Grace   Hank   Nancy   Uzi   Teague

Meghan   Slut   Bea   Esther   Ramon   Silas

Aloma   Gray   Tucker   Janine   Victoria

Lola   Littleboy   Nora   Winnie   Santosha   Matthew

Magdelena   Adolf   June   Oliver   Shiv

Harrison   Rose   Dino   Tyler   Failure   Gideon

Hazel   Colt   Tobias   Brooks   Hector

Gatling   Renault   Agnes   Donna   Jessica   Jared

Enrico   Tavi   Beryl   Scott   Edgar

Connor   Archer   Dagger   Xenia   Ian   Sven

Ruth   Corey   Caitlin   Pele   Yolanda

Dolores   Goldie   Gena   Murray   Leroy   Blake

Ethel   Rifle   Savannah   Madison   Devlin

Maury   Chase   Yuriko   Ivan   Mortar   Gunnar

Nell   Gennadi   Fenton   Grenade   Charles

Francesca   Abigail   Sadie   Marek   Bomb   Christopher

Dean   Denise   Gus   Kike   Stephan

Spencer   Howitzer   Lauren   Noelle   Phillip   Gustav

Thelonius   Spike   Emily   Hayes   Lyle

Micah   Duncan   Nina   Giovanni   Gilles   Mabel

Bridget   Heidi   Cannon   Storm   Dallas

Chelsea   Robert   Jamison   Taniqua   Rita   Shari

Shane   Aster   Vadim   Molotov   Pilar

Charity   Damian   Linden   Garcia   Fatima   Van

Benjamin   Paris   Costas   Misty   Genevieve

Trey   Napalm   Robyn   Louis   Trisha   Paul

Julius   Bailey   Nigger   Marshall   Irving

Carmine   Annette   Hajji   Lisa   Trixie   Pavel

Therese   Ese   Magnus   Rita   Jonah

Arrow   Daly   Tristan   Otto   Chisel   Arkadi

Demetria   Janice   Raymond   Saul   Maeve

Garrick   Pliers   Eugene   Mariah   Pablo   Arthur

Santos   Whore   Carrie   Lorelei   Buck

Clamp   Wrench   Gwendolyn   Irina   Vito   Douglas

Stuart   Jefferson   Elias   Wendy   Eunice

Glory   Bianca   Diane   Bowie   Butterfly   Mick

Forrest   Ned   Jordan   Nicolas   Zachariah

Eunuch   Ophelia   Ginger   Ernest   Gertie   Moss

Nathan   Wiley   Rhoda   Claire   Dashiell

Joss   Elsie   Ainsley   Lardass   Kael   Djuna

Spic   Jorie   Lilith   Retard   Howard

Donnie   Tammy   Stone   Jane   Jewboy   Lisel

Una   Pasha   Katana   Billy   Prudence

Stefanie   Hank   Rae   Derringer   Winona   Ann

Rachel   Breydon   Tasha   Darryl   Luger

Margaret   Remi   Winchester   Owen   Solange

Sterling   Smith   Bitch   Ashley   Wesson   Lois

Lawrence   Tony   Veda   Drill   Sloane   File

Maddox   Horace   Django   Faggot   Renee

Natalie   Hammer   Greer   Casey   Shovel   Kelly

Mort   Dunstan   Kiki   Cunt   Maxine

Spade   Judith   Theodore   Justus   Scissors   Dawn

Whip   Lucius   Victor   Verity   Scythe

Nada   Dothead   Kieran   Jade   Miguel   Blythe

Glynnis   Rock   Regina   Mac   Hymie   Patrick

Sambo   Fatman   Gabriel   Zoe   Lathe

Sickle   Art   Faith   Enola   Cynthia   Machine

amputation = echo :: dark by seven = dark by six :: cars go
home = cars go to bars :: houses hung w/ flashing bulbs ::
lit-trees = prettylittlewindowdeaths :: plastic/infant/everready
Christs (aglow, subtly, from within) :: whitekings-on-camels =
so-so-much-love :: season = pornography = pianodesperate =
tinkling keys :: baby-Jesus-not-touching-himself = avoidance
of leprosy :: frostbittentown = breastmilk-after-stillbirth ::
snow rots where it lies :: the mind with blackened limbs

NOVEMBER.

The first night back in York, Lark had joined Byrne in his bed—a simple platform with a thin, hard mattress, no springs—large enough for two people, if they made a concerted effort, not to touch. Byrne had fallen in love with her little girl. He liked Drew. And Lark loved Drew: they had a little girl. So Byrne and Lark had not slept together. Other than to sleep.

The second night, after a grueling day in the chambers, they came back and she, wordlessly, grabbed a flannel blanket from his one closet and curled into the sunken sofa Byrne had inherited from the landlord. The next morning, he took the top sheet from his bed and set it on the already-folded blanket. Lark spent the next four weeks, ten hours a day, working in the chambers. Twice, she'd said for him to go home without her, and she'd slept at the studio. A large, zebra-striped sectional dominated the Kepler lounge. Dizzying pattern—sleek, retro lines. He'd passed out there often enough during rehearsals. Daymares.

On several occasions he overheard Lark tell West she didn't know how to begin drawing a sleight. She said it defiantly. And each time West answered, "Whatever you need." So she trained. Byrne had been watching sleightists all his life, closely now for three months, and he had not seen anyone go at the practice—go at themselves—so ruthlessly.

Monk and Kepler would begin each day in chamber one, warming up. Some arrived a half hour before class, to prime their bodies for priming. Others came into the chamber only when called. Lark was among the former. In her unrelieved intensity, she stood out. Although the other sleightists worked through class in seeming unison, each focused on his or her unique body. Kitchen began his exercises loose and small, at a lower level and with eyes closed, for balance. Clef was nursing an ankle, lifting and circling her foot until the joint cracked or, alternately, bending her knee to elongate a powerfully articulated calf. T, easily the most flexible sleightist in Kepler, maybe Monk too, spent the mornings testing the outermost limits of her contortions. Byrne had noticed, previously, that although sleightists spent a great deal of time on the weak areas of their technique, they invested even more in pushing their strengths to summation. In this regard, Lark's practice was different. Her effort nondiscriminatory. She applied equal energy to each exercise, each body part, each quality of movement. To watch her was to be exhausted. She might not be as talented as the others, he couldn't tell, and certainly she was out of practice—but she saved nothing.

Sometimes Byrne would stand in the back first thing in his sweats, doing what he could, which wasn't much. Spine articulations, grounding exercises, some joint release. Once they began the larger motor movements—stridings or redemptions or flailings[26]—he'd slip out the back, into his shoes, and head to Jersey's for breakfast and to think, write. Lark didn't eat breakfast, and she didn't like his coffee. On the way in each day they stopped to get her something stronger. His hosting abilities were lacking, he wasn't reciprocating her family's generosity—but how could he? He wasn't a family. He didn't have the depth of bench for graciousness. He kept thinking she'd leave to stay with her sister, but Clef only had the motel room she shared with Kitchen, and Lark said Byrne's was fine. When he came back from his

[26] Each sleightist has a unique method of training, distilled from endless hours with multiple instructors. The classes taken prior to rehearsal and performance are, strictly speaking, not for the individual, but indispensable to forging a troupe identity. Without practice flocking and schooling, without a unified sense of what constitutes foray, absolution, swarm, and congress, the members of a troupe would be suspended and then dissolved. Prey in their own webs.

Denver omelet each day, the sleightists were separated into three chambers, perfecting the animal work they'd begun just before he and Lark had arrived in York.

The pair had pulled into the parking lot that first afternoon, beat. They'd walked up to the dented steel door, the back entrance Byrne knew would be unbolted. Entering, covered in the film of a twelve-hour drive begun before dawn, they immediately sensed it—the multiple, nearly constant wicking. Though they could see nothing from the lounge, the air was charged, popping. They couldn't look at each other. Making contact in that air would have been, Byrne thought, intolerable.

When Lark dropped her bag and keys onto the loud couch, he'd looked at her, but not into her face. Although the lounge was well heated—a blast of warmth had hit them when they'd come in—she'd grabbed herself, maybe to confirm she was still there. The air was fanatical. It was like the air at book burnings perhaps, or cockfights, maybe prisons. The air had color the way Lark's Souls had it—erratic and palpable. It was how the air must have been at Marvel's studio in Kenosha, when he was still making rent. His brother had asked him, more than once, but Byrne could never bring himself to go.

She'd stood, shaken her body from its cold pose, and moved toward the closest door—the door to chamber two. When Byrne didn't follow, she walked over and took his hand, to lead him. Her fingers were artic-ulate; whenever she spoke, they went to her head or fluttered and tapped one another, as if counting. He had imagined their touch: abra-sive—a fine sandpaper. But they were water. She took his rock hand and together they entered the chamber. They'd stayed that way, watching the menagerie unfold. For an afternoon, they were statued witness—two hands enveloping stone. Flesh, grown around a pit.

Each day since, when the sleightists separated to work on the crea-tural links, Lark went to chamber four, kept open for her use. And after Jersey's, Byrne went into the office to watch her. West was often there, laughing at him.

"T's been missing you, Byrne."

"T still has you, at least occasionally. She told me. She also has a husband."

"As do many of the women who spark your interest, it would seem."

"Screw you."

"Screw whomever you like, as long as you're writing."

"I'm writing."

"Good. It's why I keep you around."

West spent some of these weeks on the phone, putting the tour in order, doubling hotel arrangements and bus rentals to accommodate two troupes instead of one—they were to leave seven days into the new year. With the rest of the time, he observed the links, occasionally entering a chamber to suggest a different entrance into a structure, a different path through a manipulation. Byrne had known West was talented, but in these weeks he saw just how. West would walk into the room, take a sleightist aside, quietly conferring for a minute or two. Invariably the sleightist would nod, or her eyes would light up and she'd excitedly move to rejoin the link, explaining West's insight to the others as she did so. It was fine-tuning, but without West's eye, these novel configurations wouldn't blossom. They would startle, yes, so full of promise. But seeds—they would not, without him, become something beyond themselves. West was chef, gardener, alchemist. He would harvest.

Meanwhile, Monk's director roamed at the level of the chambers, bumbling. And then suddenly, he'd needed to be gone. He told West, who told the troupes. There were familial matters, he'd be back before tour. Byrne thought, probably not. He might have felt sorry for the man. He didn't. For one thing, Monk seemed more at ease; not everyone liked West, but they didn't doubt him. Only Kitchen seemed sad. He sometimes ran rehearsal from his customary perch atop a stool in the corner. He liked a balconist's perspective, he'd explained to Byrne—the cheaper seats. He mentioned Monk's missing director whenever there was a question of line. The man had an eye, it couldn't be denied, for the organics. How to prepare the shell for immolation. Lark noted none of the troupe politics, or didn't care to speak of it. She rarely spoke at all—a little, if prompted, over late dinners. They ordered in, or she cooked, and at her suggestion he bought a case of wine. He liked vodka better, but drank as he was asked. She was a good, quick cook, and Byrne ate better than he could remember. She talked to Drew and Nene over the phone each evening, but about day-to-day stuff. Filler. Lark asked questions while stirring a white sauce or chopping scallions; she didn't mention her own work. Byrne's apartment was dim, and her forced cheer fluorescent. Of course she both loved and missed them, but the way the telephone coerced language was simply wrong. Byrne cringed at the bright, heavy assurances. Though it was done with rocks, not electric, not wireless, he was reminded of the medieval torture used on witches and during the Inquisition—called what? Pressing.

It didn't surprise Byrne then, the way Lark worked alone in chamber four during the day. As if coming out from under something. She hadn't yet the stamina of the rest of them, but she moved her sphinx-like musculature with vicious will. The other sleightists worked steadily for hours, repeating links eighty or ninety times before letting up, but Lark rarely repeated anything. She would go through a whole series of gestures with an architecture, twenty minutes worth, then hurl the thing across the room and fall to the floor, heaving. Byrne, the first few days, thought she was frustrated, that it had been too long since she'd been in a chamber. Soon, however, he realized what she was doing: not wicking. If she left her manipulations rough, threw down the architectures when she felt it coming on, she could keep from going out.

She worked that way, in fits, getting to know each of Clef's seventeen architectures. Sometimes she'd go get Clef. They would bundle up—Lark in the parka Byrne had loaned her, Clef with her ridiculous scarf—and walk out into the bleak, perpetual threat of snow that hung over York. In the chambers, Lark kept mostly to herself. A few times she left to grab a sandwich or a second coffee with Yael and Manny, two sleightists she knew from before. And when she and Kitchen passed by one another, they exchanged a strained nod. Byrne was beginning to find Kitchen's style of sleight irritatingly cerebral.

Lark had been up four nights in a row, sketching. It made Byrne's sleep fitful, the light and the scratching sound from the living room/kitchen. His bedroom was small and at the back of the second-floor apartment he rented. He thought of blocking the large gap beneath the door with a pillow, but that would have impeded the heat from the one working radiator, the one that clanked and spat. Many tenants previous, that radiator had been painted, like the room, the color of clotted cream. Now, the paint was chipping in flakes so heavy they must contain lead. Still, the place had charm: a high ceiling with crown molding and French windows, and in the corner next to the fire escape—cobwebs, safely out of reach, alive in the rising heat.

Dirt was usually a comfort to Byrne; he'd been shocked when Drew and Lark's house, in its cleanliness, had failed to make him uneasy. In fact, he'd admired how they combined a poverty of goods with deep care: dishes, mismatched but hand-washed and dried immediately following each meal; dustless, secondhand books; open windows and the freshly laundered, repurposed bedsheets that graced them. In his own apartment, Byrne had no broom nor any desire to knock the friendly wisps down, and he refused to spray. Oversanitation hid things more sinister than germs. Ammonia, turpentine, bleach, paint: chemicals made his eyes water, made his meager chest tense and knit together across the sternum.

After half an hour of covering and uncovering his head with a pillow, he walked out. Lark was sitting at the poker table where they ate, leaning into her paler left hand. Her right was held poised above the graph-paper notebook she'd bought on their way up from Georgia but had only begun using in the past few days. Her bluish hand swept back and forth above the windshield of blank page. Suddenly, she stabbed the grid. Then dropped the pencil and looked at Byrne.

"I have one. Inside of me right now."

"What?" He thought he knew what she meant, but he hadn't been prepared to hear it, and it sounded . . . mad.

"Since we saw the new links that first day. I've had a Need inside of me. But it's different, it doesn't know what it wants."

"Lark, what are you talking about?"

She rifled one-handedly back through the notebook. She must have gone through twenty sheets, maybe more. Byrne was shocked to see so much work, all of it crawling with detail. Strings of ink not quite adhering to the pages.

"Look. Look here. She pointed to one. He moved closer, walked around to her side of the table. It was swingsets or seesaws, catapults or trebuchets. There was a transfer between the playground equipment and siege weaponry. This wasn't ambiguity, like the drawings he knew from her book—it was actual movement. A trick picture, like the two silhouetted faces that became a goblet or vice versa, only it wasn't about positive and negative space. He couldn't control how he was seeing it, couldn't force one image over to another. Each time the catapult shifted into seesaw, it shifted itself. And there was something else. On the way, the drawing passed through gallows. Byrne followed the lack: missing pitch, missing condemned, missing child. And back again, and repeat. Pitch, again. Child. Condemned, and . . . Repeat. It was chilling.

"I don't. I don't know what this is."

"Here, look at this one."

She was sweating, he noticed. There was an acrid smell; it was a caffeinated sweat. Her ring finger scratched rhythmically at her scalp. She had not raised herself from her slumped position, only pushed the book toward him and turned the page. There. An exhaustive analysis of a human eye was also a veined egg, swollen, with a tic in what was sometimes the cornea, sometimes not. Looking at the transmuting form, Byrne knew whatever was undeveloped, inside, would not have the strength to tear through. This depiction of unachieved birth was also a representation of vision. Byrne thought, *This is how she sees.*

She closed the notebook. Byrne listed toward the fire escape for a hit of cold air and the vodka he kept there. He quickly let in then shut out the night—the palpitating bass from a passing Buick, a siren moving away. He walked over, put the vodka on the stove, and reached up to the cabinet above for two mugs. He poured them each a fair helping, four fingers. Lark was shoving the book into the duffel at her feet. "No," he said. "No. I need to see them all."

NOVEMBER.

On Lark's first evening in York, after the episode in the chambers, the sisters had hugged and exchanged a few sentences about Lark's family, Clef's recovery. Lark had remembered pictures of Nene this time, three of them. A reading Nene on the porch swing, Drew beside her. Ankle-deep Nene in the lake. A Halloween Nene, her tinman a wrapped-in-foil, heart-in-hand affair. The child was arresting. In each picture, the day reflected in her eyes starkly, but not vacant. It wasn't their color but something else, something in another register, that marked her unmistakably as Lark's. Clef made noises, ahhs and cooings, noises she supposed one made about an only niece. The sisters had been uncomfortable, too, during the couple of weeks Lark had spent in New York. When they'd spoken at all, it had been about Lark's Needs. They had avoided the personal, or at least the frictional. After the photographs, a long silence played between them. They said good-night. Lark left with Byrne, Clef with Kitchen.

Lark's second day in York, she'd asked Clef outside. Clef had stepped into her tall boots, zippered them up the length of her calves, and swung a multicolored scarf three times around her neck. Kitchen had given it to her the previous Christmas; he'd had it made in purples, oranges, and magentas to clash irreverently with her hair. Kitchen loved that about Clef. Her hair. How it moved. "On its own," he'd say, "like an animal." And of course the color. In Tokyo, he told her, the girls were always trying to get to red, and that they shouldn't.

After walking the first quarter mile in silence, Clef, impatient—determined not to let nothing happen again—turned to her older sister.

"Lark, when did you stop loving me?"

"Don't do this." Lark was cold. She hadn't brought clothes worthy of the weather. Maybe Byrne would lend her something.

"Well, when?"

"You were my touchstone, Clef. My rosary, my worry doll, my abacus. How could I stop loving you?" Lark was teasing only the tiniest bit. She looked at the fingers on her left hand, tapped the thumb against each of the others in turn. In the gray afternoon, they were a vibrant, quaint blue: five faded virgins. "I just . . . I learned to stop counting on you." That was funny; she would remember that.

"Lark, what are we doing?"

"I don't know. I'm here because nothing else has worked."

"And me? Why am I here?"

"Because this does?" Lark was guessing.

"It doesn't. It promises to, and then . . ."

"What about Kitchen? Does he work?" Lark didn't expect an answer. This was the first jab. It was small, a swipe at the side, and she expected Clef to block.

"Why, does Drew?" Clef paused, then softened. "He . . . he looks kind—I mean, with Nene, in the picture." They were stopped at a crosswalk. Finding herself suddenly shy, Clef studied the red palm's blinking DON'T. DON'T. She asked, "What is marriage . . . like?" DON'T. The red hand became a white body and shone frozenly at them: STEP.

Lark and Clef started across. Before the far curb, a pothole floating diseased yellow leaves gaped; they leapt across it in tandem. Lark hadn't anticipated this question, her and Drew. It pleased her—also, hurt. That morning she had felt his absence in pangs. When she'd woken in Byrne's bed. When he'd called to her from the kitchen. His offer of weak coffee. Stupid.

How long had it been since she'd talked with another woman? This was Clef, her sister. But a lifetime had grown up between them—her daughter's. Lark would try to describe her marriage honestly.

"Every day, someone asks you for a piece of yourself. So you, I, I cut it off and hand it over. Partly because Drew, he has the only balm that works on the wound." Lark thought for a moment. "The one he's continually asking me to self-inflict."

"Why are you *like* that?" Clef's timidity was gone. She looked disgusted. Lark remembered the look.

"Like what?"

Clef started walking a little faster, as if to distance herself from Lark's influence. Her sister could pollute anything with description.

"So narcissistic, so focused on your own darkness. You're incapable of letting anything be . . . simple."

"Something's simple?" Lark felt like taunting. It was one of the minor brutalities once expected of her. They used to do this banter with humor. No more.

"Love is supposed to be."

"And you've found that to be true?" Unspoken was their overlap: Kitchen. *Don't go messing 'round another woman's Kitchen*—Drew had made that joke once. Clef must've thought it was why they hadn't spoken. Hell, it *had* been Clef's reason. Was she still ashamed? Probably. What had Lark felt? Undeserving. Of fidelity, love—all of it. It was she who should apologize, for underplaying her part in Clef's defining drama. No. Another lie. Lark could easily work up anger at Clef. Her little sister had always dismissed the damage she caused as warranted; Kitchen just wasn't the worst she'd done. Lark pushed. "Well, how about it Clef, is love simple?"

"Yeah. No. Some days." Clef slowed again and tossed her unruly scarf back over her shoulder. "But you don't have those days."

They were walking beside an old townhouse. Lark remembered the style—Federal—from one of Fern's lectures. The house was well-preserved: two rows of windows evenly divided a plain brick façade, five on top, four below; a fan-light spanned the central door; slatted shutters; white trim; simple wrought-iron fence. Civility. Restraint. Graciousness. Bullshit, bullshit, bullshit.

"You didn't call, Clef. Not once in six years. You didn't come to clean up after Mom. You haven't met my husband or my daughter. How can you presume to know what kinds of days I've had?"

And there it was.

Two months after Lark had left Monk, their mother hanged herself. Their father had passed away four years earlier, while the sisters had still been at the academy. Heart attack. They'd gone home for a week, worn navy. Their mother insisted: no black for them. The day after his funeral, they received casseroles at the front door and invited the elderly and middle-aged neighbors who carried them to come into the dining room for ever-brewing Darjeeling. Relieved of their red beans and rice, their thrice-baked macaroni, their green bean almondine, the women who had spent years scowling at the girls weeding the front yard in their Sunday denim had taken their hands and patted them. They'd said, "Take care of your poor, poor mother." Some of them said pawh. Pawh muthah. Lark mocked them once they'd gone. She was good at "the Southern," and had done it since grade school to make Newton howl. Clef's laughter was, after a few seconds, mildly hysterical. That night, Lark had brushed and braided her sister's hair as if they were little. They were not: Clef was fifteen, Lark nineteen. And they were on their own—their mother, after the cemetery, had tucked herself away in her room. Very away. The girls had headed back to Boston that Wednesday, although not before bagging, labeling, and freezing all the womanly kindness in meal-sized portions.

Within six months, their mother had committed herself to an expensive institution in the mountains of North Georgia—a spa for the inconsolable. Twice, they'd borrowed a car to make the sixteen-hour trip. Twice, she'd refused to see them.

Clef and Lark's parents were perhaps enigmatic. Lark didn't know. They'd transplanted themselves from Pittsburgh when Newton had gotten his professorship. Jillian Scrye had been hired as a research assistant by a friend in his department a year later. She had a PhD, but it was the seventies, the South, she wanted a family. There were limits. They were solid people, and good. They loved their work. They loved each other. They found, after two successful attempts at procreation and one unsuccessful, that there was a finite amount of love to be parceled out. After the miscarriage of their third child, the boy tried for three times, they scratched up what was left for their two daughters, who grew every day more unlike them. But that it was scratch was evident. The girls tended, as the Scryes had imagined they would, toward art—and as artists, they were uninterested in the finite.

Jillian had tried. She'd faded in and out as a mother, occasionally spending a summer canoeing, helping to chart moon and stars on the attic walls, catching fireflies and smearing their luminous abdomens onto her daughters' faces like war paint, only to follow with a fall of missed performances and unsigned report cards. Newton would've done better, but wasn't expected to. Their mother regularly disappeared inside her research, and if Newton was putting together a publication, she spent nights for a month working up his figures with him, leaving the girls to themselves. She seemed relieved when sleight took to her daughters. Even appreciated it, to a point. She always said she'd like to see it all on paper—how interesting it would be without the bodies.

When she swung, Clef was on tour. Lark had been still in New York, newly unemployed. She didn't go to the institution; Jillian had prepaid her death, Lark wasn't needed. So she bought a Greyhound ticket to Atlanta. She arrived, reeking of the gin-drunk beside her, with a bag of clothes and a small boxful of dead Needs. The house of her childhood was unlivable. She didn't waste what little money she had reinstating utilities. For weeks, she combed through the dark house for things to sell. Furniture. Her mother's piano, her violin. The good china. Her parents' microscopes. The telescope. Books. She swam laps across the lake in the evenings to allay her sweat, stench, a coagulating depression. It took four months to clear away the debris of her mother's loss. She'd lived there ever since.

"You gave me your book." Clef was defending herself. She hadn't called in six years, it was true. But neither had Lark. Four years ago her sister had sent that—that Soul—with a card alerting her to Nene's birth. But Clef, who hadn't been aware of Lark's pregnancy or her marriage, read in the Soul's hollowness an accusation, and had sent it back. Then, in August, Lark had shown up in New York, ostensibly to take care of her, and had left the book, setting off this slow-motion detonation, or whatever it was. West's interest. Her own architectures. Lark, always wanting attention. Getting it.

"And you got rid of it the f-first chance you got. Okay, Clef, I admit it. Love isn't simple for me, no. I get sad."

"Are we talking about sadness?" If so, Clef would refuse. Lark had been doing sad for a long time, it was clearly not a worthwhile endeavor. She pulled a pair of gloves out of her pockets and flung them at her sister, who was by this time shaking. Lark snatched them out of the air.

"Th-thank you." Lark pulled on the gloves as they walked on, considering. "I think we are."

"Well, I don't want to." Clef bit her bottom lip, and Lark pulled up short to examine her.

Her lips were violet. That was death. Her face was porcelain. Decorum. Her eyes were wet. Guilt. Maybe the wind. Her hair was brushfire. That was Clef. Lark reached out and put her borrowed, lavender cashmere hands over her sister's ears. She pulled Clef's head close.

"You are a dear, sweet idiot with a brick will. I have always loved you." Clef could hear Lark, but pretended not to. She hadn't thought she was cold, but the sudden warmth made her head throb.

———

On her third day in York, Lark began the morning in chamber one with the others. Monk's director led, and though soft-spoken, he was thorough and the class was good. He had joined Monk a year after she'd left. In a letter from Fern, who—unasked—updated her on sleight developments, Lark had learned that her old director, Imke Kleist, had returned to Germany. As far as Lark knew, as far as Fern had shared, none of the thirty-one registered troupes currently had a female director. When Lark quit there had been only three, and they'd been in their fifties. Women vanishing, not replacing themselves. A pattern of what? Only some wrong thing.

She didn't want to like this new director, and she deduced from murmurings that he wasn't respected. He kept offering the combinations to the troupes with question marks. *And then a lateral after the missive? Yes. And then a rowing, or should we go to the grail next? The grail, right.* The questions were unnecessary and irritating; he knew what to do with their bodies.

On that day he paid particular attention to Lark. His verbal corrections were dead-on—she *was* hyperextending both legs and back to achieve a compensatory balance. She *was* forcing it, *did* need to ratchet everything down. Not that she could. She had never affected anything other than plough horse. And it was worse now that her technique was off—she worked as if a bucket of sweat could weigh in against years of stagnation, of motherhood. Nevertheless, he tried to help her. While she was struggling against a difficult floor gesture, he knelt down and placed one hand on her hipbone and another on the inside of her opposite thigh, his surprisingly strong thumb compressing the taut line of her sartorius. He opened her like a walnut—releasing, in one burst, six years' bound tension from her lumbar spine: L5, S1.

After class, Lark withdrew to an empty chamber to try out one of Clef's architectures. At rest, the design was long and strict on one side, curved and giving on the other. Harp. She'd never worked with one that so clearly embodied opposed properties. Her sister had talent. Somehow, though, the architecture was familiar. Not harp then, maybe saw?[27] Whichever, Lark knew exactly how to start the first manipulation. She picked up the tight side and stood its end on her lifted knee. But before she could scythe it across the space left by her spiraling torso, Monk's director walked in.

"Do you know what West wants?"

Lark set the architecture gently down. Uncertain what he was after, she offered, "He brought me here to draw a sleight—to try to, anyway."

The man lifted his hand to his forehead and rubbed. Erasing. "I think," he said, "you will get hurt."

Lark knew she was out of practice, but got defensive anyway. Why had he been so positive during class only to belittle her now? "I was a professional, I know my limits."

"No, no, no." Monk's director waved his hand. "Not you, but all of you, hurt . . ." He stared into the room, as if the clearer explanation were hanging in the chamber. He turned back to the door, reached for the doorknob, grasped it. His voice was slow and muddy. "Talk to Kitchen. These links are . . . too rhythmic, too thick. They hum. Do you know? You must."

It took a week before Clef told Lark about the children. She'd kept the daily papers, and she said they were still showing small clips of the video on the local news, though it had already disappeared from the national. Byrne's apartment had no TV so Lark and Clef skipped out at lunch and went to Clef's motel room. More narrow than most, it was less a room than a corridor oriented between bed and television toward bath. Escape, sleep, soak. Lark's body was beginning to lament

[27] Like the links they unite to form, architectures occasionally resemble everyday objects. It is through this metaphorical reference that they acquire nicknames. Even more important, a resemblance suggests a place to begin. A sleightist who picks up an architecture that curves like a machete will begin to arc it through the air as in a ritual murder or gleaning. Manipulations develop out of such inclinations.

Byrne's cold apartment, its coffin-sized shower. It hurt to sit down, to stand up, although a little less each day. Clef pulled out the first article from the pressed wood drawer of the bedside table. On top of the table: a lined pad, a rotary phone, a dirty-white Bible. The motel was the same motel it must have been thirty years before. This was troubling to Lark, who saw in stasis an insidious form of regression. Perched on the edge of the dark synthetic quilt—indigo, mauve, and cocoa paisley—she read the clippings as Clef fed them to her.

She tried not to, but couldn't help herself: she went, not back into her own childhood, but into her daughter's. Nene, alone and terrified and aware. Kidnapped, her daughter would've known what was going on, which would've made it worse. Killed. And she would've known why. To be killed. Because she was too smart, or black enough. Or both. It was always juxtaposition, Lark had told her, that causes fear. Beauty. Things isolated could be controlled: colors in jars, flies in test tubes. Combination, solidarity, exploration—these were what made power happen. Life happen. Forced to watch the grisly show, Nene would have known she wasn't the first. She would have seen the bones in the toys. And if they were still there, in the basement, the children too. They would've spoken to her, wouldn't they? Nene invited such confidences. Were children still as frightened, Lark wondered, after they were dead?

"I've left my daughter. Tell me, Clef. Tell me I'm not Jillian."

Her sister said nothing for too long. Then: "Jillian didn't cheat."

"What?" The words had blunted her, a baseball bat to the face. Lark felt her Need begin to shift. Swell.

"Come off it, Lark. If you aren't fucking him yet, you will be."

"You . . . you're talking about Byrne?"

"Are you blind? The way he watches you. And that first day, you were holding his hand."

"I was holding his hand." Lark said this to herself, shocked, not angry. An eleven-year-old's proof: holding hands. Her mind had been treading the water-image of her daughter, preparing for death, and Clef brought up this.

"I don't cheat, Clef." Shock lessening, anger possible. "And I've never stolen."

Clef was prepared for this. "You didn't love him. You didn't love Kitchen."

"No, I didn't," Lark admitted it slowly, then rotated it on its axis. "I loved you and you shat on me."

Clef cut back. She scalped Kitchen from the field entirely, inserting what she thought was a stick figure, a dummy. "I don't know how to be your sister. When I'm around you, I'm sick, all the time. Drew must be a fucking saint."

"All this fucking, Clef, what's happened to you?" For Lark, Drew didn't replace, didn't counterfeit: he was. Clef would lose. "Drew is no saint, but I'm Lark for him, not some gawd-awful wraith." She was slipping into her Georgia. "He expects reality from me—and guess what? I can give it." Lark was thankful for this. If she drove around, took an hour detour after manning the kiosk to go out to the reservoir, or sat in the driveway too long, car idling, Drew got pissed off. He would remind her that it was time for her to go read Rosetti to Nene, to bathe her, put her to sleep. Such prompting wasn't always necessary, not even often. But when it was, he did it. Drew nixed the stereo on days when she looped "Waltzing Matilda," "River," "Sinnerman." And did it without commentary. Maybe he should be beatified for his subtle vigilance. But she gave too. In pieces, but she gave.

Lark faced her sister squarely and said, "I need to talk to Kitchen." Clef looked ready to spit. Lark continued, "These architectures you've made, these links, these children—West is playing tea party with battery acid, and Kitchen might know."

Suddenly, Clef felt beaten. "Might know what?" she asked weakly. Lark had somehow gotten around her, bypassed their explosion. But Clef was not satisfied, and worked to produce a final dagger. "Lark, if something is wrong—it's with you."

Lark looked at her hands before she spoke. "Yes, of course, that's right. But, Clef, it isn't me making you sick. You're pregnant again."

LARK'S BOOK.

Aphasia: Loss of the quality of speech, as a result of cerebral affection. Aphemia: Loss of the power of articulation, due to cerebral affection. A form of aphasia, in which words are understood and conceived but cannot be uttered.

It's been thirteen weeks.

The day I lost myself was Nene. Terribly normal and neutral, not mangled. My body become one long throat—disgorging. And then, failed to close. Child, placenta, uterus, language. Words were gone. Or not mine to order. Not the way you do it in a restaurant: what you want, when you want, the way you want, brought to you.

The doctors insist it wasn't the birth. And wasn't the complication, flux. That trauma was not the trauma they told Drew. Just a more recent facsimile. They hunt. Peck at. Jillian has been the maze. As the primary she is a wonderfully crayola target. What did she do? My fingers, in chalky flutter. Nene's bruise-body swaddled in my blood. Cherries in rain, under glass. A spectacle. She came not out but through. Not out, through.

She left behind a Need. It was at first a comfort. I had lost parts of my body to her, its heat. And although I was comforted by the word "body," the word was always with me, and therefore, I realize, must not refer to anything actual.

Yesterday, Nene turned three months old, and I tore down her Need, the ice cathedral sculpted by her exodus. Another ridding. A bottling. What I feel is flaked, chipped, like slate. Rockfaces shirring off, tumbling into dead trees below. It is hard, burnt out, the wrong brown. She is, sometimes. The skin I gave her is ghost skin, a veil over her real skin. Her sharp eyes cast about—she laughs at the nothing behind me. In that way, one fears for her. Maybe it is me fearing.

Drew thinks Needs are blanks. Needs are not blanks. No names, but they are teeming. Cornucopias. Fruit baskets. Handbaskets. Hells.

This past week I asked him to and Drew moved inside me, slow, the first time since—a stirring, an all-day rain. But he couldn't dislodge the Need. Afterwards, my body a drain, I didn't know his name. His name and I were divorced. The husband I had when I was with my husband was nameless. Not even "husband," which re-became a verb—about use, about animals. I knew then I had to kill the Need. The trafficker, pimp. A brutal, brutal thief.

The doctors all said the words would probably come back, but didn't know how. I should tell Drew. I have had the Need out and will dismantle it. Along with the others. I will pull them apart and then pull her across. Pin Nene to this place. I have decided, she will let me.

———

Lark stayed that day with Clef, and Kitchen came back after dark. He had food. "Bad Mexican," he said when he saw the sisters doubling each other across the two beds, knees nearly grazing. They ate together: Kitchen and Clef on the one bed, the ripped white bag in front of them catching bits of shredded lettuce and dripped tomato water; Lark on the other, sitting upright and brittle, with chips. They watched a short segment on the Vogelsongs. This time, Melanie's mother. *No one thinks her daughter could kill. A son,* she said, *that's different, but I did not, no, I did not see it in Ray.* Melanie's mother, she prayed every day for the souls of those little angels. She knew they were with God, which was a comfort. Imagining them at God's table.

Lark could see it too. Pipe-cleaner haloes and clothes-hangered, tissue-papered wings. Demurely bowed heads gazing down into blue Fiestaware—the empty, bright bowls of God's table. Because angels don't require sustenance. Not oyster crackers, not even Dixie-sized swallows of grape juice, staining between the teeth, forcing quarter-hour garglings with baking soda and peroxide. Melanie's mother—you could hear it in her prim drawl—believed in the redemptive powers of bloodied floss.

Lark watched as her sister balled up the burrito foil, pitched it into the brown wastepaper basket beside the dresser. "Two points," Clef murmured. She switched off the news.

CLEF: Lark wants to talk with us.

KITCHEN: Okay.

LARK: What is West doing? This subject matter—why? Why two troupes? Why me?

KITCHEN: I've been wondering about this too.

CLEF: You have?

KITCHEN: Your new architectures, Clef—did you ever stop to think why you made them?

CLEF: You know why. Lark's book.

KITCHEN: That can't be it. Each one you wired together is a collage. Most architectures function; the inverted spiral, for example, is a funnel that can be adjusted to the size of what it funnels. It has a purpose—abstract, to be sure, but a purpose. Yours—not so much.

CLEF: (*getting off the bed*) So, my work is useless.

LARK: *Beyond* use. I played around with one that seems designed to slice without cutting. Each time I tried to bring it through the air cleanly, it swerved. I can't use your architectures, Clef. Only follow them.

CLEF: Even if that's true—so what?

KITCHEN: Why would West want us to work with what we can't control? How can he hope to make a full sleight?

LARK: I think he's counting on me for that.

CLEF: (*walking toward the bathroom*) Of course he is.

LARK: This isn't ego. The architectures came from my book, the links came from the architectures . . . maybe he thinks a sleight drawn by me would unite the two. (*Clef runs water, Lark raises her voice*) He doesn't realize you put something in them, Clef. Something feral.

CLEF: (*walking back in*) You're wrong. Everything I did was from your book, Lark. Things resisting their natures—that's not me.

LARK: Because you don't fight yourself.

• CLEF: You shut your mouth.

KITCHEN: Are you drawing for him now?

LARK: No, but . . . I will be soon. I have a new Need, and it's odd— it's not about anything.

KITCHEN: Excuse me?

CLEF: Her Needs—they always have a . . . what? A defect, tragic flaw . . . a cavity?

LARK: A bit like that.

KITCHEN: And this one?

LARK: This one isn't reaching, except for an identity. Right now it's trying on forms, but I think it just wants to be what it is.

KITCHEN: And what is it?

CLEF: I can't fucking believe this. They aren't real, Kitchen.

KITCHEN: Hold on a second, Clef. Didn't you tell me you touched one?

CLEF: Just because you can see or smell or fuck something, that doesn't mean it's actually, meaningfully there.

LARK: She has a point.

KITCHEN: Christ, you two are *The Shining* sometimes. I didn't remember.

LARK: Kitchen, where do you think you go?

KITCHEN: What?

LARK: When you wick—where do you go?

KITCHEN: It's like sleeping, isn't it?

CLEF: You're such a goddamn liar.

KITCHEN: You two think we die—Clef's said it before. It's deranged.

LARK: No. Death has permanence. Wicking is playing dead. We roll over, the audience claps. But West knows.

KITCHEN: Knows what?

LARK: How to use it. How to wrench the audience from comfort, which we all want. But he wants something else too. I don't trust him.

KITCHEN: None of us trust him.

LARK: So why are we doing this? Why should I give him my drawings?

CLEF: Because he knows how to make something happen. I hate him, but more than anything else—that's what we want. Isn't it? We want to be inside something that makes something happen.

LARK: Look, I'll do it. I'll draw out this Need and give it to him. But we watch, okay?

CLEF: (*starts straightening the room*) I don't know what you think he can do. I'll admit it feels wrong somehow to use those children. But West's just mucking around, right? (*drops into a chair beside the dresser, looks down at her lap, then up at Lark*) Right?

LARK: Do you even know what sleight is? Do any of us? For all we know, it could be saltpeter.

CLEF: What?

KITCHEN: Saltpeter, Clef. Add a little sulfur, a little charcoal—gunpowder.

LARK: A propellant, a chemical delivery system. But for a long time its main use—

CLEF: Unknown, I get it.

KITCHEN: No. It was fireworks.

———

The rest of November was difficult. Clef swore Lark to secrecy until she figured out what to do about the pregnancy. Lark spent all day every day at the chambers, making her way back to Byrne's to eat and sleep and, in between, study her new Need. She couldn't always feel it. Needs were sporadic, like allergies. Sometimes in the middle of the night, instead of an itchy throat, white pain would shark beneath her sternum, circling the space where her ribcage opened like a curtain. Not a good time to assess the Need. Typically, the form of a waking Need was blind, a bodied migraine. Sometimes she could get a general outline, but mostly just pain without visuals. Or if she did get visuals, they were unrelated to the Need: replayed scenarios of regretted actions—boring. But skull-boring, unbanishable. So she'd polish off whatever wine was open, or open a new bottle, and go back to the couch to wait it out. This was what the History Channel was for, but Byrne only had a laptop he kept in his bedroom.

When she was awake, Lark liked to stand. It helped to make room for the Need's alterations. Cooking, she could feel the Need in her torso. It always stayed within her core—the only trait it shared with pregnancy. She would concentrate on its dimensions, the way it was currently extending its intrusive fingers or antennae through her viscera, while keeping other parts of her mind occupied. She'd cook, or talk on the phone. Of course, when the Need got to be too much, she'd say goodbye to Nene and Drew. When it was too much, quiet was blessing. Byrne, it seemed, had a sixth sense for these moments— and chose them for pointless conversation. *How'd it go today? Which architecture was that I saw you with? You go out to lunch with Yael again?* Sometimes, with that rock, it was as if the boy were crippled.

She knew he had a crush, of course she did. Clef wasn't crazy, or even unperceptive. It calmed Lark, to be looked at in that way. Intact. Byrne was funny though, and obviously disconcerted by this dynamic—him, wanting. He was awkward and sweet and made faces he didn't know he made. When she phoned Drew and Nene, Byrne always said to say hello, and then he'd wince. It was a hairline wince: a hard blink followed by a squint, lasting no more than a second, and then he'd bounce his rock off the front of his thigh. Every time. One morning, three weeks into her stay, his beige towel slit high up his leg as he walked from shower to bedroom, and Lark caught sight of a dark green oval a few inches above the knee. It looked nasty, a bruise with roots. He was a very skinny boy.

By the end of the month, she knew the Need would have to come out soon, and she set to work capturing its forms on paper before the expulsion. It taxed her—contending with its mutations, the echoes of Clef's pregnancy, the pain of retraining her body. She lacked buttress:

Nene's arms around her neck, her sticky mouth against her cheek reciting some new exotic fact, some list, some poem. Drew's palms on her shoulder blades, fingers kneading her even as she resisted them, compelling her return to her skin.

Byrne and Lark got drunk. The notebook lay open on the card table. They'd gone through it page by page. Her explaining. Him asking questions she had no explanations for. He brought out his computer. The glowing fields of precursor at first startled her. Then, truly frightened. They drank more. Byrne's words began to waver, the screen trembled— a colorless, countryless flag. They scrolled down through the names. It was all names, just names. Names, and their terrible surrogates.

NOVEMBER.

It took the media two weeks to forget the Vogelsong children. Mr. Vogelsong had worked for twelve years in the Commonwealth's Department of Youth and Family Services. He was missed. At work, his supervisors scrambled first to discover how he'd managed the evil, then how he'd managed the office. The man had known his way around their bureaucracy. With great attention to detail, he and his wife had gathered and reordered children hard to place: some with medical issues, some abused, some the children of addiction, some a less-popular mix of races. He'd forged and lost documents in all the right ways. So. No follow-up stories with grieving suburban parents and numb, ground-scanning siblings. No new laws introduced by the bereaved and their congressional representatives. No names. Revealing the victims' names, it was agreed, would have been wrong. The press instead had decided to call them the Vogelsong children—in a final consummation of the adoptive process—before calling them nothing at all.

faceted :: winterlesions :: question-kind of marks :: bloodsum ::
ruby footprints :: joy-divided :: love is a condition tethered to
the said :: pox on both :: ore-houses :: lives-of-the-mined ::
diamond-nibs :: written hard &put away, etc. :: no praise like
some :: no homelike place :: none

SCHOOLED.

Above him she was sky. Wide face, wider eyes, broad shoulders—but thin. Hers was the atmosphere of sky, of horizon. His hands were on her narrow hips, thumbs in front on the flats of the bone, fingers digging into the hard muscle of her backside. With iron wrists, he could wave her above him like prairie grass. Did. She had a thing about being moved— the tendons of her neck eased when she wasn't in control, although she liked, they both liked, her to start on top. When she came, she would lean forward, place her hands on his chest, exhale. She wouldn't groan, offer a prayer, say West's name. Sound, she'd told him, was energy, and she would put that energy where it belonged—into intensification, not dispersal. When she did orgasm, her inner walls held their convulsion, gripping him as the current ran up her torso, and her extended arms, instinctively preserving the small distance between them, locked. As if in preparation for collision. It was only then, after T's first orgasm of an evening or an afternoon, that West truly woke to her. There was a vein that pulsed at her temple, and a flush, and a violence.

West loved physiognomy. He'd even call himself a practitioner. He could read faces and the bodies that held them aloft, and not only by carriage or countenance. The character of a person was evident in musculature, coloring, bone structure. Believing this didn't make him a racist, because of the individualized nature of his readings. High cheekbones didn't indicate passion or haughtiness in a people as a whole, but the highest Romany cheekbone did evidence something about the particular gypsy woman who wore it. His own dark features said nothing about him unless the genetic background from which they emerged could be read as template. America—the movement of populations in general—made the reading of faces problematic. West preferred more homogeneous environs, where furrows, wrinkles, hues, and angles told stories that could be trusted. It was one of the reasons he loved tour.

Until he'd known T for over a year, West hadn't known that her Mongolian features had Mongolian precedent, that her great-great-great-grandfather had been a Chinese railroad man who'd married a Scotch prostitute in Arizona, then moved to the Big Easy to start up a specialty house—her as madame to Asiatics he recruited. When T told this story she giggled, listing her attributes. "Strawberry-brown hair, high breasts, a welterweight's shoulders, boy hips and boy legs, freckled moon face, ice tea eyes, creaseless lids. I make very little sense." But to West, T embodied the most intriguing part of her history: the cross-breeding. Her calm face, its sweet placidity, was easy to read once he knew it was a mask. When they made love, it was the mask lifting he waited for, the finding of seeds bitter as those of any other orange.

This was the first time since Halloween that West and T had been together. She climaxed three times. In the terms of their friendly competition, he'd won. They felt the cold air, after, on their wet skin. T ventured to the bathroom, then to the hallway closet for an extra quilt. With her body gone, in the raft-time of the bed, West allowed himself to drift.

Since Byrne and Lark had shown up at the studio, he'd been waiting for Byrne to return to T. It hadn't happened. Otherwise, all was as predicted. Lark was doing her thing. He doubted that anyone other than Byrne noticed her flinching in class, or massaging the interstices of her ribs. T certainly hadn't. Sleightists, obsessed with their own hurts, could catalogue another member's weight, build, muscle density, flexibility, color and texture of skin, musk, hair length to the quarter inch, life story, and sexual history. But pain was personal. And Lark suffered an internal trigger, not the more normal aches and ills

West saw in the others. Whether or not her Needs were psychosomatic was beside the point. He wanted her afflicted. He wanted her to write whatever she had down in the midst of its onslaught. His work was the work of the cloud chamber: agitation. Enough true artists, given the right conditions, would start going off: hailstorm, fission, machine gun, schizophrenia, applause, Jonestown, popcorn, rapture. Lark was all over the place—obliging. But the boy was more worrisome. He hadn't shown West a word in the month he'd been back, and he was bent on Lark, ignoring T. T minded.

When she returned to bed with her black Amish quilt, West provoked her.

"So what do you think of Byrne and Lark?"

"I'd like to know what she's done to him." T curled into West, her ear on his shoulder.

"As far as I can tell, they aren't *doing* anything."

"Then why do you think he hasn't been over?"

"Are you so starved?" West stroked her upper arm. "I'm so inadequate? Josh is?" West's questions partly feigned hurt, partly purred.

"West, sex is why I let you in the house." Her calloused palm scraped across the skin of his stomach. She pulled up the quilt and settled into him. "That, plus you're my boss."

"Funny. So what is it you need from Byrne?"

"I don't need anything at all from you boys." T spoke airily, absently. "I like giving, and he strikes me as particularly needy."

"Really?" West dug a little. "Seems to me a bit of a loner."

"You're smarter than that." T was smiling; West could feel the muscles of her face against his bicep. "Maybe he'd like to be, but he's wedded to that stone, isn't he? Say what you want, Josh and I have kept some independence."

"Fair enough. When you and Byrne were still . . ." He noticed that she had turned on the ceiling fan despite the chill. "Did he ever say anything to you about the stone?" West needed to know how deep it went. If Byrne had ever released his story, West was hoping T was the one.

"Only that it's changed hands."

This was news. "What's that?"

"He switches it from one hand to the other every new year."

"Did he tell you why?"

"I asked him, before you two went down for that—Lark. He said that if he could only be half a man, he wanted to be both halves."

"Sounds practiced."

"Oh yes. He's careful with himself." T propped herself up on her elbow. "Why'd you send me after him anyway?"

"I did nothing of the kind." Dust edged the fan in gray fur.

"Ah, West. You can't maneuver me so easily anymore. Or at least, I'm not unaware. I took it as a challenge, thought I'd make you jealous as a bonus." Her dry hand went to his cheek, and when he kept his eyes on the ceiling, left it. "We're over?"

"Byrne seems to intrigue you more than I do." West was disturbed at his own petulance. They'd never *been* anything. "But, I didn't realize—you enjoy jealousy?"

"It's like tarragon. There's enough, and there's way too much."

West looked at her. She was undeniably, thoroughly, beautiful. Her eyes were thinning, aiming—yes, some anger there.

She went on. "With Byrne, there's a possibility of repair. But that woman you brought up, she's not interested."

"Not like you are." He wanted more from her. Rancor, spite.

T ignored the bait. "Why do you want him to go all puppy over her?"

"I don't think he's ever done it before. I think . . . well, that it might prove educational for him."

"Ah. The precursors." Her face opened, softened. She relaxed back into the bed, into him. T knew this part of West. The work. They both lay there, eyes open. They let themselves be quiet together. In the slanted late afternoon light, the blades of the fan were skimming their discarded skin from the top of the room, like cream.

"T, I just had a thought. Would you like to meet his brother?"

While Byrne had been in Georgia recovering Lark, West had called Rachel Dunne. She was listed on Byrne's employment forms as next of kin. No sleuthing required, just a lack of the normal editing mechanisms, some cajoling. West had been worried that Byrne wouldn't come back, and he needed him. T wasn't enough of a lure. She was too kind for Byrne, and despite the husband, maybe a little too accessible. West needed Byrne to be attached to Kepler—sewn in—to have him risk what was needed.

It had to be in the rock.

Byrne's mother had sounded older than she should. Was surprised to hear Byrne was involved in sleight, almost pleased. A little unbelieving. No, Byrne's father wasn't around. Yes, dead. It had all been settled at the time, there was no more to say. Yes, as a matter of fact, Byrne did. Marvel, younger, by just thirteen months—an artist. She had, a few weeks ago. Byrne had been to see him in Philadelphia, told him to call. Byrne was good at checking up, a good boy. Graduated in the top ten percent of his college class—a smart boy, hard worker. A number, yes. Marvel was staying with friends, not to call unless it was an emergency. *Is* it an emergency—not something wrong with Byrne? No? Fine, then. Fine. If you talk to Marvel, tell him his mother's just fine, to keep on painting. He's a special one, that boy—you get him on the line, you'll see.

———

What? She did? She's a bird, isn't she? Crazy bitch, gotta love her. Yeah, I can talk. Let me light up, man, hold on. Okay. What are you about again? Right, Byrne. He's a beaut, my brother. You'll want to hear about his rock. If I could count the times some cunt wanted to know before she'd fuck him. But you're his boss? Okay. So this was, what, eight years back. He'd just gone to State. Left me alone with Gil and Rachel. It was only gonna be a year, no big fuck. Gil didn't get to me the way he did Byrne anyway. I was applying to art school. New York, Seattle. The hell away, yeah? I was working on an installation. Something conceptual. Hold on—I'll get to the rock, but you need the background. I decided to do specimens. Deformities, fetuses, brains in jars, you know. I built this long light box—black display, fiberglass top, bulbs inside. This was at school, materials from some art teacher who had the hots for me, but the rest I was getting together in my room. Attic really, Byrne's and mine until he left. I raided the cafeteria trash for econo-sized mason jars. Really skewed scale, yeah? I had close to fifty and was filling them. For each one I got a rock. And not normal rocks—huge motherfucking wampum stones. Rough and sharp, some worn. Granite, quartz, and sandstone. White, gray, speckled, striped, every possible kind. Took me the whole September Byrne was leaving, skipping school, shooting up to Waukesha—the quarry—on my bike. Good place to smoke up. Nah, no, not Byrne. Never did that shit. I could only carry back maybe five at a time, if I could find five, but that wasn't the problem. The problem was the liquid. I was gonna call the piece "Blood Farm"—about extraction, yeah? I was pulling color from these fuckers with chemicals. First I raided the kitchen to get enough—vinegar, Palmolive, Windex, bleach. Nail polish remover from the linen closet. Turpentine from the basement. I took Gil's key to the VA to get some ammonia, ended up taking some IV solutions and blood and a couple bagfuls of urine. Then his weekend job at Mott's Garage. I hit them for motor oil and gasoline, mineral spirits, antifreeze. I want to stress how this was months. Months. Gil wasn't the brightest, and if the window weren't painted shut Mom would never have smelled it to say something. Stupid crow. Byrne was home for winter break. Gil was riled. I'd seen him like that maybe once or twice, with Mom. The hospital times. Really fucking, you know, livid. I stole from his work. He said it was like—get this—like it was him stealing. That's a fucking stretch, no? Started throwing the jars down off the bookshelf and dresser onto the floor. Those jars were so fucking thick the first two didn't break. He had to pick them back up to throw them, like, overhead them, hard at the floor. They broke then, and the fumes were insane—mustard gas or some shit. The room was the size of a toilet. I nearly passed out, and Gil . . . he either did or slipped, because after six or so jars, he was on the floor. Skull wrecked, him bleeding everywhere. And twitching. I went over and picked up the rock closest to his head. I don't know, maybe I was gonna finish him—who the fuck knows? Then

Byrne ran up. Just stood there. Gil jerked a couple more times and then he didn't. And then Byrne stepped over it, the body, took the rock out of my hand. Told me not to say a word. The police, they stayed in the house awhile, they'd been before. Byrne said he was there in the room, and Rachel, not the mess you'd think, she backed him up. So. An accident. Byrne thinks I spilled the old man's brains. And, twisted as he is, it's his fault I'm a killer. He's such an old woman—if you're his boss, you know what I'm saying. Me? Nah, no school. Took my split of the insurance and rented a loft a couple towns over, on the water. I eventually did the installation but changed the name. "Fossil," I called it. It was written up somewhere. They especially liked the jar I'd glued back together. Filled it with tar and left it leak, put a hot bulb under it, set the table on a slant. By the end of the night the display box was covered in black sludge, except where the jars were. The light shot up through some four dozen jars, spotlighting the specie like a flashlight under your chin. The light moved different through the different media—slow green, watery blue, fog red. And the jar, the one with the tar, that was Byrne's rock jar, but he still had it, still does, so that jar was empty and veined black where the cracks were. It tripped everyone out—cause at the end, tar gone, it was like the rock went molten. I tell you, it was fucking primordial.

West had wanted information, but once he had it, he realized it wasn't enough. This Marvel had to be brought in. So many things needed to be juggled, woven, collected, and set in the correct box. West was thankful for his own patience, a native attribute. He made some calls, got Marvel into rehab—he knew a program outside Philly. He hadn't spent a life in sleight without watching a few try to re-create wicking chemically. When Fern ran Kepler, she was good at seeing those signs, getting her charges into counseling early, leaving them a chance of returning to the art. Since West had been running things, he'd lost three to drugs. The thing about sleightists on speed, or coke, or even heroin, was they actually burned brighter for a little while, on the stage.[28] So for November and two weeks into December, Marvel would be drying out on the wooded edge of Germantown, bill footed by the Vice Corps. He'd agreed to it once West had explained the commission, only mildly shocked that Byrne had talked up his talent with such fervor. *Tell you the truth, man, I thought Byrne hated my shit. Too elemental for him.*

Marvel should be nearly straight by now. West would take T to retrieve him. Byrne's brother was a character and, absent Byrne, she could mother him. It was what she wanted. West liked T. He wanted to give her something, a gift.

Marvel was in the front hall to greet them. Behind him, the staircase swept up in a ballroom arc to a landing with a window that looked down on two wintering gardens, English and Japanese. Most of the patients here were affluent, but for the ones who weren't, the return to their normal surroundings no doubt made sobriety a fleeting affair. Marvel was a slender boy-man like Byrne, his hair a loose crown of brown and gold. He grinned when they entered, magnetic. Proffered his hand.

"You're West, my benefactor. And that makes you T."

"Nice to meet you."

T was immediately taken. How could she not be? The way they were smiling at each other—first day of kindergarten. West coughed.

"You must be ready to get out of here. Do you have things?"

Marvel turned his head to appraise West. A junkie, studying his face like a pro. "I do have *things,* in fact. I left them in the room because I'm already working. Thought you might want to see."

"By all means, lead the way."

---

[28] Sleight makes hybrids of its practitioners: without the art, they are no longer themselves. The art form, too, is polluted by its participants. The only possible way for sleight (or a sleightist) to manifest purely would be in the removal of one or the other. The performers know this. Retired sleightists, if they do not continue in a related profession, often sequester themselves from society. A few have spent the remainder of their lives as addicts in weekly hotels. Others have joined religious orders, suicided.

As T followed Marvel up the wide and tapestried stairs past a small, elaborately framed Degas sketch, she couldn't stop herself.

"This house, it's hard to believe—"

She caught herself there, but Marvel helped her out. "Hard to believe they let people like me in. Yeah, I wondered about that too. Mrs. Heim lost a daughter to the pipe a few years back, and since then she's gotten all soft. You know, in the head." Marvel rapped knuckles on his own.

West smiled. The boy was like a fungus.

The paucity of his room was shocking. The wooden floor supported a Shaker-style twin bed, impeccably made up with a canvas bag at its foot, and an equally simple chair and desk by the tall window. Bamboo blinds closed off the ascetic quarters from gardens and daylight. A low-hung pendulum fixture supplied a more concentrated brightness. West ducked to clear it on his way to the desk. Marvel gestured to a stack of papers and stepped back.

"That's what I have so far."

It was a boast. West paged through the nudes, T at his shoulder. He asked the obvious question. "How did you get these colors?" Each sketch was a single contortion of the female form. The bodies were in impossible positions, even for sleightists, and the positions were—there was no other way to put it—ugly. Not a seductive ugliness either, not merely the ugliness of the unfamiliar. West felt T tensing up beside him. The pictures were hateful.

Except for the colors.

"Ah. Glad you asked." Marvel maneuvered around them to the single drawer that ran the length of the desk. He pulled out a box of Crayolas, sharpener on the back, and the lid of a shoebox that had clearly served as a mixing palette. "Mrs. Heim—she doesn't approve of us having lighters, because of cigarettes. She says replacing one addiction with another is a sorry way to health, but I'm very convincing. I melted the colors together." Marvel opened the box, and the crayons, solidified in various stages of liquefaction, looked like the last day—a festival day—in Gomorrah. "I also used a black ballpoint pen, Q-tips, and spit."

"Resourceful." T could only get the one word out.

"The colors are perfect." West was thrilled, but cautious. "And the patterns too—but will you be able to re-create this on skin?"

"Before I started working, I'd have said no way. But I'll find one. This is sordid shit, my man. You do realize? If I paint their bodies, they won't be able to breathe."

"What are you talking about?" T's voice quavered.

"I'm talking about reptile breath, about connection to the world. You already have the stage, the stylized movements. You're already halfway to machine with your crazy little batons and your sealed-up doll faces. I'll be cutting you off even more. Instead of putting on your face, I'll be putting on your skin—emphasizing muscles that aren't there. Minimizing or maximizing your breasts, thighs, hips." He scanned T as he spoke. "Regulating you. I'll be making the audience see what I see: color." Marvel was positively merry. And he was speaking to T as if she should approve, applaud even.

"But these designs, they aren't regular—the patterns are all different." This was T, grasping at air.

"West told me the audience shouldn't be able to see the calculus until it bites them in the ass."

"Bravo." This was West. Clapping.

CHURCHED.

Clef didn't want to be there anymore. She was exhausted, and her sister's presence had taken what joy she had in sleight and smothered it. That didn't mean she wasn't obsessed with her architectures; the new links had started to replicate themselves, but differently each time—an evolution. It was as if the two troupes were manning a zoo. The wicking was happening more often. Sometimes a few sleightists would go out simultaneously, and for longer. Every day was precarious, explosive. And West was experimenting with numbers. He had twelve of them stand like pillars in the chamber, anchors for the other twelve working coupling links around them. Only the hands of the still occasionally twisted, allowing their architectures to follow those of the wilder movers. Clef saw in this exercise the potential for equilibrium: yin/yang. But West's tasks lacked balance. The dynamics were unequal, the emphasis on passivity. Couples or trios, quintets or septets, number didn't matter—what Clef saw in West's scenarios over and over again was an exploration of the idea *victim*.

Clef didn't want to work this terrain. But she did. Each day, she left rehearsal a little more drained than the last, furious that her signature rage had deserted her. She didn't have it in her to confront West, but she would not be used in this way. She had to do something. Act. If she had a baby, she thought, that would be acting. She had discarded the thought of walking out—West would just replace her with someone who didn't care. Besides, she'd tried it before. What troubled her was that the other sleightists were excited, not disturbed. All they talked of was West on fire. To them, his heat was an opportunity. Even members of Kepler were in awe, saying he had outdone himself. This work would be historic. They were making history.

Clef assessed her body—not worn, not thin, not like she felt. It was beginning to retain what it might need for the next months. Her fingers along her stomach no longer strummed corded muscle, but impressed a soft outer layer maybe an eighth-inch thick. She was cloud-heavy, potent. Pregnancy would alter West's equation, or at least complicate it: her body, if she let it, could be something unpredictable. It wasn't exactly life she felt inside of her—it was disobedience. And a new impatience. Six months ago she had been inside a pregnancy, but this time she didn't know what to wait for, what configuration of star or crop circle or flight of bird might make it better. Might make her whole enough. To have a baby, she realized, a woman needed no one. She began intuiting a sapling woven up her spine, a vertebral knowledge. *I can be alone.* Hers would be resistance by inertia. She would allow herself to slow down, grow large, take up space. The idea didn't strike her as maternal, or even romantic, but it was attractive. Because of gravity.

She still wanted Kitchen. She wanted him tomorrow and yesterday and in the mornings. But she'd always wanted him that way. Six years before, two years after she and Lark had joined the company together, he had come to Monk. The sisters were assigned to him, to make certain he had the rep down before his first tour. The troupe was rotating through four different shows that season, six sleights total. After long days, the three of them would sit in a little Ukrainian place on Second Avenue, drinking and commiserating about their director, Imke, her hard-assed perfectionism. Clef had watched Kitchen. Above the red tablecloth, lit by candlelight refracted through thick-glassed pitchers of vodka, his face was etched with lines so subtle they withheld age. Timeless too were the faerie tales he told of his past lives—ballet and butoh. His nearly colorless lips, blackbird brows, fingers like talking: this was beauty. But not love. He had been impossibly old at the time— thirty-four. Clef had decided to ignore her crush, thinking it was a mere missing of the father. Half a semester of intro psych had alerted her to the dangers of transference. So, instead, Lark slept with Kitchen.

After a few months spent tending her growing resentment—the ungazed-at face above their red table—Clef seduced her sister's lover. It wasn't so hard. The two of them were walking back from a long dinner, abstracting war. Minus Lark and vivid with alcohol, Clef and Kitchen riffed on pacifism, isolationism, imperialism. Coyly, Clef offered an observation. "My body is a colony," she said. The connection was urgent. Clef had only ever been with boys at the academy. Kitchen had never been inside such highly articulated energy. He was embarrassed, but told her—later—that even that night he had seen their age difference not as his flaw, but as her incomparability. It should have flattered Clef, except she knew there was someone against whom he must have measured her. When her sister had returned hours later from her film—a pseudodocumentary, a woman's narrative of husband and son, musicians both, slaughtered by the Khmer Rouge—Clef had been standing in the loft the sisters shared, waiting to be honest. But it wasn't a fair match. Lark wouldn't play. She didn't seem to hear Clef's admission, apology, defense. Instead, she talked about self-dug graves, incomplete bludgeonings, children serving up parents like overripe fruit to a fist, starvation, suffocation, ideology, fear. And then she spoke of Needs. Clef thought Lark was deflecting. Crazed. The next morning, Lark had quit Monk. Clef could still replay it in her head, its black-and-white grain—grief footage she should have seen. Cambodia.

Clef took refuge in her abilities. She was the best female sleightist in the troupe, possibly in any of the nine American companies.[29]

[29] The nine American troupes were all founded by former female members of the Theater of Geometry. When they retired, Bugliesi—as she had initially pushed them into franchise—encouraged them to find masculine replacements. She explained her reasoning in a later correspondence: "Most women are not suited to direction. The best ones uphold impossible standards while the worst can think to do nothing but suckle their troupes. A priestess, not a mother, is what is required. Few women have the innate fortitude, or the skill left in their hands by providence, to interpret what the gods have seen fit to set in front of them. When they do, the work is of course unparalleled, and inevitably claimed by some man as his own."

She worked tirelessly at it, as she had since she was a girl escaping the blank space left by her parents' adoration of one another. She and Kitchen continued to see each other, but with less talking. Then, while they were on tour, Jillian killed herself and the hole left by Lark was suddenly too much. When they came back to New York, Clef quit. She told Imke to replace her. Imke hadn't.

Clef read. Lark was gone from their studio apartment, leaving it as dead and immense as a cathedral. So Clef read about God. She read books about people who had met God, and people who'd slept with him; books by St. Teresa of Avila and Meister Eckhart, books about the lives of Moses and Jesus and Siddhartha Gautama, books of Gandhi and the Dalai Lama and Nijinsky. Clef read into the night and until her eyes burned with the bright, negative impressions of the fonts. All she wanted was to be told—it was a large and severe want. The loss of a sister, she chided herself, was not the same as the loss of God. But she had never had God, and Lark had left her stranded. What was she if she wasn't on display—disappearing better than all other women disappear? She had hardly been and was no longer a daughter. She had failed at sister, a failure in which Kitchen was complicit. She was a lover, but that was a poison fruit. If there was some untainted role left for her, it would require witness—and wasn't such a witness God?

She couldn't help but be shocked to recognize while reading the different accounts what it was to see, be seen—to be pierced to the core with knowing. She discovered she *had* had God. During sleight, she'd had God maybe a dozen times a performance. God—another word for annihilation. Clef was not the vehicle of her architectures; she was their impediment. God—as Clef grew in those weeks to understand the concept—was equivalent to any dark stage: the offering-up-of, the I-submit-to, once the I has become small enough to submit. Without performance, subjugation, God did not happen.

Clef decided, over weeks of eye strain and limb atrophy, her legs folded into a stiff burgundy reading chair, that God was selfish and that she didn't like God—but also—that she was good at God and would go back. She wasn't religious. She'd been raised deep enough in the South, but by ex-Catholic atheists. She knew only that vanishing unnoticed gave her no pleasure. She needed her absence exhibited. What was piety, to her, without an audience?

Upon Clef's return, Imke had kissed her six times and then resumed a more callous direction than ever, but at least Kitchen was angry, and speaking to her. They wouldn't eat over a red table again, and so could never decide—not until they were scanning the window of a particular restaurant and bickering like rival beggars, like judges—whether or not they were going in.

Now Lark was back. Everything for Clef was still a mess, but she couldn't quit. She had to resist West. She hadn't originally wanted to think he had power. He had. She hadn't wanted to believe Lark was truly damaged. She was. Clef refused to see Kitchen as something other than her fault. Because he was her fault. There was no decision to make; she would stay. For once, she would not just do, but do good. She would stop fighting her body and let it go to seed. Her body, Clef was beginning to understand, would never not be used. The difference this time was that she was choosing whom to sustain. As world-ocean to her fetus, she would continue in the realms of the not-quite perceivable. It was okay though, it was. Since she could remember, it had been her one talent: Existence In Service To.

West, by doubling their numbers, was setting the stage for a frenzy. Although she hadn't confided this to Kitchen or Lark, Clef was thinking that the stage, even if the stage were God, wouldn't be able to contain the feeding. She had to stay. Be a mother. Try to stop it. She just didn't know how to do—not any of these things.

⸻

"Kitchen, help me."
"Help you how?"
"We need to keep West from this."

"Right. Remind me again how we're going to do that?"

"We'll make Lark give him something to work with that isn't dangerous."

"Dangerous."

"Yes. Something benign. Harmless."

"I know what benign means, Clef. Does Lark know how to make something like that?"

"I don't know, but also . . ."

"Yes?"

"I need you to leave me."

They were in the motel lobby on the other side of the desk from the space heater. Kitchen, more shell-shocked than anything else, was waiting for a key. "We've always lived together on tour, Clef, always. We've lived—"

She interrupted, "We aren't going to."

This knifed. Kitchen looked around vaguely, trying to understand something. He settled on the wall behind the desk. It was cracked, and a Toulouse-Lautrec calendar hung from a nail wedged into the fault line—December's cancan, all inky garters and suggestion.

"This is about Lark?"

"No," Clef said. "Or yes. All these things—you, her—we don't matter. Just, we need to stop West." The desk clerk's nails were cartoonishly long, curved, a metallic merlot. She dangled the key in front of Kitchen. It seemed cruel, but was probably only an attempt to protect her polish.

They got to the chambers early and turned up the furnace. It kicked on loudly. West and T were gone that morning to meet with some artist, and West had left Kitchen in charge of the half day of rehearsal—class, and then continuation of a new string of exercises. During floorwork, Kitchen barely looked at Clef. Everyone began the cold day isolated, privately bundled in multiple, multicolored layers of knitwear. Once they'd worked through the first few links, the sleight-ists began to remove article after article of false warmth, and only then did Kitchen notice that Clef's face was, for rehearsal, uncharacteristically unguarded. And that her chest, usually a field of milk, was confused with blue veins.

About halfway through the afternoon, Clef, who had been glancing into the tinted window of the short fifth wall all day, motioned to Kitchen for a break.

"Take fifteen everyone." Kitchen started to walk toward her, upturned hand inquiring, but she was already through the door to the office.

West looked up sideways from the metal desk and smiled as Clef strode in. The fluorescence of the room made him sallow. The office had a small, murky window and a door on each cork-lined wall; only the positioning of the brushed steel file cabinet and the placement of West's chair oriented it in space. Clef suddenly saw him from the other entrances simultaneously—four-headed, multiple, ghoulish: the purple sockets of his eight eyes sucking in light even as a circular band of teeth flashed, repelling it. He had been smiling too much recently.

Dizzy, Clef compensated, as she almost always did, by pouncing. "Glad you're back, West. Lark's ready."

West kept smiling. If he had been unprepared for this statement, he didn't show it. "She has a sleight for us?"

"I think so, yes." Clef was staring hard at him, waiting for a larger reaction.

"So I can stop biding time with my exercises. Is that your subtext, Clef?"

Clef bit her bottom lip. She thought she tasted blood, but that might've been her gums. "I'm just telling you she's ready. And I think you should let her navigate."

"No." West was rotating a pencil on its tip. On the legal pad in front of him, a knotty line of graphite was quickly developing into a quarter-inch tornado.

"What do you mean, no?" Clef began to work up her indignation. "Those are my architectures you've been screwing with for a month, only Lark knows what her drawings are about, and you, you—"

"You don't like me."

"No." Unexpected relief washed across Clef. Her shoulders dropped an inch below their high mark at the base of her throat.

West nodded, no longer smiling, and tapped the pencil three times in rapid succession before speaking.

"You're a smart girl, Clef. Just because I'm not likeable doesn't mean I'm not excellent at what I do. But if it makes you feel better, I'm planning to collaborate."

"With Lark?" This was better than nothing. She would have to sit down with her sister and work out a strategy. Clef had been mentally taking notes on which links and manipulations caused the most extended wickings. All the sleightists were showing wear: stiffness, injury, infighting, laughing fits, hysteria, hangovers, blackouts, weight loss/gain, general fatigue. What she feared for them, for herself, was also what she wanted: change. But change, part of any chaotic system, wasn't worth the risk when the wind felt as foul as this wind did.

"No, Clef. I want you to navigate this."

"You want *me* to navigate this."

"Yes. As you so aptly stated, these architectures are your babies. You see things in them I can't. But the collaboration won't end there."

"No?"

Behind her, a numb Clef barely felt someone enter the office. Kitchen, she assumed. But when she turned, she was facing, at close quarters, a more wayward-looking version of Lark's roommate Byrne.

"This is Marvel, Clef. He's the art director for this project. He'll tell us what he needs from us, and we will be obliging. I believe he has a vision." West was smiling again. But it was Marvel's face that hurt her. When he laid his hands on her shoulders, she staggered internally. His eyes were a rape.

"I'm of the opinion everyone has visions. Don't you agree?" He unapologetically examined her: neck, breasts, belly, eyes. "What, for instance, is it *you* see?"

School.War, brawl.West did sleight, the fag. Tomahawk fag scalp the faggot clean the ball-less hairless faggot cunt. West threw himself against the locker until he was cut, went after the big boy, eyes like a crazy nigger Injun. Seminole. West righted the big blond cock. Get it right you Nazi. The nigger Injuns were Seminole. Hand to his bleeding head, warm. Smell like locker-room low-Coney-Island-tide spice-soap his-hand-some-nights—now blood. Big blond stepped back in his dirty yellow jock. Looked around for one of his. I'll fuck you up later just wait you little faggot fuck.West didn't give a dried piece of shit for fire—later. Later, they kicked him on the ground.

Church. Sunday—garden day, a day for vegetables. Clef fed birdfeeders and Lark weeded.Worm day. Stung-by-fire-ant day. They urinate on wounds, Newton said, true piss-ants. On the porch with his paper, Newton was crosswords and commentary—row's not straight, pepper's not ripe, a four-letter word for "to aspire"? Jillian looked up from under her hat.That was church right there—the vault overhead when Clef's mother was looking at her father, the pews rubbed down with soil. Church was a thought Clef had, an envy. A connection she didn't have with Jesus, or anyone else, and it stayed with her, on her clothes like urine or myrrh."Want."

Marriage. Lark did not take his name, did not give her own name to her daughter. Names are skin—inadequately shared. Piece-of-paper, courthouse-kiss, in-laws for whom she was a slash. Dearest Drew, Our Nene and L, they wrote. Christ keep you. Lark could not be kept, or only as one keeps a secret—a wounded animal. Her child saw and heard wrong things. At three, Nene had asked her grandparents—Is Miss-Edge-Nation a pageant, is it one with swimsuits? And when they slowly shook their heads, she'd told them: I can enter. The man at the tree with the swinging feet, he said it doesn't matter if my parents were married in the church, or by a judge, or not at all.

The family. A strangle carried in the belly. A ligature—the binding and resultant growth. Like a tree swallows barbed wire, so the family. Dead father. Opaque mother—in tablet form, time-released, empty-by-now. Only Byrne's brother too vital to stomach. Jolt seeping through the system. He brings the brother up to bury elsewhere. Meanwhile, marks his eventual grave. Byrne carries the brother's death, the father's death.They are the same death. The fear: a brother who does not recognize death will use it to bury others. A brother exists in this event to prevent a brother. A brother is—because of property laws neither understand—his brother's heavy.

MONK'S DIRECTOR: Thank you for this.

FERN: No, thank you. You've been my only visitor.

MONK'S DIRECTOR: Your son?

FERN: Oh. He came once, didn't like the smell. Did you know, Luke, I loved navigating when you were in Kepler. Your group was lovely, intelligent. And you were the most talented sleightist in it.

MONK'S DIRECTOR: I'm not such a great director, I'm afraid.

FERN: No. But you do bring some wonderful work out of your people.

MONK'S DIRECTOR: I can't claim credit for Kitchen or Clef.

FERN: Well, what about that white-haired lovely—Haley, is it? Or Emmanuel?

MONK'S DIRECTOR: Maybe. Maybe Manny . . . Fern, I went to your building five times. Your doorman wouldn't tell me how to contact you. I had to tell him your grandson was in trouble.

FERN: It's so much more peaceful here than at Sloan-Kettering—why did it take me so long to call?

MONK'S DIRECTOR: Why move at all? Why not have someone come to stay with you at the apartment?

FERN: I'm auctioning it. Everything in it. I want to have complete control of my assets. Besides—lately, it's grown too bright . . .

MONK'S DIRECTOR: I don't really know how to broach this. It was hard to come to you, especially—I mean . . . you're dying, yes? Of course I'm glad—it's been too long. But my reason is West. I think he's doing something . . . making something . . .

FERN: I'm well aware.

MONK'S DIRECTOR: You are?

FERN: He's trying to engage content.

MONK'S DIRECTOR: What kind of content?

FERN: Real content. Pain. He's been working it out for a decade. Did you see the sleight he navigated for the Nicredo festival five seasons back—*Clutchwork?*

MONK'S DIRECTOR: Marvelous piece. The central structures were almost . . .

FERN: Lucid.

MONK'S DIRECTOR: Lucid. (*pause*) Okay, yes.

FERN: I have come to understand pain . . . as a sort of unmitigated clarity. Of course, he has no idea.

MONK'S DIRECTOR: That he's in pain?

FERN: Revoix had content and couldn't maintain it, not in a single language. Or consciousness, for that matter.

MONK'S DIRECTOR: I've heard this theory—fugue, isn't it called? But forgive me, I know less of the history than I should.

FERN: His was a pathological state. Not artistic. Experimental geometries drawn by a man severed—both witness and accomplice.

MONK'S DIRECTOR: Witness and accomplice to what?

FERN: (*shakes her head*) There's too much. Do you know Lark Scrye?

MONK'S DIRECTOR: I've just met her. West brought her in. He wants her to draw it—the sleight.

FERN: Such is his talent. She might actually be capable. I have something I'd like to return to her, and a letter.

MONK'S DIRECTOR: I don't know if I can go back there. I must sound like . . . like a very little man.

FERN: No. You sound awake. (*cringing, curls to her side*)

MONK'S DIRECTOR: Do you want . . . should I get someone?

FERN: No, but would you pinch me—my hand? Yes, just there at the thumbspan. A little harder. (*relaxes, slowly*) Thank you.

MONK'S DIRECTOR: They aren't giving you anything?

FERN: I've asked them not to, for as long as I can. I have letters to write—to my girls.

MONK'S DIRECTOR: The charity?

FERN: Yes, my infamous charity. Such a hot topic—my money. I know they call the compound "Fern's perversion." Funny, since all charity is perversion. Or guilt.

MONK'S DIRECTOR: Do you want to call? Lark, I mean.

FERN: No. Just take that canvas bag by the door when you leave. You'll see to it—I know you. Did you get any of my messages?

MONK'S DIRECTOR: Messages?

(*Fern grimaces, longer this time. Monk's director pinches her again, again Fern relaxes. Then, winks.*)

MONK'S DIRECTOR: Not . . . but of course they are. Of course they're yours. Fern Early. How could I not have known? You outdo yourself.

FERN: I used to. I'm rather proud of them, not that they've accomplished anything. Roadside flashcards. That is the dilemma, isn't it Luke? How to end the world-coma?

I think all my attempts were too thoughtful. Too much thought paralyzes a would-be revolutionary.

MONK'S DIRECTOR: Are you trying to say I shouldn't stop him?

FERN: How could you? I love West. My mistake. Part of me even wishes I could stay on to . . . but he wouldn't want that. I can hear him: "another insulting attempt at reparation." Or some other bullshit. No matter, I won't be staying.

MONK'S DIRECTOR: Fern, you sound . . .

FERN: I am. I am so very ready.

WEDDED.

L ark spent the evening in Clef's motel room, arguing. "West wants you to navigate? That's what we want, isn't it? I am, I told you. Done . . . No, I won't change what I have. Altering them would only be more dangerous. I have some sense of them this way, and haphazardly changing the forms would only make them—more monstrous. Where's Kitchen? He'll back me up on . . . You're not serious—Clef, you have to tell him. Now. You can't know that—you feel differently. Who? What has Marvel got to do with anything? So he's an ex-junkie . . . he does not know you're pregnant . . . because I didn't tell Byrne . . . because you asked me not to."

Clef was losing it. Lark was hurting. Because of the pregnancy, her hips were sore and she was sleepy. Or was she sore and her hips sleepy? Her legs were nearly nonresponsive outside the chambers. She felt old. And younger too—now that she'd been relieved of the drawings. She'd spent the last three weeks working her technique in the chamber all day, then meditating on her Need most of the night before pulling it onto paper. This one had been harder than the others. She'd needed tremendous energy to hold its metamorphosing forms still enough to approximate with her hand. But she'd done it. Meanwhile, her practice had improved. It seemed the less sleep she had, the more effortlessly she manipulated. She was now intimate with Clef's designs—they extended her limbs, brought her length. She'd even spent time linking with the troupes, to fully understand where West was taking them. She'd recently been letting herself wick, and it wasn't like before. It wasn't *like* anything, really. And——why deny it?——she was proud. The notebook held two dozen labyrinthine structures. Unique structures. Perhaps West's belief in her wasn't so misguided.

She slept in Clef's room that night. Marvel was at Byrne's. She'd only met Byrne's brother for a few moments that afternoon. West had been talking with him in his office when she'd come in with a question.

"West, I keep forgetting. Lack of sleep. Could you tell me the name again?"

"Vogelsong."

"Yes. The couple with the children."

She woke up not knowing where she was. But there was Clef, on the other bed, studying her notebook. The motel. Waking in her sister's room, Lark at first felt invaded, then relaxed. Clef was just working. Lark had gotten it down, this Need; reanimation was Clef's job. The whole thing seemed improbable. Frankensleight. Lark suppressed a giggle. The only thing was: the Need wasn't dead. Since Lark had finished drawing, it had been subdued, and she knew from her time at the academy that it was helping her technique. She decided not to turn on it just yet. Besides, some of her structures might not be navigable—— she might need to document more of its forms.

"Lark, are you awake?"

"I am. What time is it?"

"Five forty-five. Would you talk with me about these?"

"What do you want to know?" Lark sat up, swung her legs out from under the scratchy sheets and, despite ache, sprang across the narrow gulley between their beds. She peered over her sister's freckled shoulder in the lamplight. It was dark outside. It would be for another two hours.

"I've never worked with structures before, Lark. You should be navigating this, not me."

"No. West's right about that part. I'm too close to these. I couldn't even begin to choose the architectures."

Clef's eyes shot up from the notebook. "You're kidding, right? I'm not sure how, Lark, but I know these drawings are tailor-made for the designs I've strung. Maybe you had them in the back of your mind as you drew?" Clef asked this, searching her sister's face for recognition or deception. Finding neither. "You don't see it."

"No." Lark set her teeth. "I don't. What I draw has nothing to do with what's outside. This *thing* is inside me." She jabbed her finger down at the page. "This Need." Beneath her insistence, a rope bridge/noosed centipede was writhing. Twirling.

"Look. You'll have to be my understudy, at least until I can figure out how to do this safely." Lark wasn't with her. She sat there, but really she was galaxied elsewhere. The wicking she hated to do with her body, Lark had always done with everything else she was. Clef asked quietly, not expecting anything, "Lark, where do you go?"

"You'll do fine. I trust you." Lark had immediately forgiven the affront and put her arms around her sister, burying her face in Clef's neck. Clef's hair was everywhere—its morning state—and smelled of ginger. Lark remembered then that she'd forgotten to call home the night before. She'd call tonight, to see if Drew wanted to bring up Nene the following week for Christmas. For cookies. For cookies and snow.

When they arrived at the chambers an hour before warm-up, West was waiting.

"Clef, join me in my office."

Clef looked over at Lark, who seemed less and less herself ever since she'd been drawing the Need, more and more like Lark as a child. Clef was reminded of her once-untroubled sister, Lark before eleven, before twelve. Her sister was grinning now like she'd just escaped a paddling Clef hadn't. As Lark turned and walked almost giddily away, Clef recalled one scorching Fourth of July at the lake when the ground was so hot they had to skip to get to their matching *Star Wars* towels. Back then, Lark—so much older—had worn her hair in two bands behind her ears, the straight ends like paintbrushes, and Clef had looked like Little Orphan Annie.

When Lark reached the other side of chamber one, she immediately began to busy herself with stretching, and Clef followed West into the center of his hive.

"What do you want, West?"

"I want to know how you're planning to proceed with the navigation."

"I have some ideas."

"May I see them?"

Clef reluctantly pulled out her notebook, and Lark's, from her duffel. She was on edge at first, waiting as he paged through them for him to oppose her plans, to forcibly insert some nastiness from the earlier exercises, the grotesque links they'd been working on since Lark and Byrne had arrived, but he just pointed at specific designs on the pages, asking questions. Thoughtful questions. Specific, technical questions that separated and focused Clef's initial blur into something more like a blueprint.

"Is a seven-architecture link going to work here? Won't it cause the next one to be imbalanced? And isn't that one the more crucial?"

As she answered his questions—one, and then another, and then another, the sleight began to acquire a shape in her mind, and not just a shape, but a rhythm, and a counterpoint. After fifteen minutes, she was beginning to get excited, answering him not with simple answers, but with explanations, and with the theories suddenly bubbling forth to support them. Clef was in an element she'd never known was hers.

She stopped herself. "What are you doing, West?"

"I'm just trying to clarify a few things."

"No. You're leading me."

"I'm no attorney. Although you could be considered a witness."

Clef nodded. It was obvious he'd been waiting for this opening—he was barely suppressing a smirk. Well, she might as well give it to him. If she didn't, he'd take it anyway. She gestured, chivalrously offering him the floor. He took his time, leaning back in his chair, extending his legs. Clef half expected him to pull out a pipe in preparation for the inevitable lecture. Sermon, really. He began, as she thought he would, by using her name—his tone, paternal.

"Now Clef, I know you have reservations about the Vogelsong children. You seem to feel, and you aren't alone, that making them central to this sleight is somehow unethical." West paused. The pause got longer. He was milking its potential for emphasis. Clef wanted to let the pause go on until it was dead and dry, but she lost patience.

"Go ahead, West. Get it over with. Wait, I've got an idea—why don't you start by telling me how my feelings are wrong? Tell me how if I just stepped back and thought rationally, I'd see that appropriating these children's nightmare is actually the *most* ethical thing we could do. Then you can explain to me how, when an idea is counterintuitive, that doesn't necessarily make it a bad idea, just an unpopular one. Tell me how you know better in this particular instance not because you're smarter than I am, or naturally superior in any way, but because you have experience and the history in this field to see the whole picture, while I've spent my time thus far inside the art. Explain to me that a system cannot be completely articulated from inside the system, that no matter how fine my insight about certain aspects of my art, I'm really only dealing in details. Perhaps then you can enlighten me about the different types of intellect that exist, how yours is simply more global than mine, more about the connections between things and less about the practical nuts and bolts of the art. You can go on to assure me how my way of seeing is utterly necessary, like bread or shelter. You might even want to talk about how useless the big picture you see so clearly is for most people, how philosophy is a leisure activity—nonessential in most times and places. Except this one. Tell me how my perspective is generally more useful and *this time* a very valuable, but nonetheless *limited,* perspective. Go ahead."

West was amused, nodding and smiling, looking at his desk as she spoke. When she stopped and took a breath, he leaned forward, searching out her eyes, then examining them for a long moment. Clef held his gaze, but felt exposed.

"You're really quite a find, you know. I thought, after I saw her book, that your sister was the one, but obviously there's something in the water down in Georgia. Your architectures, Clef, these ideas for the navigation—you don't need to change what you're doing. It's you, you who are already incorporating the children. They're woven through everything you've shown me. You aren't appropriating their pain, Clef, you're giving them a voice. Look around you. Everyone is working harder, pushing. There's a sudden urgency in this process that I haven't seen since my grandmother directed *Ach Grace*. Trust me, if I'd simply wanted to shock the audience, I could've done it without recruiting so many contrary women. You're making this vision more difficult for me, but that is exactly what will make it something other than a . . . spectacle. It is your doubt that will keep this from being merely self-indulgent, or gratuitous, or obscene. This is yours, Clef. Your baby. I'm giving it to you completely."

Clef was without response. This speech wasn't at all the speech she'd expected. She tried to take in what West had just given her—complete artistic control. Direction. She would be navigating the sleight, orchestrating it, conducting it. His hand, out of the soup. Surely he didn't mean it—he'd insert himself somewhere, he'd have to. After a moment or two, thinking through how she might test his offer, she began cautiously outlining a few more ideas, ones that she'd origi-nally thought West would veto.

But he didn't.

Two hours later Lark stood among the troupes in chamber four. West and Clef were in front of the central mirror, facing the cluster of bodies—yawners, stretchers, adjusters—all variously shifting their impatience from hip to hip. West had spent half the morning in the office with Clef, leaving Kitchen to warm up the rest. West hadn't asked for her presence, and Lark was glad—she didn't want to be included in the cabal. Maybe Clef didn't understand that, but Lark just wanted out, to be done with her part. She was exhausted. Exhilarated. She'd agreed to this—agreed to vivisect her Need and then put it on display. She had not agreed to instruct others in the intricacies of its anatomy. Her drawings were observational. Analysis belonged to someone else, a West—and now, to Clef, her little sister. She was anxious to see what they would make.

Out at the kiosk with her Souls, she got what amounted to an inadequate fix with each purchase. The money was meant to compensate her for the lack of a more profound response. It didn't. If anything, the steep prices she charged for her work, while a means of support, were also revenge—exacted for the ends she imagined her art met. Stupidity and stupidity. She didn't know what happened to her Souls out in the world. They might sit on library shelves gathering mites, suffer gossip on living room coffee tables, or fill with loose and dirty bedroom change, accruing domestic value. Up until now, she had preferred a total lack of feedback to its alternative—criticism. Fern Early had sent no less than three collectors down to buy from her before Lark stopped it. Lark didn't want the Souls in a gallery or in a museum any more than she would have wanted them to hold her ashes.

Souls were empty. Fixed. Her Needs may have begun as living mutations, but once she cast them onto the wooden knots, they no longer struggled. They congealed—mail-order brides waiting to be delivered. They were not her, and so she worried for them. Twice she'd lied and said a Soul had been commissioned rather than sell it to the wrong buyer. Once a Soul was finished, she both wanted it gone and didn't. Her compromise had been to gift the ones she couldn't part with to Nene.

But her drawings of the Needs were different. Lark recognized it. Her sketches were neither complete nor static. They were stirrings, interrogatives, queries. West, Clef, the other sleightists—what would they make of them? Of her?

"I'll need Latisha, Manny, and Sarah to go with Clef. She'll start the navigation. Clef knows the architectures better than any of us, and we've come up with an initial schema for the first few structures. We'll be using a few of the links and manipulations you've developed these past weeks, of course, as well as some Clef has designed directly from Lark's drawings."

As West said this, a number of sleightists turned to look at Lark, some smiling, some not. They all knew the sleight was going to be hers—over the past weeks the rumor had ossified into fact—but this was the first official mention, confirmation. Lark was their hand. T's troubled face was one of those turned her way. Lark found herself looking directly at this woman, wondering what she had done to incur such enmity. In a countenance as serene as T's, any cloud was an omen. This was a storm. But Clef spoke next, and before Lark had reversed the trajectory of T's hostility and followed it back to Byrne, all eyes were on her sister.

"I want us to work through the next three weeks with reverence."

Clef spoke authoritatively, but to Lark she looked and sounded small. Hair, voice—both attempts at volume were silly. Weren't they? There, at the front of the room, Clef was vulnerable. Her face, mottled with some emotion Lark couldn't place, squinted out into the sleight-ists. She hadn't pulled back her hair that morning and now seemed in danger of dissolving into the red mane's white noise. Lark felt a sudden urge to take her sister from the room, feed her sweet tea, reason her hair into braids. For the first time in weeks, she didn't care about her drawings, the sleight, this new Need.

"You all saw my reaction the first day West asked us to use this tragedy. I wasn't convinced such a response was appropriate. But the material we've created in the past month has proved me wrong. Something about the story of those children has moved us, moved me, to make something new. Something extraordinary. Now we're going to pull it all together. I'll be working the links first and then sequencing the structures. But this sleight won't work without a different type of commitment than is usually asked of you."

Clef spoke clearly, coldly, corporately, and to the opposite purpose than they'd discussed that morning or during the past weeks. Lark felt hamstrung. She'd been counting on Clef to neutralize West's influence during the navigation. And now her sister, like Lark, was balking at her responsibility to check West. Beyond that, she seemed taken with his ideas. By his ideas. Hostage. Lark hadn't expected this. Neither, it seemed, had the others, who had stopped stretching, yawning, and scratching and whose attentions were trained on the newly conditioned Clef. But it was West who spoke.

"We need you to engage."

"What did you say?" Haley said in disbelief.

"Engage," he repeated. "Not suppress yourselves—emotionally, physically, or otherwise."

"You're asking us to emote?" Kitchen's question made West wince.

"No. Not emote. I want you to be there. Inside the technique. I want a sense of the individual, all of you as individuals. I want you to be empowered."

"I don't get it." Manny's voice surfaced among the others' murmurs.

Clef fielded. "We're asking you to care. To care about what this sleight is about. If we don't care, we'll just be using their nightmare for our own ends." Clef clarified: "The children's . . . their nightmare."

"But sleights aren't about anything. They're specifically not, so as to not underestimate the audience's intellect." Haley continued, "If a sleight is coherent, it condescends. Sleight itself is experience, not the mediation of experience." She rolled off the clichés like a catechism.[30]

"You don't fucking believe that shit, do you blondie?" A voice like Byrne's, but wryer, louder, from behind them. An unfamiliar made his way up through the troupes, tracking ice, ending the trail in a puddle of gray water between Clef and West. "Because if you do—the hair's perfect." Then, without taking his eyes from Haley, he slapped Clef's back. She blanched. In her face, briefly drained of its strange obedience, Lark saw loathing.

[30] Although sleight is, with the notable exception of the precursors, a predominantly nonverbal enterprise, certain tenets of sleight have been passed down word for word over generations. While some sleightists allow this dogma to bounce off them, sleet against windshields, others are scored by the sharp bytes. Most of the doctrine concerns itself with why sleights can't mean—a question students of the art form wrestle with endlessly, until one day they don't.

"This is Marvel," West said, enjoying the effect of the boy's entrance while shifting the focus back to himself. "I've hired him as art director for this project. He'll tell you what we need from you, and you will oblige us. We have a vision."

Byrne had walked in with Marvel but remained at the back of the room, arms folded in mute tantrum. He waited a few beats after West introduced his brother before heckling.

"So tell us, West. What *is* this sleight about?"

West's reversal was both flawless and overt. "Since you've been hoarding the words, Byrne, I actually thought this might be an opportunity for *you* to illuminate *us*."

And despite Byrne's perfect awareness, West began to reel another one under.

FAMILIAR.

"So. Whose bed is this?" Marvel was sprawled on the sheets, one boot on the arm of the couch, the other on the floor, hands behind his head. "And where's your TV?"

"Lark was staying here." Byrne stared down at him, having yet to fully grasp his presence. He'd learned of his brother's involvement the moment he saw Marvel, T, and West step into Kepler's lobby that afternoon. His brother had gained some needed weight since Philly. "Are you really off the shit?"

"Clean as a whistle." Marvel took the pillow out from under his head and buried his face in it. A yawning inhalation sealed his mouth and nose; its twin exhalation created a pocket of used air. After a few deep breaths—suffocation-play—he removed the pillow and looked up at his brother with mock concern. "Speaking of cleanliness, your girlfriend is a very sweaty girl. Here, smell this." He threw the pillow at Byrne.

"Shut up, Marvel." Byrne didn't catch it. He let it hit his chest and fall to the floor.

"Knew you hadn't nailed her. You should've seen your face when she came into West's office. What's happened to you anyway? You never used to be such a chickenshit." Marvel sat up and looked around. "Seriously, you don't have a TV?"

"The world. Doesn't interest me."

"Poor Byrne. But what about the beauty and wonder of nature as viewed from inside a leaf-cutter ant colony? What about pay-per-view boxing? What about British sitcoms on public television? What about the porn, man? What about the porn?"

"I said shut up, Marvel."

"Oh, dude. That's it—you're fucking smitten."

The next day, the navigation began. West introduced Marvel to a stunned Kepler and Monk, and Byrne finally handed over a copy of his precursor. West took it and withdrew into his office. After his introductory speech, he didn't emerge to help Clef with the sleight for over a week. Meanwhile, Marvel spent his days pulling sleightists from Clef's navigation in chamber one to try out different pigments and patterns on their skin. And somehow, Byrne—with nothing left to write and not wanting to leave anyone alone with Marvel—became his brother's assistant.

West told Byrne and Marvel where to find a thrift store, and there they picked up several damaged vanities. Marvel joyed in the smashing of oval faces in the parking lot, and the subsequent assembly of the shards. For each sleightist who came in, Marvel developed an individual design. Kitchen received a corset of eight-inch spikes that extended from ribs to hipbones. Marvel used weak glue for the initial fitting, and Byrne was in charge of sanding the mirrors. When Kitchen tried out a manipulation, one of his stays came loose and pierced him just below the tip of his sternum. He said nothing, and Byrne started rounding the upper edges on the rest. Marvel just laughed.

After a day or two, it became obvious that the body art wasn't working the way he wanted—the paints were too flat or too shiny, too paint-like. They didn't live. The mirrors were by far the easier part. So every hour or two, Marvel went out for a smoke and to wail at the dumpster with a tire iron, rethinking the colors. While he was gone, Byrne slipped into the back of chamber one to see how the navigation was coming along. Clef was using Lark as her stand-in.

Every day the thing had more flesh. By the end of the week, Clef had put together nearly thirty minutes worth of material from Lark's drawings—and the beginning of the sleight was unlike any Byrne knew or could piece together from his early childhood.

Opening.[31] *A single sleightist stands far upstage right, back turned to the audience. The rest, twenty-three of them scattered across the chamber on their backs, are already manipulating. Rabidity—sea churn. The vertical sleightist slowly revolves, working her architecture so slowly its configuration is perceptible. The architecture is revealed, no longer a play of light. Not pure, not reason. The architecture as awkward prosthesis, replacement for something missing. Something crucial.*

The sleightist begins speeding up the manipulation until the architecture again lacks definition, the glimpse—of crutch—immediately forgotten. She moves first downstage, then stage left, then downstage, then stage left. Hers is a step pattern, and like all step patterns, it simulates progress. She passes over the other sleightists, linking with each one in turn.

The first link begins. She gently steps between one of the sleightist's legs, carefully forcing them open. She initiates a link that pulls the sleightist working on the floor almost into a sitting position several times, but each time the seated / prone figure returns in undulation to the ground, head lolling toward the audience. It wants to be a child perhaps rousing an adult, an urgent waking, but is unsuccessful, though by the end of the duet the architectures are moving furiously—shrieking past the horizontal sleightist's face, which is blank, blind, elsewhere.

As she moves to the next position, the vertical sleightist steps on the sternum of a second prone figure. Her free leg then begins to rise, released, as if buoyed by flammable gas. The two sleightists, top and bottom, begin to pass their architectures back and forth between them—the link makes claims of superiority or subversion without ever resolving which. Meanwhile the top holds her raised leg

---

[31] Sleights begin with all sleightists on the stage. During a sleight, no sleightist leaves the stage until the last few moments. It is the empty stage that marks the sleight's completion, not blackout, not curtains. After the sleightists have left the stage, usually one by one, they do not return. There is no bow. All the elements of a sleight are meant to be constant throughout the body of the sleight, except of course during the wicking. When sleightists go "out," it is not to be speculated that they simply left the stage. A sleightist's presence, in this way, becomes a guarantor of the nature of his or her absence.

and maneuvers it in contortion close to her face. Two arms and the upraised leg fix her as lotus, while the sleightist beneath her bogs—his compressed torso echoed by thick-slow limbs that quicken only when an architecture descends, flicking it away like bottle flies.

It continues. With each link, the vertical sleightist fights to remain vertical, all the while coaxing, coercing, painfully extricating, or failing to extricate, some new thing from the prone. The vertical sleightist affects untenable shapes while stepping here on a sleightist's stomach, there on a thigh, here an upper arm, small of back, hand, side of face. Finally, she plants her foot on a neck, and this time the trodden ascends—first managing to pull her legs underneath her, then making it awkwardly onto her knees, then crouching in a push toward the upright. This sleightist, chin to chest, trembling with the weight of another woman on her neck and upper back, never ceases the manipulation of her architecture. The under-sleightist works her manipulation low—near the floor—and haltingly, and the sleightist above her cannot link with it. The result is two asynchronous orbits around an instability. Dissonance.

Then, a sudden gesture: the under-sleightist reverses her rotation, repulsing the first. Hurling her, in fact, into the other sleightists, now upwelling—rising hostility evident both in their physicality and in the threatening wall of links they wield.

The truth was, no one could manipulate the links as well as Clef, and though the navigation was moving fast, she seemed distracted and frustrated when a sleightist didn't immediately pick up the work. In the first two days, every time Byrne looked in there was a new central figure treading across the others. First Clef tried out Yael, then an elfin sleightist from Kepler named Jade, then T. When she put Haley in, she kept her there for almost three days. But Haley, though energetic and a quick study, lacked eloquence, and—necessary for this sleight—a depth to her urgency.

Byrne was there on Friday when Clef gave in to the obvious. Haley had just slipped off Montserrat's neck for a third time when Clef said, "Just please, would you please just stop." The sleightists quickly caught up their architectures. Doug and Elisa were linked at more than three points and had to rewind in order to disconnect.[32] After a few seconds though, the room was quiet. Expectant. Byrne had noticed the regard her own troupe and Kepler had been showing to Clef. He thought it was because she was, visibly, on some edge. Since the first day, she'd shown the kind of tunnel vision associated with inspiration. Her short fuse, glazed eyes, and lip biting made her appear not quite in control, and didn't that mean she was being controlled, probably by something greater? So when she spoke now, the other sleightists didn't immediately bristle at her arrogance. And Haley, the most recent target of Clef's exasperated direction, seemed relieved to be sent to the floor to join the corps.

"Lark, get over here." Clef gestured toward a kneeling Montserrat, her architecture held out in front of her like a child's winter coat or dead pet. "I'll need you to learn this so you can teach it to me over the weekend. These girls just aren't capable." Out of a peer's mouth, this was a slap.[33]

Byrne watched. Lark began to learn Clef's part as tyrant, as precarious god, as addict, as prey. The whole time she manipulated, Lark kept looking over at her sister, whose lower lip was swollen, whose teeth were pink with blood-threaded saliva. Even distracted, Lark was manipulating better than Haley had, and Clef seemed momentarily

[32] Architectural links are accomplished by one of the following methods: a) looping one architecture's fishwire through another's (spider-point) or b) keeping the fishwire untouched and sliding one tube against another with continual pressure (whet- or passion-point) or c) catching a tube from one architecture in the joint of another (cradle-point). For obvious reasons, only the most ambitious links have more than a single point of contact between any two architectures. Complexity in linking is often referred to, pejoratively, as "wit" or "cunning." As in: "Now, there's a *cunning* structure—trading on wick for *wit*."

[33] In sleight, as in many disciplines whose continued life depends on mentor-to-student transmission, certain anachronistic behaviors have outlasted their efficacy. "Girls" is a term used by directors and instructors no matter what the age or level of maturity of the female sleightist. Similarly, even if they begin their training in prepubescence or in childhood, male sleightists are "men."

appeased. The other sleightists, however, nudged one another. Kitchen's eyes were trained on Clef, and Yael seemed not unhappily surprised by her prodigal friend's abilities, but the rest glared at Lark, suspicious.

The tensions Clef kept adding to the structure were intensified by amorphous jealousies, exhaustion, mistrust. The chamber muttered. Along the wall, arms folded across chests. Shoulders raised. And the sleightists who were in actual, physical contact with Lark—their muscles tensed, making the partnering more difficult, dynamic, exciting. Because what Clef was making was undeniable, all the anger was settling upon Lark, who—summer asphalt—began to shimmer with it. Byrne was mesmerized by the implied violence. Sold. He didn't return to help his brother Marvel in chamber four. He also didn't see himself phantomed in each figure terrorized by Lark's talent that Friday afternoon. And Byrne didn't fantasize. This was not his daydream: him, bodied in the whole of the mob poised to pull her— the relentlessly vertical Lark—part from part from part.

At six, Clef called the first section done, and a dazed Byrne wandered from the chamber. He hadn't heard Marvel call T out of the navigation, so he wasn't prepared to greet her naked body, trembling at him beneath Marvel's color. If river clay was to be found in a pale, malignant yellow, T was entirely of that shade, even her hair. Then again, she wasn't. Not entirely. Marvel had drawn a thin black band across her eyes and all the way around her head. He'd drawn it again across her nipples, and at the level of her pubic bone.[34] A final one circled her leg at the narrow moment just below the knee. But—they didn't circle. The lines were so thin that even at two yards they were difficult to make out, though at that distance and beyond they retained

---

34 Female and male sleightists keep themselves, except for the head, completely hairless. The practice is customary, a nod to decorum, originally conceived as an attempt at desexualization. In the early seventies, when it first decided to discard all stagewear except for webs, the International Board insisted that sleight directors distinguish their troupes from the burgeoning au natural culture with stringent hair removal, heavy and stylized stage makeup, and impeccable personal grooming outside the theater.

their effect: disruption. T was segmented. A skull pan. Upper tips of ears to bust. From fourth rib to just below hipbone. Crotch through knee. Calf, ankle, foot. Calf, ankle, foot. There, at the bottom—her symmetry lacked a flesh bridge. Byrne, not quite steady to begin with, put his hand on the nearest mirror. T was crying. Byrne could see streaks in the yellow stain, streaks that ran perpendicular to Marvel's black divisions.

"What have you done to her?"

"Nothing you haven't." Marvel hadn't shown up at Byrne's apartment the night before. He looked insolent, but not victorious.

T's eyes blamed Byrne. He went over, picked her warm-up clothes up from off the floor at her feet, handed them to her.

"Is this who you are?" T was tearful, not pathetic. Humiliated and lovely, she was more concerned for his soul than her degradation. Byrne saw her mirrors then. They had been crushed to a glitter and were smeared across the lines that cut her. They atomized him.

"I'm not Marvel."

"No. Your brother . . . he knows what he is." T held her clothes tight to her chest as she walked toward the restroom.

Byrne could not watch her shifting lines, how her torso dissembled all that was above and below. He looked instead at his brother. Marvel had executed what Byrne could not. An admission of desire. A desire for destruction.

But, beautifully. Beautifully done.

———

West took Byrne out to dinner that night. It was swank. It was one of those places that disavows its surroundings, thinks it belongs to another town, city, country even. This place thought it was in France, maybe Arles: an elegant ceramic rooster in the center of the table eyed them thoughtfully, mustard yellow dishes sang beneath olive loaf, bold flatware weighted down the egg-blue napkins. West ordered them both Muscat and commenced his sermon.

"I need you to go back. Rewrite. The precursor is nearly there, but the balance at the end has to shift drastically." West sipped his water. "It should finish with a burial—or better, with a holocaust." Another sip.

"Okay." Byrne had accepted dinner to discuss his brother, not sleight. He no longer knew what to think of West's work—he didn't like to think of it—but having his brother around was the real impossibility. His sleeping with T was of course expected. But his vivisection of her . . . "Why did you bring Marvel here?"

"I think you know why. He's talented, he's a force. And he's not afraid to say things with his art."

"It's easy to say things when you're a psychopath." Byrne looked at the ceramic cock. It was garlanded with hand-painted flowers, white and pink. He added, "When you're not strangling on words."

"Your brother understands color, and I've known color was needed from the beginning. He just gets this, Byrne."

Byrne flinched. "You're shitting me." The waiter had come with a bottle but didn't approach the table. "Marvel, get sleight? He's always hated it."

West motioned to the waiter. The pomaded youth leaned in, made a trembling display of the label. West nodded, and he poured.

"I'm sure he still does."

"Then, what . . ."

"Do you know how to manipulate someone?" West waved the waiter off, swirled his apéritif. It looked like piss. "You find out what they want to do, and then you make it possible for them to do it."

"Genius. You *do* know Marvel wants to cut people up?" Byrne's rock rested on the table. He usually kept it down at his side when he was out, but the year was ending, and his arm was tired. "What is it you think I want to do?"

"You? You want to atone." West lifted his glass, toasted the air. "Here's to it."

"I don't know what Marvel told you—I had nothing to do with Gil's death."

West wouldn't put down his drink. His arm was extended toward Byrne, his eyes fixed on Byrne's glass. Finally, Byrne raised it, clinked.

"You didn't stop it."

"No." Byrne didn't drink. He set down the glass and began to study the short, price-less menu.

"And now you're thinking about fatherhood, but don't know how to fall in love." West was amusing himself with Byrne's discomfort. "That doesn't make it impossible, mind you, just awkward. And Lark not only is—I've heard—but has, a remarkable child." When West said this, Byrne's rock hit his water goblet. Water sloshed onto the rooster, dripping off its wattle onto the black toile tablecloth, but the goblet remained upright. "So, Byrne, is it that you think—if she'd just let you into her little family, maybe you could make up for Marvel?"

"Marvel?"

"For failing him. As a father."

"I was his brother."

"You *were* his brother?"

"Am. What the hell are you trying to prove, West?" Byrne raised his voice. "With me, with this sleight? I see two troupes, I see the new architectures, painted bodies instead of webs, I know you want me to be literal, I know you brought in Marvel to hurt me. It's all fucked up. You want all of us to work from some tortured place, but sleight's not therapy."

"I don't offer therapy."

"Clearly. It isn't goddamned witness either."

The waiter surveying the room from the corner glanced toward them nervously. West's voice took on the hushed tones of placating nurse to the fever-muddled.

"So not therapy. Not witness. I should be writing this down. Tell me Byrne—what, do you think, is sleight?"

Byrne allowed himself to be calmed, lowered almost to a mumble. "It isn't anything. It's nothing. That's why it's beautiful. You keep trying to make it hold things. It doesn't work that way. You're stripping it of emptiness. You'll kill it."

"You think the navigation's not working?" West's voice was wet with concern.

"It's working, West. It's dark and full of everyone's entrails. Mine, Lark's, now Clef's. T's. Shit—it's Sleight of the Living Dead. I'm just asking, what's left?"

West took another drink. He put the glass down, then moved both his hands out over the table and took the rooster from its perch in the center of the farm-stitched linen. He turned the bird to face him and clucked gently to it, and Byrne felt suddenly shut out. West gave his answer to the cock.

"What's left? Cluck. What should always be left. What never seems to be, cluck, left . . . aftermath."

THE OTHER QUARTET.

SETTING: *A party. Ballgowns and masks. A small child on the top steps of an offishly kept Victorian, a Victorian painted wrong colors. A spurned lover in the kitchen. A brother, loose-cannoned, on the couch. Against a far wall, petals drifting down, an open-faced woman. It's snowing. There are exactly one hundred thousand snowflakes, each falling. The small child has counted them. They are all the same.*

NENE: It is late and the adults are mostly stumbly, except the ones who didn't get that way and so are annoyed or gone. These adults are unlike other adults in that they are all beautiful in every way. They are *animalia*. You can see it in how they move. It is you who thinks this, you, the small child.

MARVEL: The girl Nene came to the party, and her daddy Drew. Byrne wants to be ground down and spat out—don't know why. But he's clearly elected himself. Everyone knows.

KITCHEN: I am in the kitchen. It's a joke we used to do.

MARVEL: I know. He's my brother. West and Clef know. When Lark looks at him, it's pity or nothing at all.

T: Sometimes I have regret.

KITCHEN: I am waiting, Kitchen in the kitchen, waiting for Clef to ask me back.

NENE: You see how they flow from room to room, like lovely grazing things. *Subsisting*. And you notice these adults, unlike other adults, touch.

T: I think Marvel was a mistake. He just sits on the divan, watching his brother, the sisters.

MARVEL: Those bitches. It's the most fucking annoying thing in the world—to be ignorant of your talents.

T: In bed, he was sweet. That should've told me something.

NENE: They touch each other and they touch walls to steady themselves and because the wallpaper is like letters Mommy wrote and sent to Fern, who was named after but before one of your Souls. They touched you when you came in, touched your braids—not many people do—touched your hand and one kissed it. That was like a prince, you thought, and *excessive*.

MARVEL: Byrne the clown, dancing with that little girl like some precious uncle.

T: He wasn't desperate in the honest way sex should be desperate, especially the first time. Desperation of discovery, of encountering the new. Instead, he watched me.

NENE: They all look like a show, which is what Daddy said they do, but who are they showing now? Maybe you, maybe you're meant to be shown, stealing up from night, meant to be seeing them this way so waltzingly. Daddy cannot stop touching Mommy, but you see she is like she is sometimes.

(Lark is made of falling. She has snow in her hair. In the crux of her left elbow, in her fingers. Between her legs—snow.)

MARVEL: Then Byrne laughed with Drew even as Drew rubbed Lark's shoulders. Byrne the slug.

T: I see it now. He was dismembering me, even then, I wasn't new to him.

MARVEL: Where's the fucking salt? Lark's in a silver slip and I'll give it to him, tonight she's the moon—and he's the moon's slimy trail.

NENE: She looks more like them than before, and talks like one. She hugged and kissed you and it was her, but then she asked you if-you-are-mad-why-are-you in one of their voices, you don't know which one.

MARVEL: I hear she's been flashing out more than anyone, Byrne said, more than three anyones.

NENE: You met so many tonight, and one who wasn't, who was Byrne's brother. Byrne twirled you, then Aunt Clef took and Rapunzeled you into a room if your hair did, but it doesn't.

KITCHEN: I will not beg her. This is my exercise in ridiculous and pointless dignity.

NENE: Byrne had been sad from watching all the others touch you and a little angry and then thinking. Maybe he was allowed too, and there was a song he knew and asked you to dance. You liked that. He didn't hurt your back with the rock like he was afraid.

KITCHEN: Dignity is even harder and smaller than the ridiculous and pointless rock that boy carries around. Shame—there can be no other reason to carry a stone through the world. And now, Clef is carrying a stone.

MARVEL: Then Lark goes to the motel to moon over her sister, who's looking like hell, like three hells.

KITCHEN: My stone. I swear, I would love it if she asked me to.

(*The weather inside is enchantment: its extra, unverifiable weight like a bullet or a bomb hidden in the body.*)

NENE: Of course there should be ballgowns now and masks and feathers . . .

KITCHEN: It's not difficult to love the ridiculous. The pointless.

NENE: . . . but instead West was *sinister* and gave you a candy cane on the way up, though you aren't supposed to after dinner.

This is his house and the walls feel pretty and the bed in the room is deep but you can't go down into it like a spoon through marshmallow. You aren't tired.

KITCHEN: Lark is as good as Clef, and it's killing Clef.

NENE: Aunt Clef held you and sang at the corner and cried she didn't know you, but you knew her.

KITCHEN: There. I've said it. I still love Clef. Her sister is taking the place she doesn't want to want anymore, except that she does.

NENE: Newt showed you Clef a hundred times.

KITCHEN: Clef won't tell me it's killing her, and the navigation is, because she thinks I don't want what she wants, except that I do. If she's going to want it, I want it.

NENE: She's older than how Newt showed her, but so like Mommy when Mommy is there.

KITCHEN: I will want it.

MARVEL: Byrne-the-fool says the sleight loves Lark, but I won't even try to take color to her—I'm waiting for Clef.

NENE: And she's red.

T: I was another woman to dismantle, another in a series, nothing differentiating us except the way he takes us apart, the color he adds.

MARVEL: What would I do with Lark?

T: West gave me away. Byrne won't look at me. I want so much to be whole tonight, and the bourbon doesn't.

MARVEL: Lark's sort of gristle-pretty, I admit. Can't really look at her without thinking of her inside my mouth.

T: The sisters, they're loved. I don't want to be jealous—a hateful, spiteful emotion. I've never been, not like now. West did this.

KITCHEN: Clef is doing exactly what West wants, what Lark's drawings demand. Require. It's mesmerizing. There has never, never been another sleight. She is the only woman who could be pulled so hard in so many directions and maintain perfection . . .

T: West's watching, but he's not watching me. He's rolled up his sleeves to grease the wheels of his party . . .

KITCHEN: . . . and take perfection and map it onto others.

T: . . . filling mugs with too-strong cider, adjusting the music to counter the mood, control it.

NENE: This is Christmas, is love . . .

MARVEL: But tonight, Lark's soft . . .

T: "What a Little Moonlight Can Do"

KITCHEN: There has never . . .

NENE: . . . is dark . . .

T: "Night and Day"

MARVEL: . . . a thirty-watt bulb.

KITCHEN: . . . never been another . . .

T: "Bluebird of Delhi"

KITCHEN: . . . woman.

NENE: . . . is peppermint is snow outside like everything is already over . . .

T: "Clap Hands," "Take Five"

NENE: . . . and stealing up from night is the way they are . . .

T: "All Along the Watchtower"

NENE: . . . at the bottom of the stairs like fish, all beautiful fish glimmery sad and *veering* and . . .

T: West knows what to do, what people want before they want it.

KITCHEN: I went behind Clef up the stairs to watch her tuck Nene into bed.

T: Byrne followed Lark all night with his eyes.

MARVEL: What would it be like, I wonder, to dissolve that kind of light, Lark light, on my tongue?

T: What was I doing with Marvel? Was it revenge?

NENE: . . . it would be perfect . . .

T: Sex has turned. It hardly helps, and the bourbon doesn't.

MARVEL: How would it taste? What color?

NENE: . . . and you wouldn't need any more words . . .

KITCHEN: Nene is no child—she's Lark's daughter. And that, I think, requires suffering.

NENE: . . . if she would just touch Daddy back.

A PAIR OF SOLOS.

Dear Lark,

You think I can't tell when you're not there. Well, you aren't quite the performer you think you are. I made love to you last night anyway, because I can't not. I love you. This morning, when you left for the chambers with Clef, I decided it was time for Nene and me to go. This isn't the right place for a four-year-old. And that's what she is, Lark— a precocious four-year-old with an imaginary friend who happens to have your father's name. That's all. I know I sent you here with my blessings, but I'm taking them back. This thing, these people—they're bankrupt somehow. I can't explain it. None of you can tell me what it is you're making, not what it means, not why it matters . . . and yet, you can't think or talk about anything else. I didn't tell you last night, but I brought up your jars. I'm leaving them with West. After Nene's birth your painting—your Souls—they seemed to help you come back to me. To us. Come back to us, Lark. Please.

Love, Drew

Drew folded the note, sealed it, left the envelope on the kitchen table. West showed them out. He gave Nene a kiss on the forehead, a candy cane for the road. He patted Drew on the back, said Clef would be relieving Lark soon, this week or next, he'd send her home. He went back into the house. In a cardboard box in the foyer, a foot below the rail of the wainscot T had helped him to restore, were the baby-jarred colors of Needs. West walked through the living room, scanned it for remnants of the party he hadn't gotten the night before. He picked up a burgundy throw from behind the couch, took two stone mugs off of the mantle, and moved toward the kitchen. He rinsed the mugs, set them in the sink, plucked the envelope from the table, opened it, and read. Then he walked over to the pantry, pushed open the door that didn't latch, stepped on the lever that opened the small silver trash can just inside, and dropped in the letter. West reached up to a high shelf for the granola—a stretch: like most Victorians, his had tall ceilings. He went to the refrigerator for soy milk, the dishwasher for a clean spoon. He sat down at the table and ate breakfast. He wasn't happy. In the bustling party preparations, he'd forgotten to buy himself dried blueberries.

FIRST DUET.

Lark was teaching Clef. Lark showed her sister, explaining with her hands, the nuances of manipulating these architectures. Clef was amazed at her own navigation. She had wanted to curtail it, to work against West, but it wouldn't be stopped. She had looked at Lark's drawings and seen through her own body. She had seen inception. This sleight was in her. Maybe actually inside of her, next to the fetus, antifetal. On the very first day of the navigation, her notion of the child became entwined with the work. She could no more limit the sleight than she could control the growth inside her. She thought about the sleight very hard. And every time she thought *sleight,* she meant *fetus.* Or *tumor.* When she concentrated on the navigation hard enough, she felt everything in her dividing. In no time at all, every cell was multi-cellular—infinite. She was mother, artist. Connected by the same thread of worry, the same desire—what might she pass on.

Some nights, after rehearsal, she thought she could sense differentiation. Soon the sleight would have a beginning, a middle, an end: she just hoped, in that order. Because of West's involvement, because of her mother, because of Lark's Needs, there was nothing Clef feared more than the monstrous. The unbounded. It was why she worked at the navigation with love. To forestall deformation. But what was unconditional—mightn't that be monstrous too? Every way open to her was fouled by a possible future.

After three hours in the cold chamber, Clef was beyond sore; she was shaking. Lark went to her.

"We should stop."

"Why?" Clef doubled over, hands on knees, catching breath. She stood up. "I can do this. It's mine to do."

"It is." But Lark didn't move to continue instruction. Since Clef had started navigating, neither sister had discussed West with the other. It helped that he had absented himself from the process. They both knew that would only last as long as the sleight being produced was the sleight he wanted.

"But?" Clef's voice was filled with air. She was still working for oxygen, her chest heaving.

"You're pregnant."

"Really? And you know what about motherhood exactly?" Clef flinched after she said it. She didn't know when she'd developed this streak, this talent for letting fly words that stung in both directions. She bent a leg beneath her, folded her body into the floor.

"I love Nene." Lark looked down at Clef before joining her, cross-legged in the middle of the chamber. They were a two-person séance. A Ouiji.

"If you love Nene, you should be with her." This time Clef meant to convince.

"Now, *now* that you've decided you can be a mother, you're going to tell me how to do it?"

"Only how not to."

They were both still. The room was still. Nothing knocking about the walls, or under the floor. No ghost, no message. Clef spoke again.

"Do you think . . . did Jillian love us?"

Lark thought. This is where an answer should provide itself, letter by letter. She looked around. A floor, walls, a door, a window, mirrors. And above the mirrors, the wall of this chamber, like all of York's chambers, had been stenciled with numbers, not the alphabet. The sleightists in Kepler laughed about it. West and his primes—one of the essential organizations of the original things. Hands often used primes to sequence their structures, but to Lark, math seemed as arbitrary as anything else. Someone had invented math too, as someone had once invented science, language, and before that God. Someone was always trying to pin things down, to corset them. What could be more breath-stealing than omniscience?

"I know she did."

SECOND DUET.

In the car.

"Daddy?"

"Yes, Nene."

"Sometimes I get mad at Mommy."

"Me too."

"But Daddy."

"What, Nene?"

"Mommy can't help it."

"Can't help what?"

"She wants this. She's hardly ever wanted anything. And it's Christmas."

"It was Christmas yesterday."

"Then it's almost New Year's."

"Meaning what exactly, Nene?"

"The year turns over."

"Turns over?"

"Yes. Newt showed me. Nothing keeps counting. Everything's at 0, 0-0-0, like a string of baby robins' mouths."

zero orders magnitude :: zero, an egg :: child is born, lives, grows, dies in bed :: zero :: ten thousand slaughtered, twenty thousand walked to death, a million gassed, a ship sunk, tsunami come to tea, a mother ground down into the earth, planet-burnt-and-empty :: all these—zero :: zero accounts for no dead :: refuses impression :: or to blister :: zero insisting on anything, insists on nothing :: on nothing absolutely

THIRD DUET.

Byrne had taken back the precursor and stared at it for days. It was New Year's Eve. White outside. Marvel was due back soon, maybe. West had gotten him new paints from somewhere, and they were working. Marvel was in whatever constituted paradise for Marvel. He returned to Byrne's apartment to eat and sleep and talk endlessly of hue and saturation and depth of field and integument and other things Byrne didn't understand and didn't care to. Byrne nodded. Byrne didn't leave the apartment. He didn't want to see Lark, he didn't want to hear about her, didn't want to think of her leaving, didn't want her to stay. Nothing was coming to Byrne. Marvel said that Clef and the rest of the sleightists were dogs. They'd had three days off at Christmas, although few had left to see family. In consideration of that short break, they'd agreed to work through New Year's. Marvel said they'd been there ten hours a day. "Dogs," he said. "Bitches."

"Marvel, why don't you shut the fuck up."

Marvel, just in the door, was shaking off huge flakes like dandruff. He smiled. "A little touchy, Byrne, with the block?"

"You have no memory? You're completely devoid?" Byrne was looking at his brother. His eyes were metal. He stood from the table and walked toward Marvel, rock in hand.

"Ah. Date, date. Who's got a date? Do you have a date tonight, brother?"

Byrne stopped. "So you haven't . . ."

"Forgotten? What, the day I killed your father?"

"Our father."

"Who aren't in heaven. Wasn't much of a father until he was dead, if you ask me, Byrne. Since then, of course, he's kept you in line." Marvel had removed his army jacket and dropped it onto the floor. "Can we have some hot chocolate, you think?"

"You want hot chocolate."

"I want to sit down and get warm. And you'll want to switch hands."

"What?"

"I've seen you now and again, Byrne—I've noticed the change. I figured a sensitive soul such as yourself would make it into a ritual. What happens when you do it? Do you get shaggy, howl at the moon? Eat women? I would."

"I forget."

"Of course, you forget."

The two brothers sat across the card table from one another. One had his hands wrapped tightly around a cup. The other sat with both palms flat on the table in front of him, the piece of granite between them. His head was lowered. The words he spoke were impenetrable to Marvel. "What are you saying?" Byrne continued. Marvel waited, though he didn't like to wait for anything. When Byrne finished, Marvel asked again.

"What were you saying?"

Byrne looked at his brother. "I made Mom teach me."

"What?" Marvel was getting agitated.

"She said it every day for eleven months," Byrne explained. "Though I was supposed to. I caught her saying it at Thanksgiving and made her teach me."

"What?" his brother was gritting his teeth.

"The kaddish."

Marvel's eyes lit up then, and he nodded to himself. "So, you *don't* know what you're saying."

Byrne looked back down at the rock. "Not really . . . She loved him, you know."

"I did know." Marvel blew into his cocoa.

Byrne's hand twitched. "They wouldn't let her come back home after he died."

Marvel sipped, swallowed. "No, why would they?"

Byrne's hand twitched again. This time it seized the rock.

———

In Cape Town it was summer. From the plane, they could see the different way the light hit the earth. Because of summer. They went straight to the hotel when they landed, a hotel connected to a mall. Haley asked the driver of their bus to interpret a familiar-looking sign along the roadway. The man's smile was sad as he slowed the bus to turn almost completely around in his seat. "It says, 'This Land You Live on Is a Cursed Land.' Or maybe more like a land of horror—I've heard you have these in America, yes?" He went back to the road. When they arrived at the hotel, he told them to stay close to the complex. "I'm worried for your group," he said, "all so new." Marvel and West, after checking in, headed straight to the hotel bar. Byrne went to bed, having not flown well. Most of the other sleightists talked and decided to stay up that afternoon, outwake the lag. They didn't have to be in the theater for two days.

While heading to their rooms to drop off luggage, they passed through a long hallway. Elaborately matted political and festival posters were mounted close together in beautifully crafted, porous wooden frames; the even spacing, equal frame size, and quick striding of guests down the hall made the series an almost entirely subliminal film. But Latisha, at the back of the group, stopped in front of one with block print and an image of a young black man carrying a limp boy, and set her immense suitcase against the wall. T stopped a little ahead, waiting for her.

"Junie—that's June. The sixteenth. This is my birthday."

"How did I forget you were a Gemini?"

"It's Bloomsday."

"What's that?"

"The day *Ulysses* takes place. June 16, 1904. Dublin."

"Ulysses?"

"James Joyce's *Ulysses*? Best novel written in the English language in the twentieth century—that *Ulysses*?"

"Never read it."

"Yeah? Well, me neither. Tried to once—my birthday and all."

"But that's what this poster's about?"

"Nope. This is that boy, Hector. Or was it Henry? It's for National Youth Day."

"What's that?"

"The uprisings in Soweto? The beginnings of the end of apartheid?"

"When was that?"

"Happened on my birthday, apparently."

"Yeah, Tisha. You just said. I mean, the year."

"You know, I have no idea."

———

Marvel shook Byrne.

"Get up. I want to go to the botanical gardens." Marvel was already dressed. Or maybe he hadn't undressed.

"What?"

"Get up. You've been passed out on top of that comforter for four-teen hours. With your shoes on. Take a goddamn shower and let's get moving."

"We're going to see flowers?"

"Don't get smart, puke-boy."

Half of the sleightists had decided to take a ferry to Robben Island, where Nelson Mandela had been imprisoned for a quarter century, and before him lepers, the chronically ill, the insane. Their driver had suggested the tour; his brother-in-law had been incarcerated and now lived and worked there. "The place," he said, "is deeply affecting—

there are postcards." The others, less inclined to the self-education available to day tourists, went to walk down by the waterfront, which housed theaters, restaurants, and a shopping district—a familiarly upscale development project that neither demanded nor promised. Marvel and Byrne went alone to the botanical gardens on the eastern slopes of Table Mountain, the large outcropping that defined the side of the city not oriented to water.

The colors at Kirstenbosch were of a quality Byrne couldn't readily identify. They were both vivid and hushed. Byrne felt as if he were looking through a tinted lens, but he wasn't sure what part of the spectrum he was being denied. The colors were compressing something inside his chest, something like a sob, or maybe it was just the traveling—he still wasn't used to it. But no, another pang. It was Marvel doing this, on purpose, with the color. Some awful kind of sharing.

The gardens weren't crowded. Most of the guests were European tourists, with impressive cameras and chic leather bags. Byrne had left his camera in York, having of late lost his taste for documentation. An Asian family in summer hats was frescoed beneath the pom-pom tree advertised on the front of the brochure they'd been handed at the entrance. It was no longer in full bloom. An older woman strolled ahead of them, humming to herself and, as if in love, stroking with the back of her hand her own downy cheek. She could've been local. A thin black man in his twenties was sketching on one of the benches—art student? Marvel kept his head down, touching plants. Byrne stopped guessing at the people and started reading names from off the little placards, names of flowers he'd never heard before—*Agapanthus* and *Vygies* and *Bloodflowers*—but Marvel didn't want them said aloud.

"You can't hear color, Byrne. Sometimes you can feel it, but you can't hear it, especially not in Latin."

"It's not all Latin. And I can hear color."

"I'm sorry, what are you babbling about?"

"All words have color. Your name, for example. What color do you think your name is?"

"My name has no color. Don't you think I'd know it if my name had color?"

"Like you knew you were Jewish?"

"I did."

"Bullshit. Your name, Marvel, happens to be persimmon."

"What the fuck?"

"The color of persimmons, the fruit."

"I know the color. My name isn't 'persimmon.' What a fucking pussy-ass word."

They walked through the gardens for another hour without talking. Marvel kept holding leaves and petals against his palm, checking them, Byrne supposed, against his flesh tone. Byrne knew he should be intrigued by the feathery grasses, that he should be admiring the slenderness of lilies and the glittering of foreign insects that weren't foreign here. But this life didn't interest him—it was what it was. There was no art in it.

Byrne had never been, not ever, in a place that wanted him. Marvel had done his own chores and then his older brother's so Byrne would go with him to the quarry on the weekends, but the pit was too white and too wide. It didn't like them there. The earth couldn't recover from such a gash, and Byrne knew it was wrong to play inside a wound. Undaunted, Marvel started riding up there alone at eleven, and eventually ended up in a pack of delinquents who hung out between the woods and the gaping. Byrne spent most of his adolescence reading in his room, enwombed, though the house hadn't wanted him either. And then, when he'd finally left, it got to be a grave.

With duct tape, he'd tacked up pages X-actoed from library books on the cinderblock walls of his dorm room in a gesture of grief or ownership. It was the beginning of a lesson: words, like places, were not to be his. Not ready to use his father's death as a pickup line, he'd said little about it after he'd gotten back to school, but carried the rock. He became an icon of stoicism in only his second semester on campus. But by early April he'd softened a little, and one night asked his roommate to find another place to sleep. He brought up a girl he'd been watching since he'd come back—violet lipstick and fishnets in his Milton class. Amelia, like the pilot. After they were done with the awkward sex—his first time with a rock—he told her about Gil in a secondary gush he thought was emotion. She'd listened, then complained about the wordy décor, that his taste in poetry was leaden. "Ezra Pound? You think being a man is hard?" She was laughing. She didn't tell him what was harder, but Byrne knew. He had no right to what he couldn't feel. He left his walls alone after Amelia. And started jotting down language, his own, which laid claim to nothing.

Byrne didn't want to examine plants. Things directly hurt. Thorns, the smell of chlorine, yellow. He kept looking instead at the muted sky, which seemed to have a warmth to its blue, as if it were reflecting the oceans that converged there, just below them, below the tip of the continent. When he called Marvel's attention to the strangeness of this one, this sky, Marvel asked him what color he thought Lark's name was. "Brown," Byrne said without hesitation. "A dull gray-brown, like you'd expect."

When they got back to the hotel, West was sitting on a leather ottoman in the lobby, reading a German newspaper. He looked up when the brothers entered, then folded the paper and stood to greet them. He was in formal mode and Italian shoes; Byrne had seen neither since their European tour.

"Did you find what you were looking for?" The question was directed at Byrne, though Byrne wasn't aware he'd been looking for anything.

"You mean, did Marvel?"

"No," said West. "I meant you. Did you find the rest of the words?"

West was still dissatisfied with the precursor. Byrne had spent the first week of the new year reworking it. But it wasn't brutal enough, and West refused to name the sleight. It was listed on the playbills of the tour as [untitled], lowercase u. Byrne was supposed to perform the words again on this tour, from up in the ropes, but the idea made him uneasy—nauseous, if he thought about it too much. He'd suggested West record the words. Since Byrne met him, West had been saying they needed to integrate more technology into the art form—why not sound? The precursor, though, West insisted, had to be reactive. This was absurd, of course; most troupes had the precursor read onstage before the curtains even opened. West was torturing him. And to be painted black by his brother? It already felt like being dipped in oil. Marvel's hand in the process would only darken it, make a seal, night him.

Since West's holiday party the brothers had been getting along well enough. Byrne assumed it was the new paints; Marvel was thrilled with his own work, and from what Byrne had seen of it he had the right. He'd started spending his evenings with West, drinking Byrne assumed, though he didn't think any other substance had entered into the relapse yet. Marvel had always been easier intoxicated. His intensity—less cruelly directed outward. That's how it had gone with Gil too, up to a point. West said Marvel should join him, and asked Byrne didn't he have work to do—an eleventh-hour revision? Byrne watched them move toward the hotel bar, then skulked to his room to ugly up his language, as per instruction.

———————

The next day was tech and dress rehearsal. The sleightists got to the theater around noon. Byrne had gotten there a little earlier. *Lake, knife, jackoff.* He was in the unlit theater as they took class onstage. *Kilter, deepwell, jill.* Since Monk's director had abandoned the project, Kitchen had been the de facto rehearsal master, but he didn't seem to enjoy it. He gave a perfunctory warm-up. Afterwards, Byrne saw him take a few sleightists aside. *Élan, Alan, nylon, pianofire.*

Somehow everyone had managed to stay healthy—at least, none of the interns/understudies had had to replace anyone from the main company[35]—but Clef's navigation was so technically demanding that the smallest lack of focus could cause disaster. *Fungus, handgun, haibun, hotcross, blush.* Several of the sleightists, after the last few weeks, were not at their most acute. Kitchen and those few stood at the edge of the wings doing a centering exercise, breath-based, while the others gathered their things from the back of the stage and went on break. The troupes had been provided with a complimentary massage therapist, paid for by a friends-of-the-theater organization in Cape Town. Byrne put down his head to write in the dim light bouncing around and off the stage, but he heard Kitchen send two sleightists to the woman—her table was set up in one of the dressing rooms. He told them to visualize the last two sections while she worked on them, make certain she didn't go too hard. No rolfing. *Toothloss, haircrush, crash, seedbelt, bread, breast, locust.* Byrne had learned from T that sleightists preferred deep muscle work—but Kitchen knew it could cause discrepancies of reach and balance too close to a performance.

Cleo, clit, bender, gypped, sum, alcohol, heal, stiletto, fealty, tittybar, yard, improperty, confestation, insectual.

Byrne noticed that Kitchen hadn't taken Clef aside, though there was something off in her form. She worked alone onstage after everyone had gone, marking through the sleight. Byrne was ravenous. He had nothing with him—his desire for jerky was gone—but he stayed to watch her go through a three-hour performance in forty-five minutes,

[35] Most troupes have between two and four unpaid apprentices working at any given time both in the office and as understudies. These young men and women rarely make it into the troupes, though there have been exceptions. The work asked of them is grueling and thankless, though the sleightists are generally kind. When interns have to go on for the injured, the lack of integrated rehearsal time makes them perform at a much lower level than they would be capable of under normal circumstances. This shouldn't be, but is, generally held against them by the directors when they join an open audition pool. A sleight student asked to become an apprentice would be wise to refuse. None do.

without architectures, without other sleightists. It was just her and the changing lights as stagehands maneuvered around her, checking gels and foci. When the stage got completely dark, she moved through it, and when the lights came up, her eyes were closed. Watching Lark's sister catstepping, watching different points on her body interact with architectures he was left to imagine, Byrne remembered what he loved in this, and it wasn't Lark. The knot inside him gave way in the dark theater. A deep breath, a sob let loose, tears strung out, hungry zeroes.

Every other year he could cry. It was always a surprise.

The words were drumming: *dogged, godding, annie, does, boers, conscription, deficiency, foreign-hand, lesion, twine.* He wrote them down in his notebook. With his new hand, he had been incorporating too much meaning, sometimes autobiography, even syntax. He tore out the page. He wrote them down again. He crossed out *boers,* then *godding.* The paper was wet. Byrne's face was flooding, but he turned the page. He wrote down *fingers, bird, blew, flown.* He wrote *lossed.* He wrote *lark.* Down. He wrote *I,* wrote *crawl.*

OPENING.

The debut of this sleight has earned the troupes international attention. The audience is full of tourists and critics. The crowd is standing-room only, and over a hundred have chosen to stand. Because West violated a dozen conventions without so much as a nod to recognized authority, those who follow sleight politics expect the International Board to revoke Kepler and Monk's charters and put pressure on their sponsors to drop the troupes. However, the sleightists know nothing will be decided until board members see how the sleight is received. And Monk and Kepler believe in West. They believe in the way he doesn't give a fuck. They believe if there were reason to, he would.

Clef stands far upstage right, her back to the audience. She slowly turns. Lark is breathing through each movement with her, the same breaths. She is crouching backstage, behind a tree of lights. When Clef leaves her sister's line of sight, Lark moves to keep visual contact. Before Clef finishes the first duet, she has already wicked twice, once at the very beginning, once as the link was dissolved. The flickers were brief—badly spliced film. Clef is blue, blue as flame, with upward strokes like flame, all blue except her hair, which Marvel left alone. He mirrored her in small rectangles placed so close together the effect is zipper, patterned in a large *Y* on her torso, with one line down the underbelly of each limb. In her palms are two larger mirrors, and on the inside of Clef's high arches, two more. Lark doesn't care about color. She's watching her sister for breaks in concentration. And she's counting Clef's wickings. Timing them.

When, after two days of close contractions, they finally took Nene out of her, Lark had been cold. They'd put the baby under the lights on the silver platter. A little roaster, her mouth so large and red. Nene looked as if she were supposed to eat and also be eaten. And the blood wouldn't stop. After the doctors took her uterus out, before Lark could speak again, after Drew brought his wife and child home, Drew's mother came. She didn't understand her son's wife, or her silence, but showed Lark how to braid. Lark had known how to braid before, but hair—the part of a woman she keeps even though it is dead—like words, had become foreign to Lark.

In the theater, Lark hardly registers Byrne's words as he releases his precursor into the space above the sleightists. She hasn't seen it in a month. He's never rehearsed it aloud, not even at last night's dress rehearsal, and only twice did he come into the chambers in York to mutter it to himself as they ran through the structures. West wanted it that way. West told them that despite the precision required for linking, this sleight needed at least one raw element. The week before they left for Africa, the sleightists worked for the first time in the paint and mirrors—then complained of chafing, of the steel wool and abrasive soaps needed to remove the new colors. And West increased his estimate of necessary raw elements to two.

A preoccupied Lark doesn't hear Byrne's recent changes. The sleightists onstage who do focus on his voice slackening in and around them like rope—they've never heard these words at all. Lark watches Clef so intently she doesn't note it when a name loops around the ankle of one of the others. But Byrne's precursor doesn't trip them. Only a subtle tightening of their limbs, a minor constriction of air. When the sleightists hear a name that means, their nerves react—stiffening, bracing them for the next. It is only sometimes weapon. After a few near misses, the sleightists begin to wonder if they've lost one. Where is the name of their childhood friend, their nephew, lover? Is this a list of the doomed or the saved? Is their own name included? If not, where is their name? Under what replacement?

Lark is heedless. Intent. Lark is willing her sister through the sleight—names are a luxury.

Clef's wickings grow longer and closer together. Lark is disgusted with herself. Clef began the performance more exhausted than necessary because they'd been up arguing. Lark had come on tour as Clef's plan B—no one else was capable of understudying her—and because Lark had somehow misplaced her husband and daughter and didn't know how to find them. Since then, she'd played splinter-fetching mouse to Clef's lion, and nursemaid: giving her sister nightly foot-rubs, plaiting her hair, bringing Clef's favorite coffee through customs and brewing it in the hotel room despite caffeine, coaching her through the monolithic sleight. And—except onstage—Clef had been passive through it all. Not herself, not fierce. But when Lark saw her in dress rehearsal, it was over. She made up her mind: her sister wouldn't perform on opening night. Maybe no one would.

Last night's dress rehearsal was the first time they'd run the piece in full makeup and without a stop—and the wicking strobed. First, not Clef. Not Clef. Not Clef again. Again not Clef. Ten, maybe eleven times. Then not Clef with Mikaela. Those two not again. And more. Not Clef with Jade and Kitchen. Each wicking happened nearly thirty seconds apart, and the intervals seemed regular until Lark realized— at over an hour into the rehearsal—that they were growing incrementally closer. And Clef had missed none. When the wicking was happening at a heartbeat's pace and Clef was out for three, sometimes four at a time, there was still a half hour to go, and Lark fought her instinct to rip Clef from the stage. At the end, Lark's throat was sore with bile and her tendons were clenched in hornets' nests throughout her body.

Clef had come offstage and immediately lost consciousness. Lark couldn't speak then, but after physically pushing Kitchen back and waving the others off, she brought Clef around and took her backstage. Meanwhile, West gave an hour's worth of rehearsal notes to the other sleightists—all in various stages of collapse, but still coherent. Lark had a stagehand call her a cab while she showered and dressed her sister. She took her back to the hotel and asked the concierge to have a broth brought up. Broth was not English he knew. "Broth." Lark said flatly, "Soup without anything in it. Empty soup." That seemed to do it, and he picked up the phone.

When they got back to the room, Lark had been firm.

"You can't."

"I can."

"Look at you. You can barely speak."

"So don't argue with me."

"What about the baby?"

"The baby is fine."

"How can you know that? No one has wicked so much pregnant."

"If it isn't hurting me, it won't hurt the baby."

"You call this not hurting?"

"I'm fine. I want to do this. It's only seven cities, a twelve-day tour. I can do that on my head."

"Didn't you feel it, Clef? You weren't there half the time, and this was only dress rehearsal. It's so much worse than in the chambers. Too many go out at once."

"How many?"

"It never got all of you—but at the end there was a moment when I thought it would."

"So?"

"After all of you . . . who then?"

"Lark."

"I'm serious. Outside of this project, how many have you ever seen out at once?"

"Three. Four . . . five tops."

"And that's coincidence, not design. This is mechanical, Clef. And we made it. It's not a good thing."

"How can you know that?"

"I barely *saw* you."

They continued in this vein for two hours. They didn't know, was one end of it. They couldn't believe, the other. After all, what was this they were making? It was a sleight. Sleight possesses and sleight consumes, but sleight accomplishes nothing. They hated this, but West couldn't change it. He wasn't capable. No one was. In this way, they assuaged their guilt for their complicity—complicity, hell, they were cocreators. And this thing, it was a project aimed at, and locked onto, wrong. They had to believe it wouldn't reach its target. No matter how badly West might want the wicking to jump from the stage, Clef and Lark didn't truly believe it could.

Clef won the argument because they doubted, and because Lark saw that her sister was too frail to finish it.

———

Onstage, it is opening night. The sleight is pulsing, and Clef. Lark whispers, *Come on, come on.* Then, *Come back.* She doesn't register the colors and the lighting, and from backstage she cannot fully fathom what Marvel has achieved. After being disappointed by the dress rehearsal, Marvel spent all day battling the lighting designer with West's help, and he has his effect. The sleightists are jungle, engine. The sleightists are aether, beaded with plasma. The sleightists are more than anything else that they are, beasts. It's color that has done this—color that divests them of something human, but offers what is essential. Each—distilled to his or her most basic attributes. Purified.

Kitchen is so royal, so plum in his torso plated with knives, that when he links with Clef, it is war. Haley is pink, tequila on its way to salmon, slippery on the eye—sweet, peppery—her entire face mirrored. Montserrat is willow streaked with sage: to watch her is to understand where grief lives in the body—her mirrors, all in hidden places. Manny is gold, a Toltec idol, a starlet. The mirrors inside Manny's hands are twin compacts, the oval ones on his inner thighs a vulgar gold.

T is still yellow. With his new palette, the only change Marvel made in T's coloring was to divide her not with black but with a red indistinguishable from black. It is the same color he chose to hide Byrne from the audience. Up in his ropes, Byrne wears a black bodysuit, but Marvel has made his brother's face and hands entirely scabrous, the blood-black of a tick, fingers like leeches. As he sways above Marvel and West's circus, Byrne would give anything—his rock—to have a bit of flesh in which to bury his throbbing head.

Lark isn't looking at Byrne. No one is. She's fixated on her tiny sister, colossal in her blue skin, alone. Clef wicks and wicks. One in a hundred sleightists have ever felt the wicking—Lark was one. When she was younger, it was ice. An incapacity to hold warmth in the marrow, below the level of bone. She clings to her belief in this sensation, which is a six-year-old shadow now. Clef is going to freeze. Clef's baby will turn blue inside her, and the blue will not be the blue of chemical fire but the blue of blood pooling just below the surface of motion—molecules forgetting momentum. Clef has done nothing to protect herself. She doesn't know how to flush her system of desire. To separate herself. She denies hurt even as it eats her.

Lark is crouched in the wings, pleading in a hoarse whisper for her sister's return, when her body starts heaving. It rocks back, forth. Her body contracts like anything else shedding its skin. The ripple starts at the base of her, moves up and around the rims of her pelvis, and then becomes a rolling pressure, pulling her organs up, slamming them against the floor of her diaphragm, and Lark is not breathing. She's heaving, but nothing is coming in. It's all trained on out. Out.

On the floor in front of Lark is broth and bile and the remnants of a banana, black bread, some salad. On the floor in front of her is a husk. A small blue thing. She picks it up. She is tender, her two hands a cradle.

It is wet, and does not move.

"[UNTITLED]" REVIEW

BY ALDEN KEIRNAN, REUTERS
JANUARY 2001, 10:16 GMT

CAPE TOWN (REUTERS) — Revolution. There is no other way to say it.
The two most lauded American sleight troupes, Kepler and Monk,
joined forces yesterday in a performance that must be seen to be
comprehended, and perhaps not even then. There is no question that
the achievement is extraordinary, but how to parse it? I shall work
chronologically, as I can think of no other method of organization,
although after my experience at the theatre last night, time strikes me
as largely irrelevant.

I entered the lobby. I was anxious, as the hype for this performance was
unprecedented. The questions in my head, however, were petty: Would
West continue to get away with his experimentation? Would the bad boy
of sleight produce something that would finally get his troupe ousted by
the International Board? Would his endless novelty sport any substance?

And what did I receive for my skepticism? A novel substance. An
actual "original thing."

First, I took a playbill from an usher, noting as I did that the sleight
had no title. I was initially put off by West's pretension, but the work
earned this lack. Conversely, he supplied the audience with the names
of the sleightists—unheard of! And beside each name was printed the
name of a color. Although he didn't divide the sleightists into their
respective troupes, this level of identification alone was astounding.
Since its inception, sleight has operated as an art form of coordinated
anonymity. West color-coated his sleightists like Easter candy, and the
effect was nothing less than psychedelic—if that word has retained a

meaning other than its quaint reference to lava lamps and LSD. How he kept the color from separating them into various provinces of action I do not know, but the sleightists continued to function singly. They were rush-hour headlights in rain, an urban blur of neon trails, phantasmagoria.

I suppose this is the moment to recognize the stand-out sleightists, though I've never before had the occasion nor the information available to me to do so. Clef Scrye performed a central role, almost a solo (!), although the other twenty-three sleightists remained on the stage. Her technique was unparalleled, and thus rarely visible. With flaming hair, when she wasn't wicking, she was a blue matchstick setting fire to the other sleightists, who—because of the doubling of their number—had to deal with more complex structures than have ever been seen on a sleight stage. To be commended are: Kenichi Baba, Emmanual Vega and Montserrat Jones, for their superb work in purple, gold and green.

The links' cunning surpassed that of all sleights heretofore witnessed by this reviewer. But the wicking, as always, was the measure of the experience. No other sleight performance has ever supported such sustained, simultaneous wicking. The illusion's effect was breathtaking. Somehow, the visual removal of webs from the sleight was accompanied by a reduction in the white noise normally produced onstage, but in its place, the pattern of silences became the score. Incidental noise faded in and out through the evening, and as the silences grew closer, the noise between seemed to grow louder, until by the end of [untitled], I felt as if I had been trapped in one of those horrifically thumping clubs that have infested major cosmopolitan centers since the early seventies. Even as it was happening, I wondered why I didn't hate the phenomenon, the racing sensation in my chest—most especially that. But I felt only young. And it was during this violent rejuvenation that I realized that the links and the precursor, both separately and together, were heartrending. I was at the tip of myself, worried for the work's resolution. I was twenty again. Moved.

I have finally arrived at the center: West's *[untitled]* tells a story (sacrilege!)—the fable of the art form's inefficacy. West has heralded the death of sleight. I watched a Mardi Gras dirge last night, and was transported by its displaced percussion—its trumpeting of sleight's poverty. I felt, but could and cannot say for what. West has made a blaring, pounding triumph out of his art form's inability to speak to the modern audience. West has shown us the Carnival of what is not possible. Sleight can go nowhere from here. And this great turning in on itself—this is revolution.

———

West was devastated. It did not. Had not. He had watched from the light-box as all went according. The seven roving spots had worked. The side-lights and gobos. The cyc, perfectly modulated. The timing. The colors blindingly ratcheted. No sleightist faltered. The precursor gouged. Clef's navigation couldn't have been more. But the audience had been floored, not flickered. Their ovation—the typical pindrop. They sat and sat and sat after, except the ones standing, and those ones stood a long time, and no one exited. At that moment he knew failure, but didn't know the extent.

West had been fourteen when Fern had put him, at the end of one summer, in the academy performance against his will. He wasn't good. He shouldn't have been there at all, let alone been trusted to work with others, but she'd said there weren't enough men—he had no choice. Within the first minute of the forty-five-minute work, he had dropped his architecture. A sleightist does not. Does Not. He dropped it once. Twice. Then, he dropped it while linking. While *linking*. All the parents of the other, deserving students tried not to look away. Four. Five drops. Six. But he saw their faces—they weren't angry that he'd ruined their daughter's or son's performance. They pitied him. Fern made him stay after, during the meet-and-greet. She said to him firmly, no—he was wrong, they didn't pity. So many came up with their cookies, with their punch, to tell him how well he'd done. So very many. More than for any other student. He was Fern's grandson. She was right—these parents weren't showing concern. They were taking, from his humiliation, their glee.

Cape Town had not drunk. Cape Town's aristocrats and tourists. Critics and students. They picked up purses and playbills and started mumbling until the mumbling was a roar and a leaving, and he watched them exit the theater. Common, common. Whores. From it, he watched them, all their walking, whorish walking, away. They'd shown up for spectacle: an evening, a dinner, a movie, and gone. A fix. Napkin refolded. But during—during they had been there, flaunting their absence. Zombie, zombie. Television. He had done no damage. Not a single audience member was altered, hurt, woken, freed. It was incomprehensible. All he'd poured, and they'd chosen against. It had been any other sleight to them. Like all the rest, if a bit more. A little bigger. More American maybe. Excess of the same.

The cowboy was guffawing at West from under his ten-gallon. Slapping his great big American knees, leaving streaks of blood and bits of flesh on the white chaps. Only his mouth was dark with tobacco. Only his fingers and his teeth decaying. It was his face and hands that had ever frightened West. Worse and worse as he drew close. And West—curled helplessly on the floor with his rattle, his rattle. His noisemaker.

———

The sleightists knew West was unhappy. That Clef was tired. They knew something had happened to Lark—she'd stopped speaking. She hadn't come to the second and third performances in Cape Town. Lark had stayed at the hotel. When they boarded the bus to Johannesburg, she sat alone in the very back with a small wooden box in her lap.

After Johannesburg, they were to fly on to Athens. West had tried with no luck, because of security, to get a booking in Tel-Aviv. Next would be Florence, Rome, and Barcelona. They were scheduled to appear in Lisbon. West would give interviews, go on cultural talk shows. He would smile a great deal, but after Cape Town there were no more stage notes, and he soon abandoned his evenings with Marvel.

Marvel was high. For him, nothing could have gone better—and it made him unbearable. In Cape Town, each night he painted the sleightists, it was more painfully. Their surfaces were overwrought. Backstage after the show, they removed the paint and then lotioned and oiled and mint-jellied, they vitamin E-d and aloed, but nothing helped. Where mirrors were glued, some of the sleightists developed sores.

As they deboarded the bus in Johannesburg, a young girl, maybe eight, ten, walked right up to Haley. The girl was tall, almost up to Haley's shoulder, but curved like a bow. She wore a white cotton sundress with brown flowers embroidered at the hem. She was beautiful, withered. Her skin was dusty, her eyes large, almond shaped, and dull. "Excuse me, but are you American?" The girl spoke English with a melodic lilt. Haley nodded yes. The girl slowly reached up then, and barely brushed the lesion on Haley's left cheek with two impossibly long fingers. The girl's hand drifted down and Haley noticed just then that the sides of the girl's mouth were swollen and cracked. "Why, if you're an American," the girl asked her, "do they let you have AIDS?"

It wasn't until their second night in Florence that T brought Byrne back to her room. It was unexpected. The tour was getting dimmer and dimmer, and that night she took his arm and he went. She bathed him, soaped him clean of his blackblood, and he applied an ineffective balm to her thin abrasions. It was as if she'd been bound with the aluminum lashings of real tinsel. Her body, in its so-many pieces, made him uncomfortable. But she was kind. They took care: he pretended to make love to her, and she pretended to not notice him pretending. They cross-soothed—a sexual civility. The two of them, after all, didn't dislike one another. T disliked Marvel, who hurt her with color. For handing her over to Marvel, she loathed West. Her husband was a lawyer who fucked other women. But she liked Byrne, or had once.

Byrne only wanted Lark. For that night, T and Byrne were each other's safest and softest choice.

In Rome, in a café, Kitchen tried to talk with Clef.

"I know you're pregnant."

"So? I want this espresso."

"Clef, let me be with you."

"Why?"

"I love you."

"That doesn't help."

"What do you mean?"

"I love Lark. Lark loves Nene. How is it helpful?"

They had debuted [untitled] in Cape Town. They'd gone to Johannesburg, then to Athens, Florence, Rome. When Marvel asked why not Israel, West reminded him—there was a war. War was, of course, an inconvenience to an American artist, an unpleasant limitation. Marvel nodded. Why not Scandinavia then? Everywhere they went, the sleight was acclaimed, and something new: they were asked for autographs. The sleightists were disconcerted. It was big, but it wasn't what they thought, and West's disappointment was contagious. The troupes flew to Spain but didn't perform there.

In Barcelona, West received a phone call. They were at the airport, standing around the luggage carousel. He spoke for only a few moments. Hung up. He turned to the troupes.

"Fern's dead."

He retrieved his bags and walked swiftly toward ticketing. They stood around the carousel, feeble, unable to do anything with their loss but grope. All of them except Kitchen had at one time or another been her students at the academy. She was, in many ways, their heart—the kind of teacher whose sharp vitality focuses others' passions. Some of them tried to lessen the way their arms suddenly felt emptied of blood and bone by picking up their suitcases. Others stared at the slatted rubber curtains, the mostly empty conveyor belt, an unclaimed floral carpetbag cycling through over and over. There were weak attempts at comfort/contact. Haley put unanswered arms around Clef. T looked to Byrne, but Byrne hadn't known the woman. She went over to Lark, but Lark's eyes told her not to touch.

West canceled the rest of the tour. They were supposed to appear in Barcelona the next night and for the rest of that weekend, then go on to Lisbon. They never left the airport. West found them seats on four separate flights, and they went home.

NEW YORK CITY (AP) — The Grande Dame of sleight, Fern Early, one-time director of the sleight troupe Kepler, mentor to two generations of sleight performers, and daughter of produce distribution mogul Chester Early, died yesterday. She was 88. She is survived by her son, Calder, 65, and grandson, West, 41, the current artistic director of Kepler.

Ms. Early died in Sanctuary Hospice, in Manhattan. She had been in residence there a little over three months. "She passed in her sleep," a hospice worker said. "She didn't have many visitors. She asked that we not disclose her presence to callers during these last weeks."

Ms. Early's lawyer, Cecily Holmes, said Ms. Early had been battling cancer for some time. "She was ill, but she remained involved up to the very end with her philanthropy," she said. In the late nineties, Ms. Early helped to found a women's center for factory workers outside the city of Juarez, Mexico. In an interview, she explained, "It is a place where young women can live and take night classes while earning money to send back to their families in rural villages across Mexico. Many of these women have left loved ones behind in order to support them."

The beloved Ms. Early performed as a sleightist for a decade in the forties before returning to the academy to study and become one of the few female hands in sleight's history. The five sleights she drew— *Womaning, Ach Grace, Deployed, Paroxysm Station,* and *Ungotten*—are some of the best-loved and most often performed works of her era. In 1959 she took over direction of Kepler and over the next 35 years solidified her reputation as a female pioneer in her art.

After handing over direction of Kepler to her grandson West, who moved the troupe to Pennsylvania, she continued for several years to teach at the academy in Boston during the summers. During the rest of the year she resided in Manhattan, a highly visible patron of the arts.

Fern Early was born Fern Trethorne Early on November 13, 1922, in San Diego, California. The only child of Chester Early, a distribution giant infamous for his ruthless quashing of migrant-labor organizations during the twenties and thirties, she and her mother spent most of their time on the East Coast, where Fern was provided with tutors, took private lessons of all kinds and developed a lifelong love of music, art and theater.

Ms. Early never married and never disclosed the name of her son Calder's father, causing a scandal for her parents during his youth. Calder Early was raised mostly by his grandparents, Chester and Veronica, as Ms. Early continued to perform, touring extensively in the years after her son's birth. Despite much speculation to the contrary, when they passed, the Earlys left the bulk of their fortune to their daughter.

Ms. Holmes says that her client requested that there be no formal memorial service. Those who wish to pay their respects may do so by donating to the Dormitory, Ms. Early's charitable organization in Mexico.

———

The sleight was all over the papers. It had struck notes in the media, especially coupled with Fern's death. The no-longer-anonymous sleightists, Fern, Fern's charity, West: so many opportunities for profiles, for human interest. Clef, because of the initial reviews, had been approached by several reporters just as she deboarded at Dulles. Rather than chance encountering herself on cable news, that night she'd charged a movie to her motel room—*Casablanca,* her father's favorite. After Rick put Elsa on the plane, evidencing his nascent or latent conscience, Clef looked over at Lark. Her sister hadn't made it to the end. Clef tucked her in.

West had flown straight to New York. There was a dinner in Fern's honor at a penthouse suite on Fifth Avenue: an opportunity to secure future funding. The International Board wouldn't be sanctioning him now.

Everything in York was disarray. The troupes left hastily, returned more hastily. The chambers weren't scheduled to be cleaned for another week. Winged impressions of sweaty backs and kidneyed palm prints still muddied the mirrors, forgotten warm-ups lay in dung piles throughout the studios, and there was a musty smell—the detritus of the body, shut up for ten days, reintroduced to heat.

Clef had gotten them donuts and brought Lark to the chambers. No one else was there. Clef had suggested the trip to the studio; she wanted what light was available in January, and to talk. Lark let herself be guided, shuffled. She didn't want to be disagreeable—she just wanted to escape, for a small while, expression. The last time she had lost words, they had been ripped from her. This time, she was cleansing herself. Words were dirt, endless like dirt, turning and returning, and she needed to be free of them.

She hadn't spoken since Cape Town, and she hadn't shown Clef her Need, though it was in the box. Clef and Lark sat in the center of the chamber—the box in Lark's lap, the doughnuts in their hands. Lark was staring at Clef through the mirror, witnessing their one-sided communication collapse. She watched her sister intently, fascinated by the distance that had reestablished itself between them. Only Clef spoke. Lark's eyes shot back and forth between her sister's reflection and her own, analyzing. As the daughters of scientists, they had been raised to maintain a certain relationship with failure. Lark knew that in order to learn, to really learn, she couldn't simply avoid past actions. To make a failed experiment work, she had to repeat it with small variations, and then rinse and repeat. Artistic, scientific, familial, cultural, historical: all errors required her persistent efforts at repetition. What had gone wrong was too often left alone. She knew better. Although it wasn't comfortable, she embraced failure—took it inside. It filled the space left by her Needs. *I fail. I fail. I fail.* Said enough times in a row it sounded almost like she felt.

"It's over, Lark. And nothing happened, just a success. The audience didn't care. Why should they? I wanted . . . it doesn't matter. I thought that West, that we, had really done something. And now, Fern's gone, and . . ."

Lark watched her sister's left hand as she spoke. It kept pushing her hair back from her face, and the other hand never brought the doughnut to her lips. A waste. Clef could use the calories after tour; she needed to gain. Lark was prepared to take on all their losses. But her sister was going to have a baby—she should eat.

"You should go home now. I'm sure Drew and Nene miss you. I bet he left that way because he didn't think he could convince you to come with him. He was right. Right?"

They missed her? What a strange thing to say. Clef couldn't know—Lark didn't. They had been so far away for so long. At the party, Nene had been less like an old woman and more like a little girl; age was moving backwards through her. So much about Nene was out of the recommended order. Her daughter had blushed when Byrne asked her to dance—that, at least, was ordinary. Wait. Could she be wishing *normality* on her daughter? Yes, yes she could. When had Lark last blushed? For whom? Nene would be a woman one day, and Lark couldn't show her how that was done. Not in any conventional way, not in any way that had proved successful. Drew was perhaps right to think he could do better.

"West said in the airport that we'll still go to the Midwest—they can't replace us on such short notice, but no California and no New York. We're on to something else now, Lark. It's over. Kepler and Monk will split up. I don't know if Luke will come back, I think he was pretty demoralized. I hope he does, though it doesn't much matter for me anymore."

They heard the door creak before they saw him. It was Byrne. He was carrying a small package, balancing it on his rock hand with the other one. He didn't seem surprised to find them there.

"This was at my apartment. It's addressed to Lark. I was going to leave it in the lobby, but here you two are." Byrne looked at Lark. Clef looked at Lark. Lark was looking into the mirror. She watched herself lick glazed sugar from her blue fingers one by one.

"I'll take it." Clef stood. Her right leg hung limp as she lifted a hip— as if by pulley—and the joint popped loudly. She walked over to Byrne. He nodded his chin at the box.

"There's a note on it from your director. It says it's from Fern Early."

Lark,

Here is the Soul you gave me. I have a feeling it's not mine but yours. You shouldn't give away everything you make, I've learned. Also, I have for a few years kept some information I've gathered. I don't want to keep it any longer. At the academy you came to me, once. You asked a question that had been haunting me, unarticulated, for decades. You asked me how something that could do so much could do so little. You said it must take a lot of work to keep it cycling on empty. Who designed it this way, you asked. And you asked why.

I decided to find out. After I'd heard you quit Monk, after West started producing things I felt were pushing at the edges, after my body started overproducing things I didn't need and pushing them against the edges of me, I decided to go to Santo Domingo to research Revoix.

In my youth, I was obsessed with Antonia Bugliesi. I modeled myself after her. Rich girl, big father. I thought she was the orig- inator of sleight, but over time I have come to see her as an impassioned collector. She collected beautiful things, things she loved: documents she'd seen in Europe and known enough to become obsessed with, styles of movement, young people—

especially attractive but expendable ones—glass,[36] lace, and mirror fragments.

She once called the Theater of Geometry her "living cathedral." She saw herself as the avatar of a new religion—a religion of favorite things. I suppose there are worse. And the reality of what she created is not so far from that, I think. But her real achievement was to cloak everything she did in mystery and dogma, forging art from enigma. She single-handedly inculcated an order of novitiates. She showed them Revoix's work and said, "This is our bible and I shall explain it to you." She reinvented, or at least offered to America, the temple dancer. The vestal.

I spent enough time, sixty-five years, moving in her church, pantomiming her sermons with my body. After your question, I decided to go to the source. Antonia Bugliesi was never tremendously interested in Revoix. He was only a hand to her, a proxy. It was the drawings that mattered, how she could combine them with other media in endless associative play. She was a spiritualist, a collagist, and a crackpot—our priestess.

When I arrived at the mission, I realized that, like Antonia, sleight scholars have been so invested in his documents they've ignored the other activities in which Revoix participated. One of his main duties was to baptize the Native Americans, mostly Cherokee, brought from the Carolinas to work the sugar plantations. The traders stopped in Santo Domingo to check their cargo for disease, convert and catalogue it. Revoix had another job, too—to quarantine the sick. The abbot put him in charge of the infirmary. He kept records of all the transactions—I found them in the mission's vaults. It seems the patients who were

[36] Antonia Bugliesi admired blown glass. She was aware of the precarious process by which it was made, and she modeled the apprenticeship system within the Theater of Geometry after that of certain European glass houses. She lamented her estrangement from her father for a number of reasons, not the least of which was her disenfranchisement from certain elements of his estate. He had amassed an impressive collection of Venetian pieces during his lifetime, now on permanent display in Milan.

admitted to the infirmary were primarily between the estimated ages of six and thirteen. In the records, Revoix described these children in detail: by teeth (age), height, gender, and any other noteworthy physical characteristics. Beside each description was a number—a fee.

The infirmary had a nickname: the abbot's stable. The nickname is well documented. Local myth has it referring to smallpox, but none of the descriptions of the children include markings consistent with that disease. And Revoix listed too few deaths for smallpox. There were some, but next to these, the causes of death were not recorded. Only more numbers. Replacement costs, maybe. User penalties.

I don't think Revoix profited from the abbot's business. I think he was in the position of sending these children to nearly certain death on the plantations, or procuring them for the abbot's use and the use of his associates. Maybe Revoix saved some, let them loose in the town to fend for themselves. I don't know. I only know these were the circumstances under which he began to draw obsessively.

The abbot died not too many years after Revoix joined the mission, and another replaced him. The stable was dismantled. I believe that this was when Revoix hid his notes—the structures and the words—only to come across them decades later, after he had worked long and hard, ministering, to forget. It haunted him, what had been done. I looked again and again at the precursors, trying to decipher them. I think originally he may have been trying to translate or to encrypt translations of the children's Cherokee names. He was a linguist. But there are no names in the infirmary records against which to check my theory. This could of course just be me hoping. That he tried to save—even their names.

What I cannot decide is whether or not to remain hopeful. This art I have found all my life so astounding, so beautiful, this art I have built a life around, and West's—it came from such misery, depravity. Is this any cause for hope? Every day I have been asking myself.

My first inclination, and my second, and my third, is to say that it is not.

I am writing to you because I want you to be well, Lark. Try to be well. You have done nothing. Maybe this is why you feel sick. I envy you for knowing so early on to be sick, to want to do more. Have you? I don't know why you can't feel, but I recognize it. My grandson will only hurt you. He probably already has. I can only hope it helps in some way.

Yours, Fern

———

Hancher Auditorium, Iowa City. A frigid day. Bluer than the second day in February has any right to be. Four are walking along the river that is not completely ice. They walk a mile, less, onto the college campus. They cross a bridge, and the bridge sings to them. Two of them decide to run back and cross it again—the song is happy, and happy is addictive. The other two laugh and frozen breath escapes them in a fine, glad mist.

A group of students pass the four just on the other side of the bridge. The students are scrubbed and shining. They have exactly the right amount of flesh to fill their skin, the right amount of blood in their cheeks; they do exactly the right amount of bouncing and walking backwards as they argue physics or football, but when they see the sleightists, something happens. Perhaps for the first time in their lives, the students are envious of another way of being on the planet. They feel young and awkward, but not as they did in puberty, not ashamed of self. They feel young and awkward now because they move like humans—they lumber and fidget, they twitch and trip, they knock teeth when they try to kiss each other drunk. They are embarrassed. Once, not long ago, their natures seemed particular, but now the students share a communal shame: they would avoid having bodies if they could. Because they can't, they are learning to wage a prolonged war against them. All of them, against all of their bodies. The school gym is always full, laxative supplies at local drugstores quickly empty. The students' bodies are all around them, but they don't think to live in them any more than they would think to study at the library.

The students note the stylized walk in three of the four they pass, knees soft, heels never grounded. They unconsciously mark the posture, in which the shoulder blades are dropped and opened across the back, so that, thin as these sleightists are, they take up more space. How their faces, when animated, don't end at the chin like masks but are integrated into movements of neck and chest—the entire torso, a speaking thing. Every movement, no matter how unconscious, is large and alive and purposive. *This is what beauty is,* one of the girls suddenly understands, *to be what is meant. And it is*—the girl is the philosopher of her group, and so follows one thought with another—*what I will never be.* The students look at the lovelies, each other, and then down at the new snow that covers everything this February morning. They want to crawl down under it. They want to leave the blue of this day to these deer, these willows, whose movements don't give them away, whose bodies are trained to deserve it.

The talk has been all over campus. Even the few that have never seen a sleight performance are trying to get tickets. Their school has, by accident, hit platinum: an Event. The sleight, in the three weeks since it debuted in South Africa, has received more local and national media attention than this year's bowl game—a good one, Dorito or Toshiba—which they won. Parents are coming. Alumni, and those aficionados on the coasts whose tickets have been voided, are flying into Chicago and renting cars for the three-hour trek across 80. As they pass the sleightists, the students give them a wide berth. To make room for everything that surrounds them. The tallest boy of the group thinks one of the four is not so amazing looking, not so very other. Byrne smiles at this Ichabod, waves his stone at him. Indeed, he remembers this scene from the opposite vantage point, and knows he is not so very other—although he is, a little.

HALEY: How far are we going for coffee?

T: That kid backstage said there's a student union building a block farther up.

MARCUS: That's never real coffee.

HALEY: Sometimes it is.

MARCUS: It never is.

T: How'd you think tech went?

HALEY: Okay I guess.

BYRNE: Is West using slides on the scrim?

MARCUS: I don't think so. Why?

BYRNE: I thought I saw them testing stuff from up in the ropes.

T: What kind of stuff?

BYRNE: Old film stills maybe—I was too close, but it was black and white.

HALEY: I'm glad we didn't do dress.

MARCUS: West said the lighting here is set. He can punch in all the cues digitally. Not like Europe. He's been strange—you know, since Fern. Says he doesn't want to hurt our skin.

HALEY: "Any more than is absolutely necessary." What a crock.

BYRNE: So why doesn't he get rid of Marvel?

HALEY: I guess Marvel's absolutely necessary.

BYRNE: He's a monster.

T: He's your brother.

BYRNE: So? It isn't hard to love a monster, just exhausting.

T: This I know.

The four arrive at the student union. They go in. The distinct and not unpleasing smell of popcorn fills the warm air, and cannot be disentangled from it.

theater :: ship-of-dark :: not nightdark nor dark-of-dead-day

:: not-time, because of no sky :: makeshift-time, rigged ::

sidelights as late sun :: scrims as drag horizons :: curtains

faking little mortalities :: floorlights—baptism, circumcision

:: washups over dolly-eyes :: blinkless :: time un-world-rooted ::

wedded to machine :: jealous vessel :: fashioning-anew-what-

world-discards :: hours, days :: stitched-to-sail :: time&skin&sin

:: original, &not-at-all

CLOSING.

Marvel started painting them at three in the afternoon. That morning they'd rehearsed, then broken for lunch. A deli tray in the lobby. West wouldn't let him paint for the tech, said it wreaked havoc on the sleightists. Marvel knew that, of course—it shouldn't matter. These freaks did plenty of nasty shit to their bodies. In fact, their bodies were agonizing to look at without the paint. He'd always thought so. No flesh, no imagination: all tendon and muscle and technique. Only his paints made them visually bearable. Not that he hadn't fucked two or three these past weeks, but he hadn't had much choice, had he? His junkie girlfriends may have been thin, but they weren't so bristly, so aware at the level of their skin of other eyes on them, so in need of shellacking.

He usually started with the men. Doug's paint job was a pinkish red. Maraschino. Marvel applied the first daubs to his torso—Doug's pattern he'd developed in spots, almost stippling, like a rash that's won—then moved to his legs. A minute later, when Marvel looked up, the torso was avalanched in cherry blossom. Reddish-whitish—pink. He stirred the paint jar, went back over the area, but now it was bleaching out even as the color hit the skin. Marvel let loose a string of words that turned Doug's face red, but nothing else. By this time Manny, Marcus, Kitchen, Tomas, and Vic were looking over.

"What's going wrong, do you think?" Kitchen tried to be calm, sensing that Marvel was perhaps not good in emergencies.

"What the fuck does it look like, man—the paint's malfunctioning."

"How about you try me?" Tomas offered an arm. "Maybe it's just that one."

"Why in shit's name would it be the others?"

But even as he said it, Marvel was pulling another can from under the table where he was working. He opened it, stirred, and slapped some paint on Tomas. The deep, pacific teal started going pastel immediately. Marvel leaned over, searched frantically through the cans. In the next two minutes, he tried out each man's colors on different parts of their bodies: arms, backs, legs, faces, feet. Then he put Marcus's paint on Kitchen. Even as he attempted the transplant, the paints grew paler and paler and cracked. The men looked as if they'd been partially foiled in dead white leaf, or ash.

Doug went to get West.

By the time West arrived from the sound booth, the scene was mild chaos. Almost all the sleightists were milling around, examining the streaky ivories and eiderdowns and ashy-semen colors of the men. Marvel was pacing in the far corner, his head down. Byrne was walking beside him, talking softly. West scanned and assessed. He clapped his hands together, and the clap echoed, and they turned.

"It's perfect."

Kitchen walked right up into West's face. "What are you *talking* about?"

Kitchen had had enough. Enough of West's machinations, enough of not knowing what they were doing and not understanding why it had been successful. If it was the sensation that it seemed, why had West canceled half the tour? He'd been curious about the project from the beginning, and—unlike the sisters—he saw darkness as necessary, a part of the scrutiny, the spelunking of sleight's potential. But he never trusted West. Now that it was done, Kitchen thought the sleight hung on the color. He was sure of it. The color and the fronting of the individual—parlor tricks, really. The links were genius, Clef's navigation was. But it was the props, vibrant nakedness, and the opportunity to attach celebrity to the sleightists that transfixed the audience. He said as much.

"If we're all white, we won't be a zoo anymore—and not-a-zoo is the opposite of [untitled], isn't it? It's not what they're coming for."

"No." West ceded the point. "But it's what they're getting." He brushed past Kitchen—he had no time for the thinker—and made his way over to Marvel, whose agitation was sparking uncontrollably in the corner. He was scuffling and muttering like someone off his meds who shouldn't be, ever. Byrne stepped protectively in front of his brother.

"Leave him alone."

"Byrne, I need Marvel to do this."

"Do what? There's nothing for him to do."

Lark, who had been invisible in the room, spoke then. Quietly. "There is."

It was the first time anyone had heard her voice in weeks. Since they'd flown back from Barcelona, she'd been at all the rehearsals in York, even stepping in when Clef's body gave out. But she didn't talk, and no one had thought she'd come on this last tour. They had assumed she'd be headed back to Georgia, hoped she would. Something was wrong with her. Even as the pressure of making the sleight had receded, Lark's presence had surfaced among them as a small dread. Many of them hardly knew her. They didn't want to deal with trauma outside their sphere, and she had the feel of trauma. She belonged elsewhere. Clef couldn't be asked to, but weren't there other people—Lark's husband, for example—better equipped to deal with her?

But T, who'd once felt threatened by Lark, hadn't since Cape Town. Lark wasn't so odd. Everyone got quiet sometimes. So she carried a box—Byrne carried a stone. Besides, it was probably a gift from her daughter, or for her. T tried to draw her out during breaks. She small-talked, asked questions. And when Lark didn't answer, she kept at it. It became important to her. The rest of her troupe, and many in Monk, shot malice in Lark's direction. Some of it was holdover from the navigation process, anger and confusion over how Lark had—after six years outside sleight and in only two months—made herself capable of things they couldn't. And this, after drawing the most astonishing sleight they'd ever been asked to perform. So, the typical accusations: ambition, insanity, witchery. T thought differently. She framed it safely, genetically: Clef's got talent—why not her sister? They were maybe born that way. T noted all the wrong energies around Lark, and realized hers had been one. In recompense, she tried to act as a buffer.

In the past weeks, T had been at Lark's side at the beginning and end of each day. She'd started bringing lunches for her and Clef. Soups, basil and balsamic and mozzarella salads, homemade breads. And talk. T had talked and talked to Lark about nothing at all: T's most recent homework—a new loft bed and built-in bookshelves for her bedroom, her New Year's resolutions, the dissolution of her marriage, the weather. She asked questions. Clef sometimes sat with the two of them, listening, answering for Lark when she knew the answers, but more often she'd gone off to catch a brief nap on the zebra couch. She seemed content to let T brood over Lark during the day. T, noting the space between the sisters, was disconcerted one morning—after arriving at the chambers a half hour earlier than normal—to find Lark brushing and painstakingly sectioning and braiding Clef's hair.

T looked at Lark now, and the small jealousy ebbed. She felt a certain modest pride. Though the two things may not be related, she'd been calling her, and Lark had come back from wherever she'd been.

Byrne had been in and out of the studios during the same two weeks. He'd been unprepared to see T and Lark together. More unprepared for how it made him feel. T looked kind. She looked good and whole and solar. He found himself thinking that Lark should be home with Nene. With Drew. He found himself drawn to T, to what she was doing. Her attention was a gift, the way she talked and listened to the way Lark didn't speak. He was beginning to pity Lark, and the pity turned his stomach, focused as it was on a woman he'd once wanted to be within. He was suddenly ashamed of conceiving of women in these terms, as homes, cars, or paper: to be inside, driving, writing on. But Byrne took comfort—he thought if he were to see T in Marvel's paints now, they wouldn't work. No one else could cut a woman into pieces. Women carried their own blades—sometimes, bandages.

Byrne looked at Lark now. She had come back from wherever she'd been. It all seemed too easy for her. His rock hand throbbed. *How selfish she is,* he thought, *to be broken.*

Lark stood in front of Marvel.

"Just paint them like you did before."

"It's not my work."

"It will be, a little of it anyway. But mostly not, no. Tell me, how did you get my jars?"

Marvel looked at her. He licked his lips. West answered.

"Drew. Drew left them at my house."

"Drew wanted to punish me?"

"To help you."

"And you . . ."

"Gave them to Marvel. Yes, yes I did that."

Marvel grunted. "I asked where he'd gotten them. Bastard wouldn't tell me. I needed more, but the colors were so fucking condensed, I mixed them with what I had. What the hell is this shit?"

"Mine. My Needs. They're almost gone—this is the last?"

"I guess. Yes. They aren't fucking working."

"No. They are. They finally are."

Marvel had little choice. There was no time to get other colors, and West—monitoring the process—seemed genuinely pleased with the white. Because it wasn't white. The paints retained a vestigial tint. The sleightists' bodies were crape myrtle trunks, green and terra-cotta hues beneath their wintering, or chalky riverbeds—russets and ochres promising a return with rain. The patterns were still there, though Marvel said the audience wouldn't pick up on them, that he was wasting his time. He kept whipping his brushes against the wall in frustration, but he got all of them done. All but two.

Of the sleightists, Clef he usually painted last because she insisted on it. Now she came up to West and Marvel and said, "I can't . . . I won't."

West didn't exhibit the surprise she expected. Instead he asked, "Is this about the fetus?"

She winced, but didn't back down. "I know where this comes from, and I'm not putting it on my skin anymore. God knows what damage I've already done."

West studied her for a long moment before saying, "I understand."

"What?" Clef tried to get her bearings. She looked around the room. Where was Kitchen, she wondered, was he already onstage?

West reiterated. "I said, okay."

Clef was still thrown, uncomprehending. Then she saw Marvel looking over at Lark, nearly salivating. West's eyes were there too. He asked, "Are you sure you're ready for this?"

Lark avoided her sister's face. "Yes."

———

Clef tried to not be angry—she didn't want to perform. Not this. Anymore. She was hurt anyway, and so couldn't stay backstage. She thought about walking along the river, but the temperature had dropped below the afternoon's eighteen degrees. This was her sleight. This was also her weakness—not being able to extricate herself. Except for Kitchen. With Kitchen, she was winning. She dressed slowly. She concentrated on that—dressing. She had nothing appropriate, and her jeans were just beginning to stop gapping the way she liked, even after a day on the bus. She found a red sweater among her things that might be passable. Then she made herself up—offstage, she didn't often. Eyes. Lips. At the last possible moment, Clef decided gaudy was better than meek and threw her scarf around her neck before heading to the lobby. It was there she saw, about to herd her family to a waiting usher, her old friend Bea.

Bea squealed.

"Clef! I was going to surprise you. Why aren't you performing? Is it your ankle?" Two of Bea's three children were weaving in and out of her legs. The third, Jay, was standing, in very adult embarrassment, next to his father.

Clef kissed and hugged them all. The two men bravely but barely endured it. It was the last thing—their reticence—and it crippled her. She put on her gala face and lied.

"No. Everything's fine. Lark's performing—I needed a break. She's back, at least for this project. But Bea, I don't have a seat and this thing is sold out."

"I know, I know. I'm so glad we got ours so early, though I'm sorry we won't get to see your 'unparalleled whatever.' I can't believe that your names are out there. I have no proof . . . the kids don't believe I used to do this. Lark's back? My god. You'll sit with us, of course. Emmy'll be in my lap the whole time, if she doesn't make me take her out to the lobby."

"Thank you."

Bea's hair was longer, and down. A soft curl nearly covered her serpentine tattoo—she'd styled it that way. The effort sickened the already lying and pregnant Clef, but she kept her tongue in her mouth.

———

The curtain opens. Lights fade up. Lark stands far upstage right, facing away, aboriginal in her white paint. On the stage between her and the audience there is a roiling—limbs and the fiberglass flash of architectures. Lark maneuvers toward. Her architecture is a word in her hands, and then she speeds it up, and it is thought. No longer under her control. Its process pulls her into dialogue with the other sleightists, and the architectures manipulating them. It is the structures moving the sleightists now—puppeting them.

Lark is alarming in her pale, painted skin, so violently, terribly naked. Her movements—angular, yanked. Marvel hasn't mirrored her in the same way he did Clef. In fact, except for Kitchen's and Haley's, he altered all the patterns. Kitchen's still encircles his waist, but because the mirrors can only bounce back black curtains or dark audience, he has no center. Haley has no face. Montserrat is without upper arms. Marcus has a reflecting worm where his spine should be. Marvel thickened two of T's lines but left off the rest, cutting her just at the knees. And Lark has no heart. Marvel, with mirror shards, has removed an asymmetrical hunk of Lark's torso: the left side of her rib cage, front and back. Clef cannot look at the disfiguration. The hack job. It is horrifically literal.

Lark's fingers are white.

The audience is hushed, as they were in Africa, Greece, Italy. The links are working without color. The bodies are still emphasized, though not singular. When Lark wicks, the architectures do not keep articulating—they spiral beyond what was meant, having lost their ballast, their plumb. Their flesh-marionette. On their own, the manipulations are too much, too open. It's then that Clef sees Byrne above the rest. He is two hands only. Face. Two white claws, one gripping black rope, one around a stone. A dark mouth in the center of a stilled, white oval—façade of a face. Clef—whose practice it has always been to let the precursor wash over her, like lyrics—looks into this mask of Byrne and listens.

FrancescaAbigailSlutMarekAjaxJackassChristopherDopeDickDeniseGilGusKike StephanSpencerHowitzer

She doesn't understand. Was this what was raining down on her? This onslaught? Suddenly Marvel's paints seem almost benevolent. But Byrne isn't saying this, is he? He's just saying it. It's nothing. Precursors are kindling—they have to catch fire. Newsprint is kindling and it too says nothing.

The wicking is growing closer, and Clef, punctured by the words, admits the beauty. Merciless. The links kaleidoscope over her—fracturing, multiplying. The architectures are lights on a radio tower, the sleightists—waves. Clef watches a structure contract a nebula, fitting it to the stage. She witnesses the molecular birth of a plastic. Clef sees a tree die, an entropic study of a cloud's dispersal. At one point, all twenty-four sleightists link to affect the glint and stab of asphalt, in serenade of a star long dead. She feels strongly—design is here. Momentous configuration. Consequence.

And then Clef remembers: this is hers, her navigation. She did this. And she had no plan, no plan at all. Just intention.

The fetus inside her flutters. It is the first time.

Two hours they watch. Bea's children are dumb. Clef looks over at the stoic older boy. Jay's mouth is hanging slightly open, his eyes are wet, tearing up—he's not blinking enough.[37] Clef thinks maybe she's hearing a siren, but it isn't a siren. Barely audible, what she is hearing beneath Byrne's wrong words she hears more clearly during the wickings. She begins to know it—the low-level song. It is the scratchy recording of a trumpet—muted. Music. It continues, fading in and out for the next ten minutes, twenty. She knows better than the rest of the audience where they are in the sleight, but even for her, time is lost here. She has been in this dark theater for a day, month. A year. She has been in this theater since her mother's death. Clef misses her parents, and is ashamed that she cannot miss them more than she did when they were both alive.

It is some time Clef spends with the horn, trailing it through the sleight, in and out of Byrne's words: *JossElsieAssholeLardassKaelDjuna SpicJorieLilithRachelRetardHowardDonnieTammyStoneJaneJewboyLiselPasha KatanaBillyPrudenceStefanieHankRaeDerringerWinonaAnnRachelLesboTasha DarrylLugerMargaretRemiWinchesterOwenSolangeSterlingBitchLawrenceVeda DrillSloaneFileMaddoxHoraceDjangoFaggotRenee.* It is some time with just the horn, the wickings deafening, and they must be nearing the end. Clef wants it to end. But West has made the end. And it is not yet.

---

[37] It is not uncommon for some audience members, attending their first sleight performance, to develop dry-eye. Because of the mind's inability to process the act of wicking, the involuntary act of blinking is retarded, or shut down altogether, in an effort to catch the sleightist mid-removal. A product called Natural Tears readily relieves the symptoms, and after a few sleight performances, the mind adjusts to sleight's opacity and the condition no longer occurs.

A flicker. On the scrim. A flicker on the scrim. The sleightists, mirrored? A flicker, nearly subliminal. The next one longer. Longer. Longer—movement. A film. Video. A strung toy. A puppet. Another. A monkey, a horse. A bird. A lion. Behind the sleightists, a film of white parts, strung together. At the top of the scrim, on the tape. A white hand in evidence. A wedding band. Above the scrim, Byrne's face. Byrne's hands clutch. A rock, a rope. The dark. Below him sleightists are spun, twirled, slapped. By architectures. Flung. The film behind them—children. The puppets are bone. Bone sleightists. Strings are architectures. Architectures, strings. Little crossed batons. Little crosses over strings hanging down. Frets. Playing. Miniature deaths. The dancing dead. The prancing, swinging, prowling, waltzing, pawing dead. The horn. Cloy. Sweet horn. A-sail above scratch. Scratch. Cadaverous lovelies. Cadavering. Staged. A preciously. Precocious. A postmortem. Baptism. A bris. Away. Adage. Skinless children are sinless children. Say it with me. Skinless children are sinless children. All gone, Mommy. All. Gone.

It takes a few minutes to register. No one in the audience has seen this section of the Vogelsong tape; it wasn't released. But the audience, all audiences, have a memory like a hunger for filth. This was, what, a few months ago? The animal puppets, the killer couple. Now, what was it they did? This film, then, on the scrim, this is children? The monkey, the horse? The bird? The lion? The audience moves. Shifts. It fidgets, uncomfortable, as if it were human.

Emmy, beside Lark in Bea's arms, claps her hands together. Points. "Mommy, look, a birdie! Mommy, look! Birdie up! Up! Mommy! Emmy want up! Emmy birdie, Mommy! Emmy birdie!" A woman behind them doubles over and vomits onto the floor.

The audience begins to leave the theater. This—this zoo—it is not what they came for.

The end. Lark is barely there. She is in and out again and she is grateful. She feels the cold again. Deep, and all through her she ices. This is what she wanted.

Out. To hate the sleight again——to remember why to hate. The word "planta-tion." Hunger. I know I love my daughter. Know it. The other sleightists begin to leave the stage. Leave like Claudia. Like Newton. Jillian. Like Clef. Goodbye. Out. Then there is sound, it is warm like burning, and behind her a black-and-white fire. A house burning down, she thinks, on the scrim. Is she homeless? It seems right. Sad. To leave one's home. Out. Necessary. Jillian needed. Nene needed. When home is sick, it's right to leave. Out. You leave pain. You leave color because it, like pain, makes you feel. There is only black, only white. Red and blue and green impossible. Brown and beige impossible. Out. Not actual. It's why she left my body. Out. Because I cannot keep color inside. I am only white parts. White parts it is right to kill. Out. Already infected. Yes, Jillian. Infected. See my red eyes. My blue fingers. White skin. It is not, Out, right to use the dead. To forget the dead. To use the dead. If I leave my body, Nene, then home, and I will be returned. Out. I will reach the other side and you can king me. The logic of it. For a moment Lark is worried——these ideas, they're perfect, and that is always a sign. But she forgets of what. Out. Utopia. The word "plantation." Out. Big house, instead of living inside the body. A body, instead of what? Out. During her next return she examines the theater. It is wrong, the theater. The theater is the test tube she has filled with disease. Out. Poor flies, glassed in. Out. The theater was rife with specimens and now is less. The people are not as much there. Wicked? Has she done it again? Were the audience hers? Did she hurt them? Out. Need them? She mustn't hate them. She mustn't hate them, though she knows she does. As herself. Out. As useless as that, Out, as needy. This is it—— what must not. Out. Must not happen. But she did, she must have hated them because the wicking is gone from the stage. Out. Her responsibility, she drew it, Out, self-leeched it, and now it is Out, Out, Out in the theater. Perfecting. She would stop it. Out. Call it to her. Lark knows how to call things, how to pin them. She will, Out. She will fix the wicking down, Out, inside her bones. She will welcome all its cold. Out. What is perfect doesn't move. It was never cold in Georgia, Out, like in Boston those summers. Out. The wicking, all inside her, all, Out, at once. The blue had always been right there, right at her fingertips. Drew understood. He had to. Out. Out. Here, finally, was something she could save.

Lark burned the house of her childhood down inside her. Lark did not mean to hurt, but needed to.

Clef stayed. It was the end of the sleight, and one by one the sleightists unlinked and left the stage. Only Kitchen and Lark were left now. And Byrne's words:

Judith You Theodore Now Justus You The Scissors Now Diane You Now Byron You Whip Lucius Now You Victor You You Verity Now You The Scythe Now You Dothead You Hurt Kieran Now Jada You Miguel Blythely Now Glynis You Take The Rock To Regina Now Now Mac You Fuck Up The Hymie Patrick Now The Stick To Sambo Now Now Fatman Fallon Hideo Now Zoe The Lathe Now Die Die Die Now Please The Sickle You Alette Now Me Take Byrne Now Art Now Faith Now Them All of Them Take Them Down You Enola Down It Drop It Now Now You Cynthia Now Cynthia Your Turn You Be Machine

Lark flickery. Kitchen fully. She was in his arms when she was there at all, the link a cradle-point. Kitchen juggling. Bone-juggler tossing his hard scarves again and again against harder air. Art. Lark and light. Lark and light. Lark and light. Then light and light and light and light.

The architectures spun. For three seconds. Thirty. The Vogelsongs' tape kept showing, looped, in the space where once was Lark. No more words. No horn. Kitchen let his arms fall to his sides. The architectures went on weaving for another few moments. Fell. Several tubes reverberated from the stage, graceless, before settling into awkward hush. And there was a child—come out from a slow dragging through milk, held too long under too much of what gave him life: Kitchen. He stood, hands down in front of all the white animals and nothing, nothing in his face at all.

Clef rose in the dark. She said, "Kitchen. Kitchen, I'm right here."

It was the end. And Byrne, looking down and seeing Lark gone, thought to blame no one. He closed his eyes. Unclenched his hand from his rock. The sky falling hit the stage behind Kitchen. Everything, littled. As Byrne undid himself, he remembered a Mustang engine, out on the block, and Marvel only eight or ten, standing on a chair beside Gil, gazing into it.

The end. West watched from the curtain as Lark went. West watched the audience's slow hemorrhage from the theater. He spoke aloud, and loudly, and to no one in particular.

You Are Now Leaving the Site of an Atrocity—tell me, where will you go?

rising	*emptied*
wild	

if box ≈ something inside :: if not ≈ something else :: at the lake ≈ ahead of themselves :: years ahead :: precarious ≈ now :: a precipice :: to balance there ≈ pain :: also, a special box ≈ book / camera / slide :: the stage :: lenses ≈ documentation :: because you were your own horror ≈ you could not cipher another

FISHING.

They are fishing. The three of them wade out to the bone sofa of the fallen sycamore Nene dubbed Whale a decade before. Once they climb onto it, Clef, who doesn't wear boots, pulls a leech from her calf and then rinses off the spittle of blood, pointlessly. It won't stop.

It is a long time in the morning sun. They never catch anything worth keeping, but Abra is addicted to the way nothing happens, then suddenly does. Abra is their coddle, and they baby her. She leaves next week for Boston—her first summer at the academy. Nene thinks twelve is too young, she has argued it with Clef. Clef thinks Nene should get out herself. Georgia has gotten inside Nene, is making her thick. Haunted.

Nene smiles at her aunt. "It's not the place, Red. It's the ghosts."

"Why don't you go stay with Byrne and T? They've offered so many times."

"You know why."

"Nene. That was a child's crush."

"I would hurt them."

"Fine." Clef can't make way against Nene. She is hard, vain, unlike any seventeen-year-old Clef has ever known. Nene doesn't doubt herself. She graduated high school three years early, yet Clef couldn't get her to apply to college, let alone leave the house.

When they'd first moved down, Nene had spent hours shepherding a then two-year-old Abra around the edge of the lake while Clef and Kitchen looked on. They had come temporarily to help Drew, because it was a big place for a man and his daughter alone, because Clef was done with performing, because they were all hoping Lark might somehow return. It was Clef who gave up first, when she realized she wasn't hurting for no reason anymore. The men never admitted to it, but hoped longer. Then Kitchen opened a studio near the university. And Nene and Abra were riveted, fastened. Sisters. So Clef and Kitchen and Abra stayed, extending family.

Clef unlocks the tackle box and the girls take their bait—finger-thick earthworms dug out of the compost heap early this morning. When she and Lark used to come out here with their father, he'd had one rule: they couldn't fight. As a result, fishing mornings were nearly silent, barring the occasional Newtonian lecture on the perfection of fish as organism, needless of evolution. Her niece used to tell Clef stories about him—grandfather-as-child—but somewhere around her eleventh birthday, Nene had stopped. Clef had been glad. It hurt her: Nene talking of talking to the dead. Her dead. Clef threads her worm onto the barbed hook, savagely—it is now two worms. Nene never meant anything by it. Lately, Clef was wishing Nene still had an adviser, maybe an editor, even if he were spectral.

"Abra, don't go."

"But I want to, Nene. I'll be back in six weeks."

"You'll be different."

Clef has heard this litany pass between them before, and it is getting old. "Don't keep making her feel bad, Nene."

"Why not? She's going to learn how to drop off the planet. Do you want her to follow my mother?"

"We never made Abra take. She wanted to, remember? We never made you either, and you never wanted to. Sleight isn't the enemy."

"I'm going to Mexico."

"What?" Clef's head snaps toward her niece. Abra looks down at the water. Nene's secret had been making her cousin's hands itch. Now they are burning. Abra dislikes the constant, prolonged battle between her two guardians. It feels like she should stop them, but she can't think of a way. Other than Boston.

Nene explains. "West wants to train me as a hand at the Dormitory."

"He's not even sanctioned. It's not sleight. You can't go."

Since the International Board had relieved West of his stewardship of Kepler, he'd been in Juarez. No one had spoken with him in a decade, and then, last year, he'd called Drew. Said he'd been working with the girls there—that some of them had proved quite talented— but he couldn't stop thinking about what had happened to Lark. After several conversations, over months, Drew agreed to talk to him in person. West had flown up at Easter. He'd worn a ridiculous white linen suit, and Clef had wanted to strangle him until he shit himself. She'd stayed out of the house for most of the visit.

"He says we should stop ignoring the root. That it's how things get exponentially worse. He says he lost her because he didn't know enough about his materials. That he threw them against one another for flint. People. Without adequate research. He's studying. He wants to put together an all-female troupe—Slit."

"What?"

"Slit. Past tense of sleight."

"No."

"You're not my mother. Drew says yes."

"What is he thinking?"

"You know what he's thinking, Red. That of anyone, I might be able to find out what happened to her."

"You won't."

"I know that."

Abra speaks. She is shy, doe-eyed, constellated. Take away the thousand freckles, and she'd look like her father. But Clef is there, all over her skin. Abra is beautifully normal. Except she has been raised by Drew and Kitchen, Clef and Nene. And back at the house, on top of the bookcase in her room, she has four other hand-me-down parents: Newt, Fern, the Lacemaker, and Marvel, whose Soul is still red and orange but three years ago stopped breathing. She also has a box, inside of which a white knot cradles the corpse of Lark's last Need. Nene gave all these to her when she turned four. Nene said she had her own things and reasons, but that Abra, more impoverished in that arena, might need to be *amused*.

"What did happen to Nene's mom?"

"You know this. She never came back from a wicking. She stayed out."

"But how?"

"She chose to."

Nene lays her rod across the crotch of the bleached tree and walks out. Once the water hits her hips, she dives, and with piercing strokes it takes her only a few minutes to cross this slowest edge of the green lake. Mother and daughter watch her go, watch her turn, watch her head back. She stands up. As she trudges the last few steps toward them, she squeezes out her thick rope of braid, winding it around her head like a halo, or a noose.

"Forget catching anything now, Abra."

"Yep. Thanks, Nene." Abra is used to her cousin's profound shifts of mood, has found it useless to let them rile her. She's also learned how to punish. "So . . . you don't think your mom left on purpose?"

This exchange nearly breaks Clef. They are not at all replicas of her and Lark. Nothing like. Nene is self-assured, Abra is patient. But the energy they pass between them. The system of pain. She and her sister might have patented it, it was that identifiable. The lake water is bath-water, but Nene trembles.

"She didn't *choose* to leave me. It wasn't simple."

Clef can't unsay it.

"She loved you, Nene. I didn't mean . . ."

Nene stops her. "I *am* leaving. On purpose. I'm going to Mexico."

"Why Mexico?" Clef knows it's already done. Her line is slack in the water. She hates when there's no fight. She has always loved and succeeded at fight.

"Because I want to be a cowboy."

Nene and Abra apparently share this joke. First, they shake. They start rocking and cannot stop. Abra drops her line. Nene's hair comes undone, lashing out across her shoulders. Lasso. Eel. Abra's giggle is punctuated with hiccupping intakes of air. They laugh and laugh. Their bodies are wracked and reeling and no fish. They are the fish. They fall into the lake and they're leaving her, and Clef watches them flop, flash, wrestle in the silt like boys, and she works very, very hard to feel tragic. Instead—always and where it should not be—there is joy.

COLOPHON

Sleight was designed at Coffee House Press, in the historic
Grain Belt Brewery's Bottling House near downtown Minneapolis.
The text is set in Perpetua. Additional fonts include Kepler, Futura, and 20,000 Dollar Bail.

FUNDER ACKNOWLEDGMENT

Coffee House Press is an independent nonprofit literary publisher. Our books are made possible through the generous support of grants and gifts from many foundations, corporate giving programs, state and federal support, and through donations from individuals who believe in the transformational power of literature. Coffee House Press receives major operating support from the Bush Foundation, the McKnight Foundation, from Target, and from the Minnesota State Arts Board, through an appropriation from the Minnesota State Legislature and from the National Endowment for the Arts. Coffee House also receives support from: three anonymous donors; Elmer L. and Eleanor J. Andersen Foundation; Around Town Literary Media Guides; Patricia Beithon; Bill Berkson; the James L. and Nancy J. Bildner Foundation; the E. Thomas Binger and Rebecca Rand Fund of the Minneapolis Foundation; the Patrick and Aimee Butler Family Foundation; the Buuck Family Foundation; Ruth and Bruce Dayton; Dorsey & Whitney, LLP; Mary Ebert and Paul Stembler; Fredrikson & Byron, P.A.; Sally French; Jennifer Haugh; Anselm Hollo and Jane Dalrymple-Hollo; Jeffrey Hom; Stephen and Isabel Keating; the Kenneth Koch Literary Estate; the Lenfestey Family Foundation; Ethan J. Litman; Mary McDermid; Sjur Midness and Briar Andresen; the Rehael Fund of the Minneapolis Foundation; Deborah Reynolds; Schwegman, Lundberg & Woessner, P.A.; John Sjoberg; David Smith; Mary Strand and Tom Fraser; Jeffrey Sugerman; Patricia Tilton; the Archie D. & Bertha H. Walker Foundation; Stu Wilson and Mel Barker; the Woessner Freeman Family Foundation; and many other generous individual donors.

This activity is made possible in part by a grant from the Minnesota State Arts Board, through an appropriation by the Minnesota State Legislature and a grant from the National Endowment for the Arts.

NATIONAL ENDOWMENT FOR THE ARTS

MINNESOTA STATE ARTS BOARD

TARGET.

To you and our many readers across the country,
we send our thanks for your continuing support.

Good books are brewing at www.coffeehousepress.org